TO THE STARS

THROUGH

DIFFICULTIES

TO THE STARS

THROUGH

DIFFICULTIES

ROMALYN TILGHMAN

17-18

17-18 Ing

Published 2017
Printed in the United States of America
ISBN: 978-1-63152-233-8
EISBN: 978-1-63152-232-1
Library of Congress Control Number: 2016954659

For information, address:
She Writes Press
1563 Solano Ave #546
Berkeley, CA 94707

She Writes Press is a division of SparkPoint Studio, LLC.

CARNEGIE LIBRARY, MANHATTAN, KANS.

"A library outranks any other one thing a community can do to benefit its people. It is a never failing spring in the desert."

—Andrew Carnegie

"Gild Edged Mikado Club (GEM) members were appointed to solicit books, periodicals, magazines, illustrated papers, pictures, etc. from the citizens for The Cherryvale Public Library. A public library is something Cherryvale is very much in need of and calling on citizens for donations during the week, and from time to time in the future, this can be started without any great expense to any one individual. The ladies of the club desire it understood that they are only the custodians of the property donated to the library, it being the common property of all, the same as all other public libraries."

—*Globe Torch*
November 24, 1886

BOOK ONE

TORNADO DEMOLISHES KANSAS TOWN

NEW HOPE, Ks. (AP)—The entire community of Prairie Hill, Kansas (population 2754) was demolished Saturday evening by a tornado the National Weather Bureau rated EF-5, the highest rating on the Enhanced Fujita Scale. The twister was 1.7 miles wide, on the ground non-stop for 24 miles and 29 minutes, with a wind velocity of 200 mph.

Over 100 injuries have been treated at the nearby makeshift clinic in New Hope. The town was leveled, with churches, schools, businesses and homes reduced to ruins.

"Exactly one wall is standing," said Mayor Wade Brown. "The front, just the façade, of the old Carnegie library is the only vertical object in the entire town. Otherwise, everywhere I look, there's nothing but sky. Flattened debris and sky. We're lucky; we had a 20-minute warning which saved hundreds of lives, but otherwise, we have nothing."

New Hope Gazette
May 31, 2008

ANGELINA

No mountains in the way. That's what my father used to say. Nothing between you and the horizon. Which spans forever. It's frightening to some people, afraid they'll fall off the edge of the earth. Kansans believe it takes a sophisticated traveler to appreciate its beauty.

The empty skyline matches the blank spiral notebook digging into my back hip. Speeding along I-70, there is nothing, and everything, ahead. One hundred days to finish my dissertation so I can submit it before the last extension on my last deadline. The time is now, or never. My advisor has been absolutely clear on that point. I can pull it all together, or … or what? Not much future for a penniless dropout in a dismal economy.

Time to get to New Hope. And fast. No more diversions. No more distractions. Time to stand on the steps that inspired me to write about the libraries Andrew Carnegie built. If the library the next town over was destroyed, what about *my* library? The library that changed my life by giving me the love of books. Time to soak in its history and salute its glory, while it's still standing, although as an arts center.

It wasn't easy to make arrangements; I had my moments of absolute terror. If I hadn't just devoured *Eat, Pray, Love*, I might not have summoned my courage. I couldn't sleep the entire week as I contemplated what it would mean to walk out of my mother's Philadelphia house, alone, to take the steps I should've taken a decade ago. What it would mean to let go of a routine, in which I knew every single thing that needed to be done and when and why and how. I couldn't breathe a word of my fear so pretended I was nine years old, brave, and ready to set out. Defiance guided my steps, and my will to achieve a dream pulled me forward.

I've been fascinated by Carnegie libraries since my first and only visit to Kansas, that trip to visit my father's mother, over three decades ago. What I remember most is reading *Little House on the Prairie* with my father. We sat close to look at the drawings. My memories smell of sunshine, because when we were in Kansas, my father always changed his shirt before he read to us, and that shirt had always spent the day flying on a clothesline outside. What I remember about the book are Conestoga wagons. Conestoga wagons filled with families leaving everything behind to start anew. Back then, more than anything, I wanted to *be* Laura—to wear pigtails, play with corncob dolls, drink from a tin cup, and win spelling bees. The Halloween after our visit, I convinced my teacher to help me construct a pioneer girl's costume— a bonnet made from a round Quaker oatmeal carton and a calico skirt held in place with a hula hoop. I could hardly walk in that hoop skirt, and I wanted to run. Run away from home. When I dreamed of running away from home, I dreamed of running to Kansas.

And now I've done it. It's taken over thirty years but now I'm on my way. My boxed set of the *Little House* books in the trunk of the car.

When I announced my decision to leave, Mother threw her dishrag into the sink with the force of the tornado we'd just seen on TV. She was angrier than she'd ever been, at least since the World War she'd fought with my father after we returned from visiting his mother all those years ago. That entire autumn the house was either deadly silent or so loud we had to close the windows. By then, I'd long outgrown the magnificent days of his reading *Hop on Pop*, but I'd not been ready for his new distance from me. To cope, I sunk into my stories, pretending I was Anne of Green Gables or Mary in her Secret Garden. Not creative enough to make up my own imaginary friends, I depended on the world's greatest writers to distract me when the tension between my parents got too intense. I certainly couldn't ask real live classmates to come home with me for snickerdoodles and cocoa and shattered glass.

The one thing I knew for certain was my father lost his job for staying too long in Kansas. Mother never liked Kansas, largely because Kansas, in the form of her mother-in-law, had never liked her. Our return ignited a firestorm that was never extinguished, smoldering even after my father died.

"Don't bother to call, Ms. Smarty-Pants," were Mother's parting words as I closed the door yesterday. She swore she didn't want to hear from me and told me not to count on another penny from her, now or forever. Yes, I may have to flip the proverbial burgers after I've hit my credit card limit. And, yes, I may be in therapy for the rest of my life for having finally cut the umbilical cord. But right here, right now, it feels like my only choice. As clear as the wide open space in my rear view mirror.

Ten years I've been PhD, ABD: Doctor of Philosophy with All But Dissertation. Ten years wasted, not getting my own work done, nor fulfilling my promise to my father.

Ten years ago, I was determined to finish my dissertation, despondent at facing thirty candles on my birthday cake without my PhD. I was unequivocally jealous when a patron completed her thesis on the mating habits of polygamous social insects. Specifically, she was studying queens who mate with multiple males called polyandours, males who mate once and then die. In other words, I found myself envying promiscuous, murdering female insects. Or at least her study of them. I wanted to sink into the intellectual pursuit of discovery, become a Doctor of Library Science, and then run a major research library. Maybe not smart enough to know everything in that library, to have read every book in the card catalogue, but I'd be able to answer any question that came up. People would call me Dr. Sprint instead of just plain Angie.

Finishing my PhD had necessitated my moving home while I wrote, which had thrilled my father. As the only child of an only child, my not conceived until late in his life, the statute of limitations for his doting had not yet run out. He couldn't have been more delighted to have me within smothering distance or prouder of my being the first in his family to go to college. Mother didn't think I was smart enough to earn a PhD, but she promised to hold her tongue and stop using her pet names, "Dimwit" and "Clueless."

Just one week after I got home from a research trip to Scotland to visit the birthplace of Andrew Carnegie, my father died. The very next day, I went to work at Sprint's Print Shoppe, where, until last Friday, I had worked every day since. Until last Friday, when we locked the doors, believing the business to be no longer viable, knowing printing is too quickly being replaced by online communication, with little desire for paper newsletters and invitations. Thanks to my efforts, thanks to my obsessive tendencies, the business did well enough the first few years under my management. My father was a font guy, entranced by serifs and curlicues, but I thought my business acumen would actually make a go of the business. Until it didn't. The outside world—changes in social customs, environmental concerns, to say nothing of technology—made our prospects for profit nil.

In short, a decade wasted. With a printing crisis or a mother crisis each and every week, work on my dissertation was slow going indeed. Progress measured in single sentences, not pages. I tried to steal a few hours when I could, but there was always a crisis to be handled. A last-minute delivery of wedding invitations because the bride procrastinated on her decision of gloss versus matte finish. Or my mother's urgent need to return Advil to the drugstore because she'd meant to get Aleve. I was just plain stupid to have mixed up my priorities, to have been diverted from my most important goal, that of finishing my dissertation on the structures built by the "patron saint of libraries."

It was Grandmother who told me Andrew Carnegie built fifty-nine libraries in Kansas in the early 1900s. Before he was done, he'd spent $875,000 in communities that donated the land and committed to raising 10 percent of the capital costs for ongoing operations of a public library. As I look at the wide open space, it's hard to imagine how a literary movement would have taken hold here at the turn of the twentieth century.

Grandmother described Carnegie as a benevolent Johnny Appleseed kind of guy, and it was only later that I discovered his despicable treatment of mineworkers, including the murder of seven men in his attempt to break up the union. A few Kansas communities refused to take his tainted money even for the promise of a library.

Should we, or should we not, forgive and forget? Was he redeemed because he gave the country 1689 libraries that served thirty-five million people by 1919? I became fascinated by this man who was both a philanthropist and robber baron. Obsessed as if he'd been a bad boy boyfriend. On the one hand, he believed the wealthy should live without extravagance and give away their excess money to promote the welfare and happiness of the common man. On the other, he was shrewd to the point of ruthlessness.

My grandmother talked about the man as if she'd known him personally. She was as proud of the library as if she'd built it herself. Once she thumped her journal and said, "The story is in here." But she wouldn't let me read it. "Not now," she said. "It's a secret."

The next day she handed me a diary so I could keep my own secrets, but my secrets weren't that exciting. All I wanted was to write down every book I ever read. I still have that journal, and I still write down the name of a book as soon as I've finished it. There are over nine hundred books on that list now. I almost believe I'll deserve academic recognition if I can describe the movement that brought libraries to the Plains. And reach a thousand books.

A truck driver honks as he passes, startling me out of my daydream. I slow in time to notice the Historical Marker and swing off the road to read it, following the cattle truck into the turnout. Trying to ignore the stench of manure, I concentrate on copying the signage into my virgin notebook, aiming for fine penmanship to reflect the importance of my new venture, remembering how I once believed copying perfect cursive loops from the chalkboard would make me a grownup and prove I was smart. The marker reminds me the highway follows the Oregon Trail, taken in the 1800s by missionaries, soldiers, and emigrants in search of land, and 49ers in search of gold, which in fact follows trails established centuries earlier by Native Americans. All in pursuit of their dreams.

Embarrassed, the driver comes from behind his truck, zipping up his fly as he looks me over. "Just checking the tires," he tells me, kicking a wheel to prove his point. "Okay, so I just took a leak." He grins at my Phillies cap and wrinkled clothes. "What're you doing? Running away from home?" Before I can answer, he tips his hat and admonishes me, "Don't be a bookworm," with a nod at my notebook.

I whisk through the Flint Hills, loving the rolling landscape and undulating grassy mounds, yet eager to get to the expanse of the flat ground of Western Kansas. It's hot outside. Really, really hot. Even so, I turn off the air conditioner, roll down the windows, and let the sun beat on my arm, daring freckles to land there.

The dilapidated remains of a one-room schoolhouse appear on the horizon. The cupola is twisted, windows are broken, and the walls are missing a few planks. What must it have been like to go to school barefoot, to sit in those funny little wooden chairs, writing on the desk hooked to the seat in front? Would I have been the spinster schoolteacher, struggling to control kids of all ages, trying to impart a love of reading to unruly boys who'd rather be outdoors? Exhausted by gathering firewood and pumping water as well as by correcting grammar? Bad-tempered and frustrated at my loveless life? That's how people stereotype librarians too. Prejudice reigns. Cartoonists depict them as dour, tight-lipped, military police who protect their books as if those books would disintegrate if touched. Guarding those treasures as if each and every one of them were the Gutenberg Bible, created the very first time type bit into paper and gave us the magic of books. The stereotypical librarian has suspicious eyes peering over her bifocals and white hair twisted in a bun, wears orthopedic shoes, and sees children, if not all people, as the natural enemy of books. Her entire vocabulary consists of one word, *Shhhh*.

The librarian who changed my life, Miss Thompson of the New Hope library, was the antithesis of the stereotype, generous in her enthusiasm for reading. She knew absolutely everything worth knowing. When my father took me one day and said, "My daughter thinks she might be afraid of spiders," she produced *Charlotte's Web*, which remains one of my favorites. A few years later, at my Chestnut Hill Carnegie library in Philadelphia, I'd been disappointed Nancy Drew books weren't carried, learning only later they were considered "too formulaic in plot and predictable in style" to be considered literature. I was appeased only when introduced to the biographies of great women, such as Clara Barton, Jane Adams, and Harriet Tubman. To take the trolley, to discover what treasures waited at the library, was by far the most thrilling part of my childhood. The library's offerings changed as I changed; the librarian knew the exact moment when I was ready to graduate to Jane Austen and Charlotte Brontë.

It wasn't until grad school that I got a sense of the power librarians feel in making suggestions to readers or in matching researchers with their resources. One cannot help but feel smart when handing over just the right book. "Smart is more important than pretty," my father always told me. "Don't think you're so smart," was my mother's retort.

My father understood my obsession with finishing my PhD. "Your grandmother left Philadelphia for Kansas and gave up the opportunity to go to college," he told me. "I meant to get a degree in journalism and be a member of the press rather than a pressman," he said. "You, however, will get your PhD for all three of us. You'll be the one to fulfill our dreams."

TRACI

What am I doing here, right smack in the middle of Nowhere? Nothing in every direction? Only an occasional dilapidated windmill, run-down barn, or hand-painted billboard promising the world's largest prairie dog, rattlesnakes, and five-legged cow in Oakley. Otherwise, nothing. Plenty of space to see a tornado coming. I scare myself to keep awake, remembering how that monster storm blew that town to smithereens. But the sky is clear as water, and I keep drifting, imagining I've landed on the moon.

How did I, Traci Ashe, end up here, twenty-six years after I got found in a garbage bin on Times Square, right across the street from the TKTS booth? Right there on 7ᵗʰ Avenue, surrounded by drug deals, neon lights, and noisy tourists. Found alive, a little white girl, straight from the womb, kicking and screaming, buried in pizza crusts and coffee grounds and covered with hangover vomit. Otherwise naked, I've been told.

No one promised me a cushy life. I get that. Still, once I survived childhood, I didn't expect terrorists, each the size of a grain of rice, to put me back on the streets, just when I was getting my shit together. Didn't expect to pack up my stuff and head straight into Tornado Alley, thanks to an invasion of bedbugs. Three weeks of sleepless nights, eighteen-hour-days of washing every inch of my rent-subsidized apartment, broke my spirit. I sanitized, vacuumed, disinfected, and scrubbed, like I could clean up my past as well as the apartment.

But in the end, even after I got a lead on black market DDT, I knew the bedbugs had won the war. When my roommates moved out and the landlord swore he'd track me to the ends of the earth to collect money to clean the place, he wasn't messing around. He'd rather throw me back on the streets, leave me to find food in the same garbage bin where I'd been found, than fight an army of itsy-bitsy insects. It was time to get the hell out of Dodge.

And there's the irony. All I wanted was to get the hell out of Dodge, and now I'm almost there. Boot Hill, here I come. Almost to New Hope, Kansas, where I'll be "artist-in-residence" at the New Hope arts center, the repurposed Carnegie library. How in the name of Godzilla did I get myself here?

To be honest, I'm more afraid of Kansans than I am of a tornado. The top Google hits describe a wacky bunch of dangerous Right Wingnuts, led by Reverend Fred Phelps who pickets military funerals with signs saying "God Hates Fags," and politicians who want to be first in the country to do away with government support of the arts. Family values are big, so I won't tell them I was adopted by a couple hoping I could save their marriage. But I didn't. Their *real* child, a son named Jonathan, called me Trash, and reminded everyone of my origins for the sixteen years we were shuttled from one parent to the other. He blamed the disintegration of his family on me.

Partially drunk when I answered a random ad from someone looking for an artist willing to move to Kansas, I told Mrs. Rachel Smythe that I'd taught Sunday school art classes. I lied. Gave as references my roommates, "one who unfortunately was away on a mission to Bangladesh," and the other whose cellphone was sitting on the kitchen counter and I answered myself to brag about my talent and lovability. No need to let my ex-roommate know I borrowed her cellphone while she was packing the last of her stuff.

When I talked to her on the phone, Rachel Smythe, president of the New Hope arts center, seemed impressed by my "commitment to recycling," which she thought would seem groovy to green teens and practical to frugal senior citizens. In less than an hour, start to finish, we made a deal. I agreed to come and teach up to ten classes a week, in exchange for a paycheck, housing, funding for art supplies, and my very own studio. I'll pretend there's a big loopy heart to dot the "I" in Traci. So sweet they'll never guess I've removed my tongue stud and the fluorescent purple highlights in my hair.

As I turn onto the tar road, the engine sputters again, and my heart skips a beat. I'm not into the God thing, but I do pray. I do pray this cherry red Volkswagen buggy that I bought off Craig's List will get me to New Hope, Kansas, wherever the hell that turns out to be. The cherry red Volkswagen I've just named Ruby Slippers. The cherry red Volkswagen I plan to trick out with a sequined steering wheel cover if the thumping in the engine doesn't kill her first. I remember to down-shift gears and the engine re-engages. If I tap on the gas, the car speeds up, and I can just as easily slow the thing down. Have I ever had so much control over my life?

A tumbleweed, the size of a Shetland pony, skips across the road. I swerve to avoid an entanglement, just missing a barbed wire fence. I should've stopped to pick up that tumbleweed, could've woven cassette tapes through its branches to make a dark and threatening sculpture, but at 80 mph, I've missed my chance before the idea fully forms in my brain. To calm my adrenaline rush, I switch the dial of the radio, trying to find some hip hop or even good bluegrass. Only the churchy stations come through loud and clear; the rest is static. Jesus has the monopoly over airwaves in these parts.

Since a career on Wall Street wasn't for me, I took to the occupation to which I was born. I'm an artist. My medium is junk. Other people's discards. Being an artist keeps my head busy so I don't fixate on what I don't have. Instead I daydream that people will look at my art and know me. Maybe even know me, get me, and like me. But I want them to do all that through my art, without knowing me personally and certainly without knowing my sordid past.

My wish almost came true. Six months ago, I was "discovered." A guy named Freddy saw my work spread out on the sidewalk in front of MoMA. He was fascinated with my fabric pieces, said he had a fetish for neckties. Imagining bondage, I figured he wanted to tie me up on a four-poster bed, but when I met him at the Hilton coffee shop with a switchblade in my pocket, it turned out he's gay. And a gallery owner. No sex attached, he offered me my very own show at artZee Gallery in Brooklyn. A show of my quilts, made with used men's neckties. Silk. Embellished with ketchup and bubble gum and adorned with Cracker Jack prizes, bottle caps, and other found objects. Ketchup you can pick up at any McDonald's counter; bubble gum from under their tables. "Worn and Pieced," he named the show, a riff on some old Russian novel, but in my case meaning worn clothing, pieced back together.

One part of the deal I didn't like was the name he wanted to use. When Freddy heard what my brother called me, he insisted I go by TRASH. He made the most of it, telling me it should be my "brand" and would be the perfect marketing tool in the midst of the "trashion" trend of crafting clothing out of recycled materials. "TRASH, the trashionista," he called me.

All fine and good, except for one thing. I blew it with the interview I gave to a hotshot reporter at *The Village Voice*. He pushed and probed, getting into my business, asked where I'd been "schooled." "Cooper Union?" he guessed. "I definitely see Rauschenberg's influence. I'd bet Peterson was your primary instructor."

He got under my skin so I blurted out, "You're wrong. Dead wrong. My only school was that library behind the lions."

No need to tell him I went there to get warm in the winter, cool in the summer, as much as to study the art books. I fed him some bullshit, said what I shared in common with Rauschenberg was the log cabin pattern, how cool it was the center square was always red as if to represent the heart of a home. Freddy told me that part.

"C'mon, I know you're the product of one of the art schools. Tell me which one," the reporter insisted. The guy was as determined to find scraps as the rats in the subway. He didn't believe me about my lack of schooling, so I told him the truth. How I might have inherited artistic genius but I had no idea where my genes come from. How I picked up my education the same way I picked up my art supplies. On the streets.

Freddy gave me a high five when he read the article, but the way I saw it, reviewers hated the show, got totally distracted by my name and past, tried to imply I'd been seduced by neckties, in search of semen, looking for my own DNA and lost father. Came up with lame explanations of how ketchup represented blood, and bubble gum depicted my innate desire to be desired, to stick to something. Someone. Anyone. One critic even had the balls to say I'd "need to know love as well as loss" before I could create art worth seeing.

⌒℮〜

NEW HOPE. Population: 2975. I slow to take it all in. Diagonal parking down the center of the street, three blocks worth of stores, some brick, some wood, most with false fronts so they look two stories high when they're only one. Like the set of a cowboy movie. A general store, a bank, a post office, a diner. A small Methodist Church on one corner and a small Lutheran Church on the other. Both are made of limestone, both have steeples, both have cemeteries. "Jesus Loves You" is the sign on the Methodist Church. Like I believe that; he'd be the first. I do get religion when I spot the New Church of Little Hope, but turns out I read it wrong. It's the Little Church of New Hope. I prefer the New Church of Little Hope. I might've joined, Hopeless being my religion.

Even with my gawking, it doesn't take five minutes to drive the main drag. I start to make a U-turn, to drive it again in the other direction for another look, but then spot a gas station and stop for directions to the Smythes.

A tinkly bell announces my entrance, but the overweight woman wearing a chartreuse floral housedress, rocking in her chair, doesn't even bother to look up. She's reciting the Lord's Prayer. Even I know I shouldn't interrupt.

While I wait for her to finish, I glance at the *Wichita Eagle Beacon* sitting on the counter and skim the article on a meth lab that exploded in Eastern Kansas. The sheriff says he's afraid they'll spring up everywhere. "All it takes to produce methamphetamines are common household utensils—spatulas, coffee filters, mixing bowls, and soda pop bottles. Someday Kansas will be covered with them if we don't clean them up now. Every barn in the state could be a lab."

The proprietor finishes her prayer, but before I can clear my throat to announce my presence, she's started again. "Our Father, who art in heaven, hallowed be thy name." In fact, she repeats the entire Lord's Prayer three times before she gets up to take macaroni and cheese out of the microwave. Is she flipping crazy?

"Fiddlesticks!" she says, still oblivious to me. The scorched smell tells me her dinner's burnt to a crisp. "Oops. Sorry," she finally acknowledges me. "Usually, it takes three rounds of the Lord's Prayer to cook. I must've lost count."

Fiddlesticks. The new f-bomb.

When I ask for directions to Rural Route #2, she shakes her head. "Oh girlie, you must not be from around here. We don't really have addresses. Who you visitin'?"

"The Smythes. Rachel Smythe is expecting me. Can you tell me where to go?"

"Sure. Drive a few miles in the direction you're headed." She looks my car over as she points. "Then, a little bit past the four-way stop at Brown's Landing, just past the railroad tracks where the Anderson's barn burned down a couple of years ago, go east toward Prairie Hill. A couple miles down the road, you'll see the Smythe ranch."

"Are there signs?" I ask.

"Don't think so," she answers. "We all pretty much know the way around here."

Her voice is friendly enough, but with an eye on the security camera and a hand on the phone, she telegraphs her suspicion. Maybe she doesn't see many strangers. Or maybe it's just me.

GAYLE

I stand in front of my house that isn't. For the twenty-seventh day in a row, I look over a landscape of rubble, in the middle of a war zone that once was a town before there was a tornado. I sift debris through my fingers, hoping for treasure. It's been five days since I found anything worth saving, but that silver baby spoon, the one Aunt Becca gave us when Vic was born, pulls me back, day after day, with the hope that one more memory can be excavated.

Twenty-eight days ago was a normal day. Working at Yesteryears, selling three greeting cards, no antiques. Mark and I arguing about whether we had enough money to redo the kitchen, me insisting there was no way the grout on the counter could ever be properly cleaned, him swearing that a granite top would send us into bankruptcy.

What I'd do for that dirty grout now. The grout that held us together before our lives were blown apart. Some people'd say our lives were blown to the heavens, but I'm thinking they were blown straight to hell.

Every afternoon, after I've stopped by the house that isn't, I head to the Salvation Army tent. To see the neighbors I saw every day when I worked at Yesteryears and helped pick out cards for birthdays, anniversaries, and funerals. Cousin Mary doesn't understand why I choose the Salvation Army's variation of hamburger to the fresh salads she tries so hard to tempt me with. She doesn't understand the solace I take in being with other stunned victims who rattle on in half-sentences about what they've lost and what they've found. Who start each sentence with "Before" and "After." We can talk, or not, sob uncontrollably or giggle inappropriately, without looking at each other like we're insane.

Mark doesn't get it either. Why his wife can't cope. He's already back to work in the fields, madly re-seeding, trying desperately to grow life again. He corralled a Boy Scout troop from Newton who'd come to help. They walked up and down the fields picking up debris to clear the fields, so he could till. We haven't even decided what we'll do next, where we'll go live, but that doesn't keep Mark from putting down roots. Literally. He's a stubborn man, like his own father and grandfather, and the more he hurts the more he works. I may not see him again before Christmas.

Today I got lost in Prairie Hill. Could there be anything more absurd? I've lived here my entire life, but suddenly I didn't know whether I was on Elm or Oak. Disoriented, I looked for the water tower, which isn't there, and walked back to the one standing wall, the front of the Carnegie library, and wept. Someone had laid a bouquet of plastic carnations, like they do when famous people die.

Vic's fifth birthday remains his favorite. He got both a bicycle and a library card. He could ride to the library and check out as many books as he could carry home. Twenty-five years old now, he still rides and he still reads. "Those are the loves of my life, Mom," he used to tease, when I asked about a girlfriend and before he confessed his love for Jill. "It's all your fault."

I do wish he'd marry Jill, make me some grandkids. That's the only thing that would give me a reason to live.

ANGELINA

It never occurred to me I might have trouble finding a place to stay. When I pull into the only motel in New Hope, there is no vacancy. The adolescent desk clerk at the Dew Drop Inn rolls his eyes and shrugs when I ask for suggestions.

"Where's your brain?" I can hear my mother ask. "You should've figured that part out before you left home." I'm tempted to turn around and return to Kansas City but instead decide to go back to the library I passed on the way into town, to find a librarian who can give me recommendations.

The Carl Sandburg Library is part of the new consolidated school district and located several miles outside of town. Sleek and modern, made of steel and concrete. Downright sterile until I catch a glimpse of the playground—all made of gigantic rubber tires. Toddlers play in a sandbox of a recycled wheel of a tractor trailer, while older children madly pump their legs on tire swings and tumble through a jungle gym of more tires yet. All that rubber to absorb the bumps and bruises of young lives.

Inside, it's impeccably clean. And quiet. Institutional. It looks too much like a converted gymnasium, but I'm happy enough to see the books. Elena Morton meets me at the front desk and introduces herself as the librarian. Her hair is more salt than pepper, tied back, but more like a Hollywood starlet's chignon than a librarian's bun, and she wears black linen pants and a dark brown silk blouse that matches her eyes exactly. Early fifties, I'd guess, skinny, tan, and fit.

"What can I do for you?" she asks, hitting every consonant in the staccato way Kansans do. Flat vowels and staccato consonants. More than a little intimidating.

"I'm looking for a room for a couple of days. Maybe a week or two. Nothing fancy. Nothing that costs much," I add, wanting to stretch my credit card limit to the limit, time-wise. "Just a place to sleep, mostly." I stand up straight to hide my road fatigue. "I didn't know who to ask, so I came to the library."

"Bad timing. There's not a room left in the county, what with the tornado in Prairie Hill and all." She sizes me up, before picking up a pile of books. "They're putting FEMA trailers up, but insurance adjusters and construction crews are coming in. No Vacancy. Period. You won't find a place to stay any closer than Hays or Dodge." When she sees the confused look on my face, she adds, "About a hundred miles away." She carefully shelves a book, before asking, "What brings you here anyway?"

"I'm trying to finish my dissertation on Carnegie libraries. I'm researching the entire movement, Carnegie's involvement, but I thought I could do a few paragraphs on the one that inspired me." It's all I can do to keep from stammering.

"You do know the New Hope Carnegie has been an arts center for thirty years," she tells me. "You won't find any books there."

I nod that I know this, although I've tried to put the thought out of my mind.

"Too bad you didn't get here two months ago. Prairie Hill had great primary sources. All the photos and newspaper articles from when their library was built. All blown away in the tornado." She snaps her fingers for emphasis. "We always hated that they had so much. Most of the records of our own library's early years got tossed out when they converted it to an arts center."

She stops to remove Post-It notes from a book that's been returned, unaware of how devastating this news is to me.

"How did you get interested in Kansas libraries anyway?" She cross-examines me the way Miss Jamison did when she asked if I had permission to check out *Fahrenheit 451* when I was twelve. Miss Jamison was right. I was much too young. It scared the bejesus out of me, but I knew I wanted to read it because it was about books.

"I used to come here to visit my grandmother. I never forgot the Carnegie library, so I thought I'd start here." My voice sounds both desperate and defensive even to my own ears.

"Wait a minute. What did you say your name was? Angelina Sprint?" Her brows come together. "You're not Amanda Sprint's granddaughter, are you?"

"Yes ma'am. I was named by her, given the name she'd have given her daughter if she'd had one. Instead, she had my Dad, Trevor Quinn. Both names mean 'wisdom.'"

It's not like me to be so chatty; those hours in the car must be having their effect.

"Amanda Sprint? Oh my; I still miss that woman." She shuffles a stack of books, apparently alphabetizing them, as she continues the conversation. "That settles it. You're almost family. You'll stay with me. My daughter's gone and you can have her room until she comes back for her wedding, which I have my hands full planning. If you need to stay longer, you can figure something else out."

After telling a young volunteer to expect a group of 4-Hers, Elena leads me to her house. I follow her black Volvo down Main Street, where yellow irises grow wild in the median strip between the cottonwood trees, and honeysuckle comes up in the ditches. The buildings are older than I remember, but well kept. Many have window boxes with geraniums, sweet peas, and nasturtiums showing off their colors. Dandelions pop up in the median and I remember how I used to make necklaces from their stems, putting one end into the other to make chain links until my fingers got too sticky with milky goo.

We pass the old-fashioned drugstore in the middle of the block, the home of Cherry Cokes and Tin Roof sundaes, where I learned the difference between a malt, a shake, a soda, and a cream. We pass the local barbershop, Feed-and-Seed, Jack's General Store, and Farmer's Bank.

And then, right there on the corner, the Carnegie library. Except for the arts center sign in its modern Helvetica font, the building is as I remembered it, but smaller, a miniature of itself. Limestone, rectangular, one story above a raised basement, portico and columns framing the front entrance, and an elaborate cornice emphasizing the classical look of the building. "Let there be light," is inscribed over the door. I remember walking up those steps as if it were yesterday although the steps I remember are steeper. I swear I can smell the musty books and hear the creaky floors. "I'll be back," I promise the building, as I drive past.

Elena's house, a moss green Victorian at the end of Main Street, boasts a wraparound front porch with two rocking chairs and a porch swing. The Victorian widow's walk makes me laugh, as far as we are from any ocean where a whaler might be sailing. The immense rose garden scents the entire block. The roses are in full bloom, with pink, red, and yellow flowers as big as dinner plates. A woven wheat wreath with a bright burgundy bow graces the front door. In a word: idyllic.

Elena invites me into a gigantic living room, big enough for a baby grand piano, three sofas, and a loveseat. Huge windows and a beautiful stone fireplace.

"What an enormous room," I blurt, before I realize I'm stating the obvious.

"The only other owner was Gene Lubber, Sr., the funeral home director," Elena tells me, as if that explains everything. "They had viewings in this room, and the garage had to be big enough for a hearse." Seeing the look of horror on my face, she continues, "Don't worry, they never did embalming here. They had a room in back of the furniture store, which they also owned, where they built the coffins. You can see what good carpenters they were. Just look at this staircase."

Everything about the house is impeccable. The woman is nothing if not organized. Even though we've just met, I discern she is a woman who loves the library job I hate the most, organizing books by Dewey Decimal, a system conceived by some old white man whose rationale I still can't explain after all these years. Does Elena mind when she spends a whole afternoon getting books in perfect order only to have a patron shuffle them to chaos? There are two kinds of librarians. The kind who want to *know* everything in the universe and the kind who want to *categorize* everything. I am of the first kind; Elena, apparently, the second. All of us want to share our love of the written word and collection of the world's knowledge. Commonality of purpose supersedes differences.

The room Elena designates as mine is a monument to the princess who is Elena's daughter. A king-size bed, covered with a handmade starburst quilt, and twelve pillows, all of vintage lace. The walls are painted blue, which makes the crisp white lace curtains pop out and shows off a collection of milk glass ceramics carefully arranged on shelves.

The room is perfect in every way, except it's on the second floor, making it quite a challenge to drag my suitcases up to.

"How many bricks did you bring?" Elena asks, as she watches me struggle.

"Books," I confess.

"You didn't think we'd have any books in Hicksville, did you?" she accuses me.

Color races to my cheeks because, in fact, I'd known I could survive anything as long as I had my books. I'd brought a couple on Carnegie libraries and Truman Capote's *In Cold Blood*, for his description of Kansas, as well as *The Little House* books, which I carry as an amulet. I thought I'd shown restraint in limiting myself to so few. After quickly unpacking, I check my email. The usual announcements from the American Library Association and solicitations to buy books for Afghan women, which I can no longer do until I can support myself. A reminder that a payment on my student loan is due. As if I can pay it.

Just as I'm ready to close down my laptop, a ding announces an arriving email from my advisor, finally responding to my promise to complete a draft of my dissertation before the end of summer. He certainly did take his time in answering.

Dear Angelina,

I was glad to hear you made the decision to finish your dissertation. However, I need to inform you we have a new faculty member, Dr. Jason Young. Impressive credentials: Rice University. He's hit the ground running and very much wants to be kept in the loop on your dissertation. I must tell you, he has some concerns. He wonders if you will be contributing original research and reminds you several books have been written on the Carnegie movement since you started work on your dissertation a decade ago. (See Carnegie Libraries Across America by Theodore Jones and Free to All: Carnegie Libraries and American Culture, 1890-1920, by Abigail Ayres Van Slyck.)

We know you've worked on this topic for a very long time, but he requested I ask you if this will truly put our field ahead? Please let me know when you have more evidence of your capacity to fulfill the requirements of this degree.

Regards,

William Belvin

Bees, not butterflies, swarm my stomach. I've worked ten years and come halfway across the country to write about the Carnegie library movement. It's important. Every cell in my body knows it's important even if I haven't been effective in articulating why it's important. But now I'll have to convince Dr. Jason Young who was probably in high school when I started my PhD. And what if I can't find the evidence I need to convince him?

Elena calls me to the kitchen, where she pours me a glass of sun tea, and I wait while she pulls cold poached chicken and a quinoa salad out of the refrigerator, arranging everything perfectly on bright blue and green Fiestaware, adding a sprig of parsley, and laying out woven Mexican napkins. I suddenly find my apetite. We take our plates to the porch and I try to push Jason Young out of my mind so I can savor the tastes, especially the touch of curry. For dessert, Elena produces plump, juicy strawberries, the size of small plums. As I steal an extra spoonful of clotted cream, she sighs and does the same, telling me, "This is my Last Supper. Tomorrow, I diet."

I start to argue she's already skinny, but she interrupts. "Paula's wedding is October 1st, and I'm determined to show up ten pounds lighter. I don't want her father, and his wife, Ms. Bimbo, to see me like this. I. Am. Motivated."

Elena quickly changes the subject and talks a hundred miles a minute about how much culture there is in Kansas, still miffed about my bringing books. Tells me the highest per capita readership of *The New Yorker*, outside of New York City, is in Northwest Kansas. Tells me if I see a farmer with an ear bud on a harvester in the fields, he's undoubtedly listening to NPR.

When I can't stand any more bragging about Kansas, I ply her with questions about my grandmother. I met her just once, the summer Dad and I came out. We had such a wonderful time; he was fired from Speedy Press because we stayed three weeks.

"Your grandmother was a saint," Elena tells me, "although a lot of people won't tell you so. After your father left, she was heartbroken and pretty much kept to herself. Almost a recluse in the end, but she came to the library, to check out her limit of a dozen books every Monday morning."

"Didn't she have friends?"

"Not really, especially after that summer you were here. Your father told her afterwards he could never come back. Your mother would divorce him. After that, Amanda kept to herself." Elena stops to stack our dirty dishes onto one tray. "It's not that your grandmother didn't have friends," she continues. "There were two or three people who depended on her, recluses themselves, because she could always keep a secret. Said she wrote them all in her journal where no one would ever see them. She was close to Theresa Hopkins, a friend of your father's. She and your grandmother knitted together every Wednesday night. And Theresa did her grocery shopping and cooking when she got sick. Theresa's son bought her farm, you know."

"I thought the farmhand bought it."

"Farmhand? I guess you could call Thad 'the farmhand.' I'd have said 'friend of the family.'"

The conversation stops as we watch the cat chase a grasshopper and listen to the crickets chattering. I dare to break the silence. "Grandmother once told me there was a secret to the building of the library. Do you know what she meant?"

"Not a clue," she responds, quickly looking up to the sky.

Suddenly there's a boulder in my throat. Why has it taken so long for me to get here to search for my grandmother's journal? All the time I spent looking for primary resources in Philadelphia and Pittsburg libraries, even going to Scotland, and it never once occurred to me my own grandmother might have left footnotes for my dissertation.

Elena points out the evening's first firefly, trying to change the subject. After a second or two of silence, she says, "You know, your father was quite a ladies' man. Too old for me, but lots of girls had a crush on him. He was handsome enough, and smart and funny, but his most seductive quality was the way he paid attention. He'd look you in the eye and hold onto every word you said. Your grandmother thought he'd marry someone here and stay forever."

I consider my father as a "ladies' man," remembering the way he caught a lightning bug and made me a diamond ring. "You'll always be my girl," he said, as he stuck it on my ring finger. The light flickered for a minute or two, and the thrill was quickly replaced by disappointment. It's not hard to imagine why women loved him. He'd been gregarious and generous, quick with a compliment.

Elena interrupts to wish me goodnight, nodding toward the sky, saying my father and grandmother must be looking down.

"There must be a million stars out tonight," I say in absolute wonder. "It looks like you could touch them."

"*Ad Astra per Aspera*," she says. "The Kansas state motto. To the stars through difficulties."

TRACI

The basement of the renovated Carnegie library that has become the arts center will be my new home. Rachel Smythe is twice my age and twice my weight, has hair as white as mine is black, and might as well live on Mars for the differences in how we live. She's got a ranch, a live-in mother-in-law, three kids, six grandkids, four dogs, three cats, horses, goats, cattle, and god knows how many chickens. She worries the accommodations aren't good enough.

"Are you kidding? This place is amazing," I tell her. Way too good for me. The open space has polished concrete floors, covered with braided rag rugs, and there are vintage quilts, three of them, on the brick walls. It looks like it's straight out of a fancy home decorating magazine.

"Johnny said he could build you a partition if you want to separate your studio," she says, motioning where a wall might be built. "But since you're a New Yorker, you might prefer the loft look." Like I've ever had more than ten square feet to call my own. "At least you'll be safe if there's another tornado. This basement is the safest place in town," she tells me.

"How will I know it's coming?" I ask.

"Believe me, you'll know. Sounds like a freight train, coming right at you." She pauses, chewing her lower lip, like she's not sure whether she should tell me something. When she continues, her voice is tight. "I was in Prairie Hill the night the tornado hit. We were trying to

29

build bridges between our two churches. Like the Palestinians and the Jews, although we're all Lutherans of course. When the sirens went off, we huddled in the church basement so tight you couldn't move. I'll never forget the sound of steel ripping or people screaming. It was like the whole building was breathing. First the walls expanded and then they collapsed. One woman kept yelling 'Jesus! Jesus! Jesus! Heavenly Father!' over and over again. And my son, my six-foot-tall, two hundred pound, forty-year-old macho son, kept saying 'I love you guys, I just want you to know I love all you guys.'"

Great. I've swapped bedbugs for tornadoes.

"We'll get you a bicycle helmet," Rachel assures me. "That's what they recommend to avoid head injuries. And here's your key, with a flashlight attached; if the electricity goes out, it's pitch black down here."

Rachel says she'll give me an hour to "settle in," after asking about a hundred times if I'm sure I'll be okay, if there's anything else I need. She's put an enormous bouquet of flowers she called "peonies" on the kitchen table and stocked the fridge with strawberries, milk, butter, bacon, and eggs. She's already given me more attention than everyone's given me in my whole life put together. Not sure whether this will be comforting or claustrophobic. One thing is for sure, I'm stuck here. My getaway car, Ruby Slippers, died in the Smythes' driveway. The universe answered my prayers to get me here. Ruby went exactly as far as I prayed for her to go, but not one inch more.

After I've paced up and down my new digs about a hundred times, stopping each time to run my hands over the cold, flat, steel table that will be my worktable, Rachel comes back to talk about the classes I'll teach. She offers me lemonade from my own refrigerator, which she calls an icebox, then sits down at the worktable and pulls out a notebook, like this is a serious meeting.

"Shall we talk about what you'll be teaching? What the 'syllabus' will be for each of your classes?" she asks. She clicks her pen like she's ready to write.

Syllabus? Who said anything about a syllabus?

She continues, like she doesn't get how she's freaked me out. "There'll be an evaluation of your residency at the end and we'll need to demonstrate how many people we've reached and how we've increased 'critical thinking, problem solving, and creativity,'" she says, reading from an official piece of paper.

Time for a major punt. "I wanted to wait to see who I'll be teaching. You know, like get their input and everything. I have lots of ideas, of course," I say. Although I don't. At the moment I can't think of a single one, let alone how I can make a "syllabus." How long will it take her to figure out I lied, that I've never taught a single class? I scratch my head, suddenly itching with phantom bedbug bites.

"Okay, I guess we can wait a day or two," she says, closing her notebook, clucking her tongue while she looks at me. "You're undoubtedly exhausted from your trip."

She's disappointed but wants to be nice. "We thought it'd be good for you to work with the few quilters who meet here on Tuesday and Thursday mornings. The No Guilt Quilters. A most informal group, never the same bunch two times in a row because everyone's so busy. They're a little set in their ways, mostly like to gossip, so I'm not sure how receptive they'll be."

A teacher who can't teach and students who don't want to be taught. A winning combination. "You really call them the No Guilt Quilters?" I ask. "Isn't that kind of a weird name?"

"A bit ironic, perhaps," Rachel answers, looking mostly amused. "We all always feel guilty. Full of shoulda/coulda/wouldas. We can never do enough. That's why we declared this our safe zone, where we can be together without guilt. As long as our hands are busy, we get a pass on all the other things we're supposed to be doing."

"Makes sense," I say, although it doesn't.

"Then in the afternoon," Rachel continues, "we have the group we affectionately call 'the troublemakers.' They're not bad kids. Just feisty. Teenagers with too much time on their hands, not sure what the future holds. Too many wrong choices and bad ideas. We thought maybe you could appeal to their creative sides."

Great. I'm supposed to be a truant officer too.

"Traci, there's something else you should know." Rachel stops to stir her lemonade so I know it's important. "Not everyone thinks we should have hired you. Nothing personal. There were several other candidates with New Hope connections, and each had her own champion. Ultimately, the selection committee left the decision to me. You might be kind of careful in the beginning. You know, put your best foot forward and be gracious. I know you can win them over."

Like anyone has ever found me charming. Loveable I'm not. Why on earth did Rachel pick me?

After asking about a thousand times if I'm sure I don't need anything, Rachel leaves me to my terror, to wonder how I'm going to make everyone happy and figure out how to be warm and cuddly enough for the ladies, cool enough for the teenagers, and appealing enough to win over everyone who knows artists far more qualified than me.

To distract myself, I go to the computer. The screen is open to www.newhope.com and has photos of sunflowers and roses in front of the arts center, where I now live.

Welcome to New Hope, Kansas, USA. Some would say the Middle of Nowhere, but we prefer the Center of Everything. Three hundred days of sunshine a year, but the weather is always changing so you'll never get bored. If you need anything, Jack's delivers and the Co-op Garage will pick up your car. We have three churches, five baseball teams, and a community arts center and library. The well water is fluoridated, we've got hi-speed Internet, and the kids all walk to school. Folks look after each other— womb to tomb and cradle to grave. Cost of living is low. If you're having a baby, a doctor's visit will set you back only $58. When

you die, two cemetery plots will cost your heirs only fifty bucks—
and include perpetual care.

The description sounds positively creepy. Fine place to live if you're ready to die.

Okay, I've got this evening to try to figure out what I'll teach. Maybe the teenagers would like to knit cassette tapes? Nope. I'm not gonna share those tapes. I brought one set of chopsticks to use as knitting needles; can you even find chopsticks in Nowhereville? Pencils? What can we knit until we find more cassette tapes? Aha! A quick Internet search leads me to a demonstration on knitting ramen noodles. Rachel left some spaghetti in the pantry so that should work. Cooked spaghetti knitted on pencils. If that doesn't entertain them, nothing will. I boil a batch and spend an hour trying to manipulate slippery, slimy pasta into a swatch and then give up in utter frustration.

It's only midnight, but since there's nothing to do except worry about teaching, I go to bed. Or rather I put some blankets on the concrete floor because I certainly don't belong in a perfectly made up bed. What if I leave bedbugs or stain the sheets with my monthly blood?

It's not easy to get comfortable on concrete, especially since I am totally spooked by the quiet. There is absolutely no one around. Could anyone even hear me if I screamed? There's a sound in the kitchen, a big clunk, which scares the shit out of me—until I investigate to find an icemaker in the fridge. Another scare leads me to the air conditioner that has clicked on.

What am I going to do here for an entire year? How can I get out of town if it doesn't work out? Even if I can trick them into thinking I can teach, can I exist here? Yes, I wanted time to make art, but a person has to play too. In New York, I didn't need a TV, or books, or games. Give me my iPod and time on the streets and I am totally entertained. Here? Maybe not so much. A girl could go stark, raving mad. But I'm stuck here, at least until someone can fix Ruby Slippers.

My brain is going a thousand miles a minute, totally weirded out by what I've gotten myself into. I grab my knitting needles, just in case someone tries to break in and rape me. Could I stab him with size 15s? No one would hear my scream for help, that's for sure. In the city, the world might ignore me, but here no one would even hear.

The quieter it gets, the more noise there is. The crickets start chirping, and I hear what sounds like a coyote. Then a freight train coming right at me and my heart threatens to explode in my chest ... but it's a freight train, not a tornado. Should I hop on that freight train and get out of this town before they lynch me for lying? Might need to find me a cowboy to protect me in these parts, I'm thinking as I drift off to sleep.

GAYLE

I did not go to Prairie Hill today. The first day I haven't gone to stand in front of my house that isn't. Cousin Mary insisted I go with her to Hays to buy a few new clothes. She's tired of washing my one pair of jeans and shabby work shirt every night, having our one change of clothes ready in the morning. She won't let me help, as if I were an invalid instead of just destitute. If she weren't built like a stick, I could wear her clothes, but she is and I'm not. Although I'm stickier than I once was. I've dropped two sizes this month. The Worry Diet is much more effective for weight loss than either Grapefruit or Atkins. To think my biggest worry used to be my weight.

I worry we're overstaying our welcome but it's not like we have another place to go. More FEMA trailers are supposed to be delivered any day now, but I don't know if I want to move back. Not that New Hope could ever look better to me than Prairie Hill. I have no idea where we're supposed to land.

Last night I had another nightmare featuring another tornado. Me running as fast as I can, trying to round up the family like they were chickens, the tornado gaining, loud as a freight train, sucking the breath right out of my lungs. Another night of waking up to my own screams, drowning in sweat, afraid to open my eyes and afraid to close them. I'd sell my soul to rest in my own bed. To have one iota of control.

Yes, I know I'm lucky to be alive. And thank you very much, I don't need another person to tell me so. If you weren't there, if you haven't seen your own home shattered to smithereens, if you don't know what it's like to suddenly be afraid of everything, from mice to insurance agents to the rash that now covers your body, you have no right to tell me how I should feel. You have no right to look so smug, underlining the question we ask ourselves over and over again. "Why us?"

ANGELINA

The radio blasts forth with pork-belly futures, and from down the hall comes the sound of a familiar voice. The voice turns out to be Jane Fonda coaching sit-ups, so I join Elena for a workout session. It's good to stretch after my long drive, and I can almost keep up with the exercises. At least until she puts on a second tape, Go You Chicken Fat Go, which Elena insists was the centerpiece of her grade school physical fitness program. Lots of old-fashioned push-ups, jumping jacks, and sit-ups before we roll up on our backs to bicycle in the air. It's fast-paced, accompanied by a brass band and a vocalist admonishing "Give that chicken fat back to the chickens, and don't be chicken again." I end up giggling, nervous giggling, but Elena is all business.

Elena's all business about her food intake too, having adopted the "Three Bite Diet," as a way to lose weight before Paula's wedding. "You always taste the first and last bites most," she tells me when we've gone downstairs for breakfast. "So it's easy to give up the bites in the middle."

Elena offers only green tea, so I take off on foot to look for a tastier brew on Main Street. It's not a long search; dirty pick-up trucks parked outside of Jo's Café point to my source for caffeine. I order my coffee at the counter, disappointed they don't have soy lattes but glad the coffee's only "a buck." Jo introduces herself and tells me to take a seat.

Heading for a quiet booth in the corner, I try to ignore the group of men, all dressed in overalls or jeans and cowboy hats or baseball caps, yucking it up around a long, Formica table in the center of the room. Turn down the lights and give them beer steins instead of coffee mugs, and you'd swear it was a bar. They check me out; I feel color rush to my face and wish I had gray hair and looked more like a librarian.

"Hi stranger," one greets me. "If you want a soy latte, I can take you to Starbuck's. In Colby. It's just 150 miles away." He laughs at his own offer. "We can be back by three."

"Come tell us what you're doing here," another one says, pulling out the one empty chair. They rearrange themselves when I sit down, correcting their posture to appear taller than they are. I look around, trying to distinguish one from the next. Except for a bearded, pony-tailed man, they're all clean-shaven and crew cut. Weathered skin, sandy brown hair, the color of wheat, and a few who've turned gray. Age distinguishes them from one another, but little else.

As I take a sip of the chewable coffee, then reach for the milk pitcher, I wonder how to introduce myself. The PhD dissertation suddenly seems pretentious, so I tell them I'm here to visit my grandmother's grave.

"She from here in New Hope?" asks one of the gray-haired men.

"Yes, she had a farm between New Hope and Prairie Hill," I answer.

"Which was it?" he snarls back. "New Hope and Prairie Hill are *not* the same. Which town's she from?"

"Don't mind him," one of the younger men jumps in. "You must not be from around here, or you'd know Prairie Hill and New Hope have been fighting ever since we stole the county seat right after the Civil War. We were Free-Staters; they were Confederates. When the two counties were combined at Statehood, we had a major fight as to which would be the county seat. Both of them were within a day's buggy ride of the entire county, which you had to be to qualify, but we stole the records off Prairie Hill in the middle of the night."

Fascinating. I need to remember.

"No, before that," insists a man about my age. "It started when the settlers first declared their town to be 'Prairie Hill'—as if their sod houses were on higher land than ours. There's no hill there, unless it's a Prairie *Dog* Hill. That's what set off the feud."

"Remember our senior prank?" This from a man at least seventy years old. "How we stuffed old hamburger meat in the lockers at PH High, just before spring break, when the temperature hit a hundred degrees? When they all came back, it stunk to high heavens, with flies and maggots everywhere." He chuckles at the memory.

"C'mon guys. Let bygones be bygones. Show some Christian charity."

"Oops. I forgot," says the prankster. "Now we're supposed to be nice because Rodent Mound got wiped out by a tornado. God's wrath if you ask me. God pissed off because they'd let the town go. They think they're gonna re-build the way Greensburg did, but Greensburg had a lot of FEMA money and Leonardo DiCaprio. Things've changed. There ain't no money with the Republicans in power, and no movie star is gonna show up for the *second* green community in Kansas. That sorry town was ready to die before the tornado hit and there won't be jobs after they re-build it."

The old guy's face softens. "Well, we like it here," he insists. "Nothing fancy schmantzy about us, but we like what we got here in New Hope. Expect you'll decide your grandmother was from New Hope too. If you loved her, don't ever mention the other place again. Who was your grandmother anyway?"

Before I can answer, the old guy's cellphone honks, and the rest of the guys shake their heads. "Gotta go, crops don't wait," one of them says, and like a choreographed dance, they all get up to the tune of scraping chairs. They each throw a few dollar bills on the table, and the young, bearded, pony-tailed man winks at me. "Don't worry," he says. "We've got you covered. Hope to see you around here again."

After making my way back to Elena's, I finish unpacking, putting my things neatly away in the drawers she's provided. I give my clothes a good shake before I hang them, slacks grouped together, tops grouped together, both pairs of shoes neatly lined up. Except for one sandal that's missing. When I thrust my hand down the side pocket of my suitcase, just to make sure the odd shoe isn't trapped, I discover an old postcard, with a 12-cent stamp. The image is the world's biggest ball of twine from Cawker City, Kansas, described as 1.6 million feet of twine on an 8-foot diameter ball. The note, in a woman's hand, says simply, "I love you every inch of this. And one mile more." The signature is Honey.

The postcard is addressed to my father, at Sprint's Print Shoppe, and I can't figure out why my mother would have sent my father a Kansas postcard. But then, I realize the handwriting isn't hers, even though my father always called her "honey," and me his "honey bun." The postmark is smudged; no clues as to where it was sent from or when. Why is this postcard in my father's suitcase? Who is the third honey in his life?

TRACI

Rachel offers to give me a tour of New Hope on our way to the potluck that will welcome me to town. She talks on and on, and I flash back to the Japanese tour guides who give tours of MoMA, followed by a string of camera-wielding look-alike tourists.

"Jimmy Swenson is the pastor of the Lutheran Church. He's been here so long some people think he knew Jesus personally," she tells me, as if this is as interesting as Van Gogh cutting off his own ear. She stops and points to the other church, across the street. "Brad Lloyd is the minister of the Methodist Church, where many of our younger people are defecting because he gives a much better party. He's the sexiest thing to show up in New Hope in forever, I'll grant you that. I'd like to have you in our church, but I've got to admit people your age won't be there."

No need to mention I don't have the church habit.

As we walk along the brick sidewalk, she points to Jo's Café. "That's where the business is done. Jo keeps the percolator on all day and people come in to solve the problems of the world, or the spats in their families, or to fix something in the community. City council is just a formality. Jo's is where people tell stories." She shifts her bag on her shoulder. "And lies," she adds, like she already knows I've told her a few.

Next door to Jo's is Mike's Hardware Store, equally critical to the town's survival, according to Rachel. "Sure, some of the men have started buying supplies at the Home Depot in Great Bend, but they feel guilty about it, and still stop at Mike's for daily needs. Us women, we stay loyal to Mike. We don't have to tell him what we need, only what we need done. He'll explain what to do and sell us the right doodads. If we live by ourselves or our husbands are out harvesting, he'll drop by and make the repair himself."

I wonder if Mike can obliterate bedbugs. Not that I would tell him if I saw one. Bet that news would spread through town faster than you can say exterminator.

We pass by the local barbershop, Feed-and-Seed, and Farmer's Bank, while Rachel tells me how hard it is for local merchants to hold on. "The town felt a surge thirty-some years ago; we were designated a Main Street City and had a Bicentennial committee. That's when we renovated the library and turned it into the arts center. But in a town this size, one or two people make everything happen, and when Jane Robinson passed on, a lot of the town's pride went with her. Now people are beginning to wonder if we can afford an arts center at all. That's where you come in," she says, as she shoos me down the steps to the church basement. "You have to convince them."

Jell-O is the major theme of the potluck to welcome me to town. No one else seems to notice, but it's pretty cute the way the rainbow of Jell-O dishes matches the rainbows on Noah's Ark drawings that decorate the wall of this church basement. Green Jell-O, which I'm told is made with 7-Up, shown off in a fancy antique cut glass bowl. Orange Jell-O, which everyone else seems to know is the "traditional" five-cup salad, made with cottage cheese, Cool Whip, fruit cocktail, and coconut. A bright red Jell-O cut in cubes, with marshmallows and mandarin oranges. And a yellow Jell-O molded in a Bundt pan, with shredded carrots and chopped pecans. The only way I can stomach Jell-O is spiked with vodka, but I'd sure like to play with this food and see if I couldn't make a cool, soft, jiggly sculpture.

The main dishes are much less colorful in shades of white and beige. It's easy to overlook the tuna casserole with fried onion rings on top and go straight to the desserts. The pies look especially yummy, not perfect like store-bought pies. I help myself to slices of apple and peach, scooping ice cream for the top before I realize I've offended the woman behind me who has baked the Coca Cola cake and is dying to give me the recipe. Like I cook. I heap a slab on my overfilled paper plate as she tells me to boil the Coke and cocoa together before mixing with flour and sugar using a wooden spoon, not a mixer. "Add the marshmallows last," she tells me. "They'll float on top."

I try not to gag. When she sees my expression, she says, "Bet you've never had Poke Coke either. Pork chops, onion soup mix, and ketchup, cooked in Coke. You can use caffeine-free if you want, but don't try Diet. It's horrible."

Yeah, right. You don't need to tell me that twice.

After dinner, Rachel claps her hands to get everyone's attention and then introduces me more formally to the group. The potluck is also a fundraiser to support my salary, which is pretty embarrassing. Like holding out a cup. I smile a lot so they'll think I'm worth it. What's weirder is that these women are paying to eat the food they cooked themselves. Repeating lies I've told her (and almost forgotten myself), she says, "We are so very happy to have Traci Ash here with us this year, as artist-in-residence. She has served in that same capacity at St. John the Divine Cathedral in New York City, and she's had major shows of her textile work in galleries throughout Manhattan. That'd be Manhattan, New York, not Manhattan, Kansas." The whole room kind of chuckles. Turning to me, she continues, "Traci, we are so proud of the program we've built here. We converted our library into an arts center, and that building has changed lives ever since. We know you'll continue the tradition by expanding our minds to the creative world beyond our humble town. As much as we're determined to raise money, what with the uncertainty of state funding for the arts, you may be the last artist-in-residence we ever have. To put it bluntly, some people in town think the arts center is a luxury we can no longer afford." She's looking straight at me as she says this, then turns back to the crowd. "Traci is going to change their minds. With your support, she's going to change our world. That said, we need to raise thirty thousand dollars before the end of the summer to ensure we can keep the arts center open."

"That's a lot of money," one of the two men grumbles, as if I'm not already freaked out about her promise of my magic.

Ignoring him, she asks if anyone would be interested in heading up the fundraising committee, which would mean gathering ideas and leading the efforts to execute them. You can hear mumbles of "Paula's wedding," "Bible camp," and "4-H Fair."

After a few minutes of feet shuffling and nervous coughing, a woman named Jennifer Chase stands up. "I can't lead the whole thing," she says, "but I'll lead an effort to make a thousand potholders. If we sell them at HarvestFest for five dollars, that'll be our first five thousand dollars. We can call our campaign 'Too Hot to Handle.' It's a start."

Everyone claps, and you can tell they're relieved someone offered to do it.

When Rachel arrives the next morning to talk some more about what I'm supposed to do, she spends the first ten minutes flitting around my kitchen asking how I'll adjust. Hiding my fears, I tell her the only thing I'm worried about is the lack of carryout (not mentioning the garbage rations don't look like they'll support dumpster diving). Rachel says to help myself to leftovers at every potluck, probably because she saw me pocket oatmeal cookies last night. "Bring your own Tupperware," she tells me, "and help yourself to a few meals." She opens a cabinet door to show me the containers.

Crazy! First these women cook dinner, then they pay to eat it, then they send the food home with me, who they pay to do art. Seems like win/win/win for me and lose/lose/lose for them. They don't know I've lied and probably can't teach art.

We're about to talk about the damn syllabus again when Rachel spots someone coming up the steps of my new home. A redhead—wearing a button-down white shirt, and loafers—looking totally serious despite her utterly wild hair.

"Oh goody, it must be Angelina Sprint. I heard she was in town." Rachel moves closer to the window to get a better look. Rachel already knows everything about Angelina Sprint—that she's from Philadelphia and that she's single, as well as that she's got this thing for Carnegie libraries.

"Good heavens. How do you know all that?" Angelina asks her, after long and way-too-personal introductions in which Rachel lets Angelina know I'm from the East Coast and single too. As if we'll become BFFs.

"We know, we know, we know," Rachel assures her. "There are no secrets here. This place lives on gossip; it's the chief commodity. Traded and bartered, saved up and spent with serious intention." Angelina laughs, which eggs on Rachel. "There *are* secrets. But you'll have to dig hard to find them, using a teaspoon as a shovel to avoid suspicions. On the outside at least, this place is as dull as it is flat. Everyone's good. Conventional. God-fearing. You might even think boring," she says, looking at me.

Rachel seems to believe it's important for us to understand the rules of the town, but Angelina's already moved on. Her eyes dart around the room, taking it all in.

"This building is incredible," Angelina says, as she rubs her hand on a brick wall like she was petting a kitten. She gets tears in her eyes and mascara starts running down her freckled face. "I loved being here. I was in New Hope for just a month, but I fell over-the-top, madly in love with this place in that one month," she sniffles. "When I got back to Philadelphia, I found my own Chestnut Hill library held its own magic, but this one was my first love. The one I could never forget."

She pulls herself together, clears her throat, and starts to skip down Memory Lane. "Over there was the children's room, with little chairs, and there was the juniors room, with slightly bigger chairs, and then the rest of library was for adults only. Over there were enormous tables, where grownups sat to read magazines and newspapers. I thought it was like the Three Bears and people played a kind of musical chairs. I imagined a bell might ring when you went from kiddie lit to young adult."

She walks over to the atrium, where there's a built-in desk. "I loved it when you checked out a book, you signed a card so everyone would always know you checked that book out, you were part of that book's history, with the due date stamped next to your name." She opens her notebook to the back page to demonstrate as she talks. "They slipped another little card with the due date into a little brown pocket of the book. The librarian sat behind the desk with this hinged board that she lifted to get in and out. The gate to her inner sanctum. A drawbridge."

Angelina doesn't seem capable of stopping herself. It's like she's meeting an old boyfriend she's never stopped loving. "Isn't it amazing how they built this place over a hundred years ago? How Andrew Carnegie decided to give money to make libraries grow on the Plains? If only the ghosts could talk."

"We swept out the ghosts when we renovated," Rachel interrupts. "You should've seen it when we first took it over. The library had been closed for ten years, and what a mess. I'll never forget the first time I jiggled the handles to let myself in. I got inside and before my eyes adjusted to the dark, something flew overhead."

We all look up at the ceiling like some flying object will still be there.

"I never did know whether it was a bat or a pigeon," she sighs. "But even then, I could see what could happen. I knew this would be the reception area, and that we could make studio spaces there, and a gallery there. A few hundred fundraisers and a few thousand hours of cleanup later and we'd done it. Better than a mortuary and funeral home, don't you think? That's what some people in town wanted to do with it. The Lubbers wanted to buy this building and make it a funeral home. Still would."

Angelina pulls out a notebook and starts scribbling, like she's recording every word, like she could get any smarter than she already seems to be. She's already told us how almost any city in the United States could get a library building from Andrew Carnegie in the early part of the twentieth century. Just for asking. Andrew Carnegie liked to help people who helped themselves, because his own folks were poor. His father couldn't make a living as a weaver, and his mother fixed old shoes to support the family in Scotland. They came to America, and he made a gazillion dollars, which he decided to give away to libraries around the world. The town needed to provide the ground and to promise operating funds, according to Angelina. Deals like that don't happen anymore.

Angelina wants to see everything, so I offer to show her my space downstairs. It's still neat and clean, which it won't be once I start working.

"Boy, was I scared of the basement when I was a girl," she tells me as we start down the creaky steps. "That's where the restrooms were, and you needed a special key to use them. Sometimes I could make the key work, sometimes I had to call the janitor, which was embarrassing. Once inside, I could never reach the light switch, and I was terrorized by the thought I could be locked in overnight. Mostly, I just held it all in. But the minute I decided to hold it all in, I had to go worse than ever. It's remarkable I survived the trauma and decided to be a librarian." Her cheeks get red when she laughs at herself.

When we come back upstairs, Rachel pulls out an old scrapbook and Angelina gets excited. Until she realizes it's about the renovation of the library as an arts center, not its being built in the first place.

"You wouldn't believe the war we had over this scrapbook," Rachel tells Angelina, as she cradles the scrapbook like it was a baby. "We'd appointed Elena to be historian, to keep the scrapbook, but she left in a huff when we insisted it be left here. Funny, all these years later, you're the first one to look at it. Probably was silly to fight so hard."

I watch over their shoulders as Rachel points out a newspaper article, announcing the decision to turn the library into an arts center, despite the offer from the funeral home "to take the building off the city's hands." There's also an article about "Bushel for the Arts," in which local farmers gave a bushel of hay to the new arts center when they took their crop to the Co-op. They raised $349 that way.

Rachel is embarrassed when Angelina notices she pasted her daily horoscope into the scrapbook, each and every day. "It was all so personal for me," she says. "And I thought the answers would be in the stars. That they would tell me when it was a good day to ask for money, and when it was best to lay low."

She's about to put the scrapbook away when Angelina sees a loose piece of paper. It's been crumpled and then smoothed, like someone changed her mind and decided not to throw it away. Angelina grabs it, telling us all it's written on ecru linen paper, before she reads it aloud:

July 4, 1976

What a life I've led. Over ninety years old now, and I do believe I've seen it all. They'll dedicate the new arts center today, in the library I worked so hard to build. The library that I'd thought would be my legacy. Now what do I have to show for my life? Five thousand pages of journal notes that I don't want anyone to see. Ever. Should I burn them? But that would be like cremating my body, which I cannot do. Give them to Green Valley or Prairie Hill? No one from New Hope would ever step foot in those towns. I wish Angelina could have them, but that wouldn't be fair. If she does find them, I hope she'll take what she needs, forgive me the rest, and remember I've always loved her. I must figure it out before I die.

GAYLE

I have to get my stubborn back; that's all there is to it. Grandpa always told me Kansans required a bucketful of stubbornness to survive what Mother Nature throws our way. He'd tell me about the Dust Bowl, how there was a "snuster" one March, the combination of a snowstorm and a duster. Twenty-one inches of mud fell from the sky, so no one dared leave home without a shovel. People stopped shaking hands because the static electricity was so strong it could knock a person down. They resorted to eating canned tumbleweeds.

"Remember you've got that dogged Kansas tenacity in your blood, girl. Don't let your mother turn you into a delicate tulip," he'd warn before we went off shopping. "Fine to dress up now and again and look pretty, but don't turn soft on me. Keep your stubborn in your back pocket and you won't have much need of a handkerchief."

I don't recognize the person I've become, the scared-y cat who jumps awake at the sound of her own husband's snoring at night. That same snoring used to provide such comfort. Now it sounds like the locomotive thunder that became the tornado that devastated our lives. Grandpa wouldn't be proud of me, that's for sure.

ANGELINA

B rett Duncan, editor of the *The New Hope Gazette,* is cordial if not friendly. Elena told me his 106-year-old grandmother remembers the opening of the library in 1912, so I stop by his office to request an introduction. Although I'd like to hang out at the library, it's the old library I want, not the messy arts center. Better to get on with my research and to see if I can uncover what my own grandmother knew.

"Grandma's a bit demented," he tells me after we've chatted about the heat. He's a handsome, sandy-haired, wholesome man, a little older than me. "Hard to keep her in the present tense," he apologizes. "She often slips back in time, telling us how the first ballot her mother ever cast was for the library, long before the Nineteenth Amendment." He provides this information as he stashes some papers in a folder. "The town fathers gave women the chance to vote on the library. From what I can tell, it was the Reverend Timkin who led the cause, deciding women should also vote on his Prohibition efforts."

I scribble down every word about women's suffrage, not sure how it relates to my dissertation but knowing it's a fascinating nugget that could find its way into the story. Brett must figure I'm serious, because he concedes it might be good for his grandmother to talk to someone else about the past and offers to take me.

He gives her a quick call, and we walk to her house together. On the way, sounding like the consummate reporter, he peppers me with questions about Philadelphia and offers, "Was there just once. For a newspaper convention. Long enough to race up the Rocky steps at the art museum." He raises his arms in a victory pose and hums the *Rocky* theme. If only he knew what a cliché this is to anyone from Philly.

The Duncan family home is a museum. Filled with antique furniture and family portraits. A collection of grandfather clocks with the loudest ticks I've ever heard, all slightly out of sync. Heavy curtains, and tatted lace doilies over the backs of every chair.

His grandmother is still in bed, but she's perfectly coiffed and has put on bright red lipstick to greet me; her face itself is as wrinkled as a dried up prune but brightly rouged and heavily powdered. She smells of a honeysuckle rose perfume. A tray of iced tea and Girl Scout cookies is on her nightstand, but she doesn't offer me refreshments. Brett introduces me simply as Angelina, then busies himself organizing her books. I can't discern his methodology—colors, shapes, alphabetically by author or title? He's trying to look busy so he can eavesdrop.

"Pull up a chair," his grandmother says, put out by the distraction of her grandson. Her voice is weak, but her words distinct. "Brett says you want to know everything about the library. Not that I can remember much these days. It was my father who was involved. Mother went to all the meetings but it was Father who cared." She stops to wipe her nose, and I'm afraid that's all she'll say. "Mostly, I remember Mother yelled at him about how much publicity he was giving to the library efforts, and he kept reminding her that even in 1890, when the town had nothing, they had 'mush and milk' fundraisers to build the church. 'You got your church,' he told her. 'I want my library.'"

She stops to sip her iced tea, still not offering any refreshments. She takes so long I'm afraid she's forgotten me. At her own slow pace, she puts her tea down on the doily, wiping the sweat off the glass.

"The day the library opened—my that was a day. There was a parade downtown, with floats and everything. They wanted still more money for books, so there were lots of contests. Turtle racing, fence-building, geese-picking, butter-churning. That's what they did in those days. They made everything a contest. Me, I won the chicken-calling contest. Junior Division. Beat out Brett's grandfather and I never let him forget it." She lets out a cackle so I can see her skill. "I won one dollar but my mother made me give it all back to the library fund. Boy, was I mad."

"Do you remember how much they raised that day?" I ask.

"No, it'd be in Amanda Sprint's diary, if anyone could ever get their hands on it. She was such a snob, too good for the rest of us, but she wrote down everything. She always bragged about that."

I try not to gasp at yet another reference to my grandmother's diary. "Do you know where it might be?" I ask, trying desperately to keep my voice level.

"I'm sorry, dearie. What did you ask? Come closer so I can see you."

I lean in so my face is a few inches from hers. Close enough to watch her expression turn from confusion to pure rage. Where did the gentle grandmother go?

"I hate you. Just because I'm old doesn't mean I've forgotten you, Amanda Sprint. You have some nerve coming here, thinking I'm going to forgive you for what you did to my mother. Burn that journal. You're going to roast in hell for what you did."

She tries to spit, but the dribble runs down her chin.

Brett looks at me, embarrassed. "I'm sorry," he says, putting his hand on my shoulder. "But you'll have to leave. She must have you confused with someone else."

"You must have me confused with my grandmother," I say, desperate to save this conversation.

She looks momentarily lost and then her eyes sharpen. "I know damn good and well who you are. But I don't know what the hell you're doing here. You go home and forget this place. Bad blood. You're undoubtedly a whore too. Why don't you go back to Phillydelphia where you belong."

TRACI

Fortunately, when Angelina shows up at some ungodly hour, I'm already up and dressed since I didn't sleep worth a damn on that cold, hard, ammonia-smelly floor where I've been lying down at night so as not to contaminate the pristine bed. Hopefully, Angelina won't make a habit of dropping by so early, although I can use any friend I can get. She glances at the quilts and pretends interest in my wall hanging knit with cassette tapes, but I can't tell if she gets it. Says it reminds her of a show of outsider or visionary art she saw at the Philadelphia Art Museum, all done by self-taught artists. She's nice about it though, so when she tells me her next stop is to see the ruins of the Prairie Hill Carnegie Library, I ask to ride along, figuring it'll be a great place to uncover material for my artwork.

"Maybe we can find a bottle of wine on the way?" I suggest. She shoots me a look like I'm a drunk, because it's so damn early. "Not for now," I tell her before she gets the wrong idea. "I just can't sleep here. A little wine might take the edge off my jitters so maybe I can get a decent night's sleep." She looks like she could belt back a bottle or two herself, but I don't tell her that.

"Wine might be hard to come by," she tells me. "My father used to laugh about the liquor laws. Do you know there was a time when the airlines couldn't even serve drinks in the skies over Kansas?" she asks. "Flight attendants used to pick up glasses in Kansas City and start pouring again in Denver."

She waits while I lock the front door.

"You know I'm not much of a drinker myself, but a bottle of wine sounds good."

Just my luck there's not a single shop on our twenty-minute drive. About the most interesting thing we see are gargantuan, sixteen-legged insect-looking pieces of metal, a whole block long, that stretch out across the fields. They look like Space Invaders for sure, or a modern sculpture. "Those are for irrigation," Angie tells me. "Sprinklers. For watering the crop."

Prairie Hill is devastated. You wouldn't even know it was the town if someone hadn't propped up a cardboard sign with the name scrawled across it. The only thing standing is the front entrance of the library. Everything else looks like Ground Zero did before they hauled it away. Angelina isn't as tough as me and breaks down sobbing, so I turn away to give her some space. The place gives me the willies, but like they say, one woman's trash is another girl's treasure, and I've found my gold mine. Luckily, I long ago established the habit of never taking two steps without my backpack.

Angelina pulls herself together, her face still red as a watermelon and smeared with mascara, and starts snapping photos of her library, about a million of them. The empty windows frame a different scene of devastation depending on where you're standing. Devastation and the most beautiful sky you've ever seen. Angelina doesn't see all that, though. She's totally caught up in that one wall.

At least a thousand people must've gone through this trash, but my nose for garbage leads me to one foundation that hasn't been picked over. Under petrified apple cores and slimy banana peels, I find a silver fork piercing a wooden cutting board. A powerful statement, like a sculpture you'd see at some ritzy uptown gallery. Iron pieces that look like antiques are a total mystery, maybe kitchen tools or farm equipment. One is heart shaped, with a wooden handle at the bottom. The other looks like a tree with spikes coming off the spine. I build a little monument using the fork sculpture perched on top of a screen-less TV and try to imagine what I'll do with the heart and tree when I get home.

"What did you find?" Angelina asks, having snuck up behind me. She reaches out to take the heart, and I have to let her have it. "You know what this is?" she asks. "It's a rug beater. Grandmother had one. And that thing you're holding is a corncob dryer. They belong in a museum."

"No way. Finders keepers." I lay my claim and reach for the rug beater.

"You're looting," she says, with the sternest of looks. "It's a special kind of evil to steal from people who've lost everything," she preaches. She'll tell me I'm going to roast in hell. When she turns back to the car, I slip the treasures into my backpack.

By the time we get back to the arts center, the No Guilt Quilters have already gathered for our first session. I'll never remember who is who. All overweight, all wearing stretch pants and baggy shirts, a few variations in hair color but mostly gray and brown. A dozen faces staring at me, like I'm supposed to have something to say. Where I come from, there are never so many white women in one place. Strange how I feel so different here where everyone's skin color matches my own; I'm used to being the one white chick in the midst of a city of colors.

When they pull out their projects, I see these women are all great seamstresses but their choices of fabric are dismal: American flags, spiders, and cats. It's amazing how they can put so much time and energy into such crap. Rachel has a decent sense for design, and a woman named Jennifer dyes her own fabrics, but the rest are using synthetics that itch when you touch them. I do better by picking up scraps even the Salvation Army can't sell. Stalling for time, I ask them to tell me about their quilts, the way that reporter from *The Village Voice* asked me to tell him about my work. No one responds. Seems like about an hour of dead silence until I put my head down to cut my own fabric.

What they want to do is gossip. It's only been a week since they were together, but they're eager to talk about the aftermath of the tornado in Prairie Hill. Mostly, they talk about how Sheryl Crow donated a Mercedes to Joplin, Missouri to help rebuild the school where she once taught, and how Brad Pitt gave half a million dollars because he once lived there. "Too bad nobody from Prairie Hill never made good," a woman in a red flannel shirt says. "Nobody wants to help that sorry town rebuild. Already, nobody remembers they had a tornado too."

When they turn their attention to me again, their questions are personal, not about my artwork. *Where are your people from? Are you Italian? You look Italian. Except you're too skinny to be Italian. I love Italian food. Aren't you scared to live in New York City? I know I'd be scared. I won't even go to Topeka unless Corey comes along. But then I didn't ride an escalator until I was eighteen.* They get so busy asking questions and adding their own comments, they don't even notice I don't answer. Three hours seem more like three days but eventually they do leave, muttering how glad they were to meet me and looking forward to Thursday.

I manage to grab a cheese sandwich before the teens show up for a yet-unnamed art class. Sylvia, the leader of the group of four, has long black hair, wears a tight jersey floral dress and cowboy boots, but is best distinguished by the F-U-C-K tattoo across the knuckles of her left hand. "We're here as punishment," she announces. "We got kicked out of band, and they won't let us just hang out in the afternoon. Treat us like babies."

"We're 'runners,'" Zed announces. Zed, a way too unfortunate name since his face is covered with zits. His hair hangs over his forehead, trying to hide them, and there's one on his neck that he's picked raw. "Ran away from home, and if we run away from the foster family, we'll end up in juvy."

They think I don't get it. If only they knew.

"You'd run away too if you had toxic parents," Sylvia tells me. "Ours were insane religious fanatics who made us fast for days. Drink nothing but tomato juice and water. Forced us to hold anti-abortion signs at rallies when we were four years old. They loved giving the youngest kid the Dr. Seuss one: 'A Person's a Person, No Matter How Small.'"

"Or 'Save the Human Babies,' Zed says. "If we whined about how hot we were or tried to sneak off to sit in the shade, we got whipped until we bled."

Okay, maybe some kids did have it worse than I did. Being ignored might've been better than what they've been through.

"Them guys are our foster sibs," Sylvia says, pointing with her thumb to the clean-cut kid and the pony-tailed blonde trying her damnedest to look hip. "Sam and Madonna."

"And we're bored to d-e-a-t-h," Zed adds. "I mean we were plenty bored in Hays, but here is hell. They won't even let us have iPods unless we make C's in school. It's like we're gonna suffocate."

All four look to be about fifteen. Who would take these kids on? People like the couple who raised me, who didn't consider the consequences of taking on another child?

They stand staring at me, lined up in a row, arms crossed across their chests, hands tucked under their armpits, chewing gum like it's a weapon. Daring me to interest them.

"Shall we try to get to know each other today? Like try to figure out a great project?" I still don't have a definite plan and sound like some impotent teacher who nobody will like no matter how hard she tries.

Sylvia shrugs, giving assent for all of them. "You go first," she says.

"Okay. My name is Traci Ashe."

"Hey, Traci Ashe? Like Trash? We'll call you Trash."

It's taken Sylvia one split second to see through my disguise. "I'm from New York City; I like to make art out of things other people throw away. I know it sounds crazy, but I love making weird pieces out of garbage. Junk."

"Do you ever steal stuff?" Sylvia asks.

"Of course not," I say, although this is not entirely true. "In New York, you find stuff on the sidewalks, especially in alleys. Here, I guess you have to look harder."

Their faces open up for a nanosecond, and I run through the opening like a cat on fire. "Do you want to see my newest project? It's easier to show you the weird way my brain works." I take them to my worktable where the cassette tape wall hanging is laid out. "See, everybody's now throwing these away and downloading music instead, so I wanted to figure out what to do with the discards. I unwound them all first and then started knitting. Then, to get in the right spirit, I downloaded this exact music and put it on my iPod so I can listen while I work. There's a little Bob Dylan, Beatles, Michael Jackson in this one. So I want the overall piece to reflect that. I'm trying to figure out what to add. Maybe some denim for Bob, tweed for the Beatles, satin for Michael."

"Yeah, well what're *we* gonna do?" Sylvia asks, her eyes darting around the room. "You're supposed to be teaching *us* art."

"I saw this cool video on YouTube, and I thought maybe you'd like to knit with noodles." I swear I don't know why this comes out of my mouth.

"Right." Sylvia now directs a stare right through me. "Macaroni art. Like we did in kindergarten. Next you're gonna teach us how to Scribble Scrabble."

"Did you always know you wanted to be an artist?" Sam asks. He's a teddy bear kind of a guy, the only one not daring me to impress.

"Truthfully? Didn't have a clue. Maybe still don't. But it's pretty cool to play with junk." I pick up my project and knit another few rows of cassette tape, my clicking needles providing the only sound while Sylvia and Zed stare.

"We want to be musicians," Sylvia announces. "All of us. But not band music, not those Sousa marches the school band plays. Rap. Hip hop."

"I want to scratch old vinyls, but their folks say no way," Zed says, cracking his knuckles for emphasis.

"We want to make music videos, post them online, go viral," Sylvia continues, hands on her hips, daring anyone to disagree.

"Hey, what if we could make instruments out of junk?" I ask, suddenly inspired.

"You're fucking kidding, right?" says Sylvia.

I want to slap the girl. "I'll bet we could figure it out," I say instead, forcing myself to breathe.

"Cool." Sam dares to break away from Sylvia. Madonna curls her ponytail around her fingers, over and over again.

"Would you *please* take us seriously?" Sylvia steps forward to gain control of the situation. "If we're gonna be pros, we gotta have good instruments."

"You know I found some great stuff over at Prairie Hill."

I show them the rug beater and the corncob dryer, hoping they won't squeal on me. "If we could figure out how to get there, we could get more."

"I can drive," says Zed.

"No way," I reply. "We're doing this above the law."

It's tempting though. I'll bet I could get this kid to drive me anywhere.

"I'm legal," he says. "Been driving since I was fourteen. In Kansas, that's legal."

Hot damn! I've just found wheels.

When they leave, I realize the rug beater is gone too.

GAYLE

Looting in Prairie Hill. As if there's anything left to loot. We've been through every inch of our land, even using a metal detector, desperate to find anything we might have overlooked. It's the scum of the earth who'd come in now, looking for remnants.

Vic called again tonight, and I tried to sound like a normal mother. I can tell he's worried about me. He tried to be cheerful, telling me how well things are going between him and Jill, how much support they've been able to give each other since both have lost their childhood homes. "We're going to build new lives," he promised. "It feels like we lost a huge chunk of our past, but now we're determined to make every day count."

Mark's obviously told him what a basket case I've become. Vic kept telling me how brave I've always been. "Remember when you made a game out of losing electricity? How you lit candles and told us to pretend we were pioneers?"

I do remember those nights. We played the same game my mother always played with us when the lights went out. Marathon games of Crazy Eights. I wasn't afraid, but then nothing really awful had happened to me then.

Now I know how fast the world can turn inside out, upside down, and backwards. I worry Vic could have a car accident, Mark might get prostate cancer, I could trip on the uneven bricks of Main Street and fracture a hip.

I know horrific things happen to pretty good people.

ANGELINA

When I call Brett to thank him and ask for another meeting with his grandmother, he tells me we'll have to wait until she's feeling better. I'm impatient and wonder how long I can afford to hang out and wait. Still, I don't want to terrorize a centurion. Sensing my disappointment, Brett offers to introduce me to Jennifer and Frank Chase. "Frank comes from a family that's been here since before God," he tells me. "He can tell you stories. They're cooking dinner for me tonight. Always enough for one more."

Frank meets me at the door wearing a denim shirt and jeans. He's big, as in 250 pounds, round and jolly, with a crew cut, not the least bit suave and artsy like his wife. For the first time since I got here, I've put on a linen skirt and even painted my toenails. Definitely overdressed for the occasion. Noticing my discomfort, he says, "Pretty. Not to worry. We have an apron, so you can still churn the ice cream." He hands me a vintage red-checked pinafore, with rickrack and a heart-shaped pocket, offers a glass of wine, and puts me to work cranking a big wooden White Mountain churn, which is easy at first but turns into hard work after a few minutes. It's evident I need more Chicken Fat push-ups.

As he peppers the steaks, he plays the cordial host. "Brett said you're here to find out about your grandmother, but he didn't tell me your grandmother's name."

"Amanda Sprint. Amanda Beacon Sprint."

"Well, I'll be damned." He stops mid-shake and looks at me, as if searching for a resemblance. I wonder if he'll see it and react the way Brett's grandmother did.

"Did you know her?" I stop churning, waiting for his response.

"Well, I'll be damned," he repeats. "Sure, I knew her. You can almost see her farm from here. I've been trying to buy it for years, but Thad Hopkins won't sell. Must be waiting for one of those conglomerates to make him an offer that'll support him for life."

I tell him I've tried several times to go out there, but keep getting lost.

"Jen will take you," he assures me. "She can introduce you. Thad's pretty rough around the edges, lives like a hermit, but he likes women well enough. If you sweet-talk him, he might let you look around. Not that there's much to see. He's let the property deteriorate." Frank looks over his shoulder to make sure Jennifer isn't listening. "People wonder what he's doing over there, like whether he's growing weed or making meth. He's just weird though. Not dangerous."

While we set the table, Frank and Jennifer tell me about their courtship in DC, when Frank was interning at the Department of Agriculture and Jennifer was taking art classes at the Corcoran. "We met when she dumped an enormous bowl of green pea soup on me at the Smithsonian cafeteria one day, then made me take the shirt off so she could wash it and return it. To this day, I don't know whether it was an accident or she just wanted a date," he grins and leans down to kiss her on the top of her head. "Or maybe she wanted my shirt for a quilt," he says, as he points to a charming small wall hanging of multiple hearts, the blue heart in the middle with a conspicuous green blob.

"Well, I can tell you for sure it would've been an accident if I'd known you would give up a secure government career in the nation's capital for a struggling ranch in Podunk," she teases him back, with an edge to her voice. "You told me you had a B.S. but I didn't realize it was a bullshit degree. Literally. Earned by studying the chemical composition of cow crap."

They have rehearsed their banter many times, perhaps less light-heartedly with each telling. Their story is the story of my parents, for they too met on the East Coast. The difference being that my mother refused to move back to the farm in Kansas, and their bantering turned to bickering, which turned into World War III.

Even the memory of the manure cologne doesn't deter me from digging into a huge T-bone. It might be the best meat I've ever eaten. Juicy homegrown tomatoes on the side, baked potatoes with sour cream and chives, and a salad layered with iceberg lettuce, Cheddar cheese, green peas, and mayonnaise. All topped off with a glass of Cabernet Sauvignon. I may be poor, but I'm eating well tonight.

Brett passes on the wine but shows off his connoisseurship, none-theless. "I am noting the rich marble that permeates this hunk of meat and tasting charred boldness, with caramel undertones." He's impressive at impersonating a true snob. "This from your own private stock?" he asks, knifing his steak and waiting for the blood to ooze out.

"Yep, we're still growing two or three heifers a year for ourselves, letting them graze rather than sending them off to be finished," Frank answers.

"Finished?" I imagine cows wearing white gloves in a receiving line as if they were in finishing school. Sprint Print used to provide invitations for those families.

"'Finished' is a fancy word for fattening the cows up," Frank tells me. "Ranchers send their herds off to feedlots to eat corn for their last hundred or so days on earth. Keep them in restrictive quarters so they don't burn calories wandering around. Here, we've got a hundred acres of alfalfa, two hundred acres of brome grass, and two hundred acres of hay with capacity to run up to six hundred cows and heifers. Lots of room to absorb the shit."

"Shall we change the subject before we ruin this woman's appetite?" Brett asks. "She's a city girl."

For dessert, there's our rich and intensely strawberry homemade ice cream. Instead of Elena's three bites, I have three scoops and taste every one. Until now, my favorite flavor has been Gadzooks! Blanc— having peanut butter brownies, chocolate chunks, and a rich caramel swirl—but it's dropped to second place in my palate.

"This is delicious," I gush. "What's the secret?"

"Fresh cream from the cow a few hours ago," Frank says. "Eggs laid this morning."

Brett pumps his fist and squeezes his biceps, indicating churning is the secret.

"Jell-O," Jennifer laughs. "Strawberry Jell-O." Seeing my disbelief she goes to the kitchen and brings back a well-worn recipe and the empty Jell-O box.

We move our overstuffed bodies to overstuffed living room chairs, and I decide I've had enough food talk. A splendid free meal, but it's not what I came for.

"Tell me about my grandmother," I beg Frank. "I'm especially look-ing for stories about the library. She told me she was involved." I don't tell him about the reaction of Brett's grandmother but can't be sure Brett hasn't already filled him in.

Frank settles into a deep easy chair after he's refilled everyone's glasses. "To tell you the truth, everything I know about your grand-mother's involvement with the library I learned at her funeral. Until then, she was just an old lady who didn't like company. My father made me go to the funeral. Only six of us were there. Even your dad didn't come."

"Mother wouldn't let him," I mumble, realizing this doesn't make either one of them look good.

Brett picks up a seed catalog to peruse and Jennifer a small piece of needlework; they're not that interested. Still, I can't stop now.

"What did you learn?" I beg Frank to continue.

"Reverend Joseph officiated and he seemed to have a hard time coming up with good things to say about Amanda Sprint for the past eighty or so years. So he went back. Way back. Eighty years back. To talk about how this library wouldn't be here if it weren't for Amanda Sprint, and Amanda Sprint wouldn't have stayed if it weren't for the library." He pauses to drink his wine. "You know, I didn't get that until recently. Like now I know Jen would never stay here if it weren't for that damn arts center. This place simply isn't good enough for her, and it's her consolation prize for living here."

I look over, expecting Jennifer to disagree, but she doesn't. Instead, she says, "What can I say? It's the one place I feel accepted. If you don't go to church in this town, you don't have friends."

"More about my grandmother?" I beg.

"The Reverend went on and on about how even as a boy he'd heard how dedicated Amanda was when it came to the library. Even though she always had her baby on her hip, she'd hound people for donations. Got so people would cross the street to avoid her when they saw her coming. Like they avoid Jennifer now."

Brett starts to chuckle, but Jennifer interrupts, slurring her words a bit. "Brett, I've been meaning to ask. Don't you want to make a contribution toward our artist-in-residence? Traci is going to be great, but our membership drive is falling short and so is our cash flow. We're not sure how we're going to pay her. I've just volunteered to head a committee to make a thousand potholders to sell but it's not nearly enough."

Brett reminds her he's already met his pledge this year. He's uncomfortable at being solicited, even after such an enormous dinner.

"Good. We'll be asking for more," Jennifer assures him. "For money. Newspaper space. Blood, sweat, and tears. We're not above a bit of male prostitution. For the cause."

"If you want to see how they raised money for the library, hang around the Guilty Quilters," Frank tells me. "Nothing's changed in a century when it comes to the way women manipulate their men."

I'm afraid of starting a row, the way I often unintentionally instigated arguments between my parents, so start to take my leave. I've gotten a glimpse of my grandmother and will try to find a way to get more from Frank.

Brett says he'll run me back to Elena's, but I tell him I brought my car. Although I wouldn't mind spending a few extra minutes with him, I certainly don't want him to think I'm too stupid to hold my liquor.

"No, I'm taking you," he insists. "No argument."

I look over to Jennifer and she shrugs. "Better go," she says. "He doesn't look the part, but he's a leading member of the Women's Christian Temperance Union. I can bring you back here tomorrow to pick up your car."

Both Frank and Jennifer are looking slightly tipsy, but I really am fine. It's not like I'll be negotiating Philadelphia traffic. Frank puts his arm around my shoulder and says, "Better go with him. Before long, they'll bring back Prohibition if Brett has his way."

Jennifer shoots him a look and mimes zipping up her lips.

"Don't ruin a wonderful evening," Brett tells Frank. "As for you, young lady, don't be stubborn. Get in the car."

TRACI

The hard floor is totally uncomfortable for sleeping, but I'm grateful for its chill since the weather has been sweltering all day. I keep thinking about how much this place means to these women and how hard they work to keep it open. They spent all morning trying to decide what to make for the bazaar and how to price crocheted doodads. Rachel was here until midnight poring over the books, and I wonder if they have enough to pay me for the rest of the summer. It'd be pretty crappy if they got me here, clear across the country, with no way out. I'm also freaked by how I'm supposed to teach the Troubled Teens. If I'm honest, they remind me of myself, especially Sylvia. Unloved and defiant. Doesn't mean I want to hang around them.

A bird right outside my window repeats itself, over and over again, in cruel, high-pitched accusations. "No love, no love, no love" is what I hear, more annoying than a cackling ring tone on a cellphone.

Realizing I'm biting my cuticles, I get up, determined to make something of the night. Maybe start a new piece? Looking at the gigantic worktable, I should be thrilled to have the space to make something of scale. Time and place to work, a dream come true, but I don't have a single idea. Rachel told me there's supposed to be a supply budget, but not yet, not until they figure out their cash flow crisis. She asked if there was anything she could scrounge for me, and I told her no, the only thing I want is a camera. That's the one thing I couldn't find on the sidewalks of New York and it looks next to impossible to find something like that in the garbage here. With a camera, I could transfer images to fabric, giving them a whole new dimension.

Surface design reminds me of screen-printing, which leads me to potato printing, which could work for both the Quilters and the Teens. The Quilters can make napkins, placemats, and dishtowels. Even potholders if they want. The teens can make t-shirts. Milton's General Store was selling "big fat spuds" for $3.49 in five-pound sacks. Problem solved.

Rachel left me apples in the fridge, and since I don't have potatoes, I spend the rest of the night carving out shapes in apples, blending colors from the tempera paints someone left behind, using a toothpick to add details. By morning I've made a whole roll of wrapping paper covered with geometric shapes. Sliced in half one way, with the seeds taken out, the apples make circles, all of them slightly different. Sliced the other way, the apples look like apples. Or even hearts. I make a few of them into hearts, just for the helluvit.

You'd think I was a genius the way they fall all over themselves when I announce we'll be doing potato printing. Sally saw an article in some Martha Stewart home-decorating magazine, so she is impressed, and Jennifer says all the cool, young urban hipsters are doing it. She saw hundreds of examples when she visited DC last month. Pillowcases in high-end shops caught her eye, and she's now inspired to make some herself after she whips out a few potholders.

We start by tearing a pale blue sheet into four-inch squares. Then the gals (as they call themselves) start carving potatoes. They all begin with hearts. They always begin with hearts, like they own all the love in the world. It's interesting though, how each heart takes on its own personality. No two hearts alike. Then they get brave, a little creative, making stars, then other geometric shapes. Once they have half a dozen stamps apiece, we get out the tempera paint, and they concentrate on applying color. The pieces turn the most incredible shades of teal and violet, depending on the intensity of the application.

When they've made a few hundred pieces, we put them in the middle of the room and pass around a kaleidoscope as we change the position of the fabric to see the infinite possibilities. The women start giggling, almost hysterical in their excitement over the changing patterns. Like I've been dealing drugs instead of creativity. Twenty minutes after the class is supposed to be over, they're still on their hands and knees, rearranging, arguing about the differences between magenta, merlot, and fuchsia. Moving onto the blues and greens, Angelina says, "This reminds me of a Renoir painting at the Barnes Museum. Called 'La Prairie,' it always reminded me of Kansas." Suddenly I'm transported, like time travel, back to the days I sat in front of those Monet paintings at MoMA, daydreaming, wishing I could be somewhere calm and quiet and peaceful.

When they get ready to leave, Rachel pats my shoulder and says, "You really are a miracle worker. Now if we could get more people involved. We're going to need the numbers to show how good you are, or ..." Her voice trails off before she can tell me again how dicey my situation is.

Because they stick around so long, I hardly have time to scarf down a peanut butter and jelly sandwich before the Troubled Teens arrive for their afternoon class.

"You're bullshitting us, right, bitch?" Sylvia says when I tell her the potato-printing plan, after they've defiantly thrown their backpacks on the floor. Her playmates shuffle their feet when I glare at her. "Man, I told you being here was our punishment. You know we hate you, right?" she asks, to make sure there's no question about it.

"You can participate or not," I tell her. "Printing is really big in SoHo, but maybe it's too far out for you guys. Too cool for Kansas kids."

That gets her attention, and she reaches for a knife to begin carving, just as I'm wondering if she should be allowed to hold sharp objects.

I show them photos from a fashion magazine, how we can make patches for clothes, and soon they are totally into carving skull and crossbones, spiders, swastikas, and what are supposed to be dragons. When they run out of potatoes, Sylvia helps herself to celery in my refrigerator, slices off the bottom, to make a brilliant design of concentric circles. As for printing, they'll have nothing to do with the pastel fabrics the Quilters left but want to do everything in black, which is the last piece of fabric in my stash. Not easy for the colors to show up, so I bring out bleach I found in the laundry room, and they have a great time "painting" with it. They would. Bleaching color out of fabric is the desecration that would appeal.

GAYLE

I still can't believe I'm living in New Hope. Literally adding insult to injury. I can count on one hand the number of times I've been here since our high school basketball games and can't help but wish Cousin Mary lived anywhere else on earth. It's not like everyone hasn't tried to be kind, but that smugness prevails. They're such a *tight* community, all caught up in their activities. Church, Scouts, 4-H, that arts center they're so damn proud of. I can't even walk into Jo's without everyone staring at me like I'm a Martian.

Prairie Hill was tight too. Mark keeps saying we'll be tight again. I wonder if we'd have been any more gracious about accepting Hopians if they'd been devastated instead of us. We would have taken in Mary and her kids. They're family. And we would have invited everyone to church. But, if I'm honest, we'd have stared too.

ANGELINA

I tossed and turned all night—disturbed by a cat in heat howling for her mate, a creaky sound in the attic, and then the distant whoo-whoo of a train whistle—and tried to uncover clues to Brett's character. The hints were few. He doesn't drink. A fundamentalist Christian? Or a recovering alcoholic? He has a story; I want to know it.

Now that it's morning, it's hotter than Hades, so I decide to take advantage of Elena's offer to use her personal library. Which is air conditioned.

I lay out my set of colored index cards to see if I can put order into my notes on Andrew Carnegie. Devoting myself to the first chapter—the role of libraries in promoting democracy in the early twentieth century—I scribble notes on how libraries started as an urban phenomenon and were seen as a way to combat new social and moral problems such as crime, alcoholism, gambling, prostitution, and juvenile delinquency. Copying directly from George S. Bobinski's excellent book, published by the American Library Association, I note details to demonstrate what the landscape looked like before Andrew Carnegie stepped in, when libraries were located in the nooks and crannies of small towns:

> "A millinery shop in Clay Center, Nebraska; a decrepit wooden shack in Dillon, Montana; the hospital in Dunkirk, New York; a printing shop at Grandview, Indiana; the balcony office of a drugstore in Malta, Montana; a building housing the horses of the

fire department at Marysville, Ohio; a physician's reception room in Olathe, Kansas; an old, abandoned church at Onawa, Iowa; a room in the opera house of Sanborn, Iowa; three small rooms over a meat market at Vienna, Illinois—all were typical examples of the ingenuity of townspeople in their efforts to establish local libraries."

The research intimidates me. Bobinski has discovered so much, but he still hasn't told the story I want to tell. How did the communities do it? Yes, they wrote to Carnegie, and yes, Carnegie sent the money, but who was responsible for writing those letters and overseeing construction? What was happening way out here?

When I look up, I catch sight of a biography of Carrie Nation on Elena's bookshelf. Carrie Nation, the six-foot-tall, tomahawk-wielding, temperance crusader who destroyed bars across Kansas in her battle against the Demon Rum. She described herself as a bulldog running along at the feet of Jesus, barking at what He doesn't like, crying out against the Devil's hand. Her slogan was "Smash, women, smash!" which she cried as she raided saloons, shattering bottles and demolishing furniture. Her own marketing guru, she trademarked her name as Carry A. Nation for its value as a temperance slogan. Changed her name from Carrie to Carry to make it work.

Suddenly the day's almost over, and I haven't accomplished a single thing in regards to my dissertation. Okay, maybe some background information, but nothing concrete. No progress. Tomorrow I'll measure the rooms of the library and see if they match the template of the other Carnegies. Tomorrow will be better, I promise myself, as I open my laptop to check my email.

My email is as listless as the day is hot. Mostly spam, offers of insurance and Viagra. I open one by mistake and realize it's not spam at all. Instead a notice from my credit card company saying they've lowered my credit card limit to $3000. Due to my change in employment. How can they lower your credit card limit at the exact moment you need it most? Haven't I paid my bill in full for the last twenty-odd years? Did my mother really call them to report my "change in employment"? How else could they know? Most important, how long can I live on $3,000? Which is probably now $2,000. Elena's daughter will be back in two weeks, and I'll need to find a place to stay.

Heat or not, I go out for a walk, this time to Grand, which parallels Main, and is hardly thriving. Desolate would be the word. It's not a slum like you'd see in Philly. No trash. No graffiti. The bright late afternoon sunlight gives the whole street a bleached look, even though a layer of dust covers every horizontal surface. Windows are boarded up and buildings in need of paint. You expect to see a cow's skull in the middle of the road with vultures circling overhead.

A woman could lose her mind here. Away from her loved ones, in pursuit of a crazy dream, a woman could forget who she is and what she's meant to do. I have enormous empathy for the women who came out in covered wagons, risking drought and disease, in pursuit of better lives for their children. My foremothers were among them. Why didn't they all go mad? There's so little here now, but back then, there was nothing.

TRACI

The Troubled Teens show up late, but they already have a plan. They want to drive to the Walmart Supercenter in Great Bend for "art supplies," as in more fabric for potato printing. Like I believe that. They're determined to take me along and since Sylvia's t-shirt reads, "Give Peace a Chance," I pretend they're trying to make a fresh start. After all, in the end, they'd been pretty proud of their printmaking.

Besides, I'm desperate to get out of town to do some shopping myself, to check out cameras, and to get personal items. In NYC, I never had a second thought about buying tampons from Mohammed, a man from a country where women are stoned for the immodesty of showing their ankles. Still, I cannot bear to show my personal purchases to Mr. Jack at Jack's General Store on Main Street, New Hope, Kansas, USA—Mr. Jack, who wouldn't even let me buy a tube of toothpaste without commenting, "So you're a Crest girl." This place is so damn personal.

"Will Walmart even be open?" I ask, noting it's already 5 p.m. and remembering how dead New Hope becomes at dusk. "We roll up the sidewalks," is how Rachel put it.

"Oh yeah, Walmart's open, like, 24/7," Zed says. "It's, like, bigger than this whole town. You can get your tires changed, if you want. My mom used to get her eyeglasses fitted after she shopped for beer. You can even get your hair colored," he says, reaching over to pick up a strand from my head, examining my roots. "Wait till you see."

"Do they have cameras?" I ask.

"Sure," Sam says. "They've got hundreds of them."

"Why do you want a camera anyway?" Sylvia asks. "Use your smart phone."

No need to tell her I don't own even a stupid phone. No one to call. We all pile into the pickup, Sylvia's low-cut jeans giving me full view of the butterfly tattoo on her bare buttock, with "BUTTFLY" in calligraphy, as if we would miss the pun. She, Madonna, and I climb into the back of the truck, our seats made of hay. Scratchy, smelly hay.

"Quit your bitchin'," Sylvia says, when I mention my discomfort. "You got your clothes on, donchya? This whole state lost their virginity slobbering in a hayloft."

She takes out her cellphone to play some game, ignoring the world, except for flipping the bird at a car sporting a bumper sticker reading: "Choose Life: Your Mom Did." If only Zed were as concerned about my life. He whips the truck around curves, as if to call attention to the roadside memorials of crosses and flowers marking the death spots of other carefree and careless teens.

Terrified, I distract myself like I always do when I'm scared shitless. Try to make art in my head. Reflect on the spiked corncob dryer and realize it could make a cool candelabra with votive candles from Walmart and some kind of non-flammable wire that I can knit to decorate the tree. Cement it into a flowerpot to keep it upright.

Walmart is guarded by a decrepit old woman who calls me "Ma'am" when I ask where the toilet is. I need to ask because, like the kids warned me, Walmart is its own city. A city bigger than New Hope and full of oversized people wearing plaid Bermuda shorts and t-shirts, who turn blue because it's suddenly freezing. It's like being inside one gigantic refrigerator, with kids screaming for Ding Dongs.

The entrance is stacked floor to ceiling with thirty-two-roll packages of toilet paper, more toilet paper than I've used in my entire life.

Probably more toilet paper than on the entire island of Manhattan. Makes me remember my roommate who used to restrict us to one roll a week, or buying a single roll from Mohammed, or the times I grabbed a roll or two from a public restroom when they weren't chained down. I'd stick them in my oversize backpack—not stealing, more like taking a doggie bag when I couldn't finish my lunch.

By the time I've finished my business, I've lost the teens, so I head for the aisle marked feminine hygiene. Sanitary napkins. What a weird term for women's blood diapers. There's a whole street's worth of shelves of nothing but ways to catch the monthly waste. Regular/super/ultra absorbency. More space devoted to them than exists in Mohammed's entire store. I grab what I need before colliding with Sylvia, who's checking out early pregnancy tests. She looks quickly away, then tells me it's part of a class assignment. They have to pretend they're pregnant, then have a child. They'll carry an egg around for a week and pretend it's a baby.

"Supposed to scare us into celibacy," she says, rolling her eyes. "What. Ever."

She can't get away from me fast enough, and in her rush bumps into a woman from about two centuries ago, a woman wearing a plaid full-length dress and black cap. "Mennonite," Sylvia mutters disdainfully.

The fabric aisle is abysmal; this must be the source for the No Guilt Quilters. No subtlety whatsoever. Everything is primary colors, like clown clothing, or sweet pastels. Nothing as charming as the vintage fabric hanging as quilts in my room, that's for sure.

Beyond the bolts of cloth are guns. The sign says you must be sixteen or older to buy air rifles, eighteen to buy pistols. Thank God. Surely they require ID so the Troubled Teens can't buy. Although they could if they wanted to. They'd find a way.

Looking for votive candles, I get lost in the wax. There must be a thousand different kinds of candles but not a single votive. I always thought when I could afford to shop in stores, rather than scrounge stuff from the sidewalk, I would make better art. Have more options. Maybe not so much.

There may not be votive candles, but there are cameras galore. The hardest decision is whether to hope for the compact one that will fit into my jeans pocket, no matter how tight, or the one that gives me better picture quality. A nice clerk helps me find one that provides both zoom and panoramic vision. The change in perspective is more thrilling than a roller coaster. With it, I could get awesome shots of the tornado debris and capture both scale and detail. It would be amazing if Rachel could buy me a camera like this. I write down the make and number of the Nikon.

I take my purchases to the checkout counter, let a clerk show me how to scan them, stuff my bills into the machine, and bag my things. Then I start looking around for the gang. After twenty minutes, I cruise the parking lot and realize the truck is gone.

What kind of joke is this? I go back inside, ask the guy in charge to page the teens, and wait while "Will the parties meeting Traci Ashe please come to the courtesy desk?" bounces through the store. But I already know the truth. They've left me stranded. I spent my last few bucks on Tampax, don't have a cellphone, and there's not one person in the world who cares enough to come get me.

GAYLE

The Martinsons have put up the first new structure in Prairie Hill. A carport. They were beside themselves with delight when several of us appeared with a bottle of champagne to celebrate. You have to admire their optimism. They're going to rebuild the house that's been in Pete's family for three generations. Correction: they're going to build on a lot that's been in Pete's family, because there's not a thing there to rebuild.

We agreed to start meeting in their carport three times a week and try to decide what comes next. We're calling it the "Carport Café" and will bring our own thermoses of coffee. I probably shouldn't be there since we haven't decided to rebuild, but these are my friends, the people I grew up with, and I can't stand not to be a part of it. Their old house holds memories for me too. It's where we hung out as kids. Pete's mother knew how to do everything. It was in their living room that I learned to knit, the same afternoon I watched Armstrong take his first steps on the moon.

On the way to the Salvation Army tent where lunch is still served every day, I passed the one remaining wall of the library and remembered what it was like to curl up with a good book, something I hadn't done since before the tornado. Then when I got to the Salvation Army tent, I found someone had started a lending library there. "Take one, leave one. Have a good read." Up until today, there'd only been a Bible.

I took *The Knitting Circle*, by Ann Hood, and devoured it this evening. She lost a young daughter and found solace in knitting with friends, which is the story of her novel. I cannot imagine what it'd be like to lose a child, and for the first time since the tornado I realize I really am lucky. Lucky to be alive and luckier still that Vic and Mark are alive. Grief is to be lived through, one day at a time. Not sure knitting's my answer, as it brings back memories of the blue blanket I made for Vic before he was born, another thing lost, but I see how loss is the price we pay for being alive.

Donna's back from Lawrence; I ran into her at Jo's. They've decided to stay with her sister's family in New Hope while they decide what to do. "It's too hard to be away," she told me. "Even though there's nothing here, everything's here. Know what I mean?"

Of course I do. There's no way of running away from our lives even when nothing's left. Donna sounds like they'll rebuild, which helps me lean in that direction too. It's so hard though. Don't people know tornadoes make their own paths? Tornado alleys? The fact that once a tornado has forged a path, other tornadoes follow? I'm sure if I heard another one coming, I'd simply have a heart attack, knowing now what devastation is. Mark has another perspective: "We've lived through the worst, now we can survive anything."

Is he brave? Foolish? Putting on an act for me?

Every morning he reminds me you can be either a victim or a survivor. You get to choose which you're going to be. A victim who lies down and dies? Who sits around and whines? Or a survivor who brushes herself off and gets back to work?

Mark's never had much patience for victims, believing people should pull themselves up by their bootstraps and do the work God intended for them to do.

ANGELINA

What I want to do more than anything is to see Grandmother's house, but Frank insisted Jen should be the one to take me, to introduce me to Thad Hopkins. She and Frank are taking off for Wichita, so I'll have to wait. Instead, I agree to help Elena with wedding plans. It's the least I can do to thank her for her hospitality.

After breakfast, Elena hands me a stack of *Brides* magazines and a pair of scissors, so I can snip articles and pictures and file them in pink folders neatly marked "Mother of the Bride Dresses," "Wedding Cakes," "Flowers," and "Miscellaneous." I assure her the invitations won't be difficult, that Brett is perfectly capable of printing her elegant invitations and she needn't outsource them to Kansas City, and tell her traditional fonts for weddings are Copperplate Gothic, Snell Roman, and Garamond. Paula is lucky to have such a supportive mother. "You really do want this to be the best wedding ever invented, don't you?" I ask. My own fantasy of marrying in a library is an act my own mother would never support. She might not even attend my wedding, let alone plan it.

Elena stops to show me a picture of an enormous bouquet of nylon net flowers and suggests they could make a colorful centerpiece for a bridal shower. "If you take the blossoms off the stems, they become pot scrubbers," she says, "so they can double as party favors."

Elena excuses herself and brings back two tall glasses of iced tea and a small bowl of baby carrots. "I didn't have a wedding, getting my chronology wrong and all, being pregnant before marriage," she continues, as if there hadn't been a pause. "Everyone thought the golden boy was doing me a favor by marrying me, and he's never let me forget it. As if I stole his sperm while he was passing the collection plate at church."

By the end of the afternoon, we've found fifteen photos of dresses that might look good on the mother of the bride. Elena's still going strong, but I've had enough of weddings and decide to visit the cemetery and pay respects to my grandmother.

"Pick some roses to take to her. She loved my roses," Elena offers.

Roses in hand, my fingers well plucked by thorns, I make my way to the cemetery behind the Lutheran Church. It's the kind of place anyone would want to be buried. Peaceful, with large maple trees. Jasmine permeating the air. Old stones, but well kept. Picturesque. A few of the graves haven't been tended in a while, but many were remembered at Memorial Day, with wilted flowers and brighter plastic ones. On the far side of the cemetery is a section of gravestones from the early 1900s, and I'm especially touched by the number of infants who are buried here. I've already shed a few tears before I spot the grave I came to see.

"Amanda Beacon Sprint, 1890–1979, Wife, Mother, Grandmother." Next to her lies my grandfather, who didn't live long enough to meet his own son, my father. "Ned Sprint, 1880–1910, Husband" is all it says.

I sit down on a nearby bench to consider what questions I would ask my grandmother. What had she wanted out of life? Did she regret leaving cultured Philadelphia and the possibility of college? What were the toughest parts of raising a son alone on the prairie at the beginning of the last century? I do love this woman, although I'm pretty frustrated at how hard she's made it to find her journals. What could she tell me about building the library?

A mosquito takes a bite out of my ankle, underlining how late it is. I rearrange the roses one more time and promise to visit again soon.

As I head back to the main gate, I notice a man, shoulders slumped, also having a conversation with a loved one. I try to slip by unnoticed, but when he looks up, I realize it's Brett. One glance at the tombstones tells me what he hasn't. Constance May Higgins Duncan, born the same year I was, died two years ago. "Wife. Mother." The neighboring smaller headstone bears the name William Allen Duncan, who also died in 2006, before he was two years old.

"Oh my God." I'm not fast enough to catch my words before they fall out of my mouth. "I didn't know. I'm so sorry. Why didn't you tell me?" Tears pour out before my thoughts are fully formed. Brett starts to hand me his handkerchief and realizes it's already spent, so I reach into my pocket for my own shredded Kleenex.

"I would've. I was going to," he stutters. "If I didn't, someone else would have. Elena. Or Jennifer." He pauses and takes a deep breath. "Okay, here's the deal. You're the first woman I've talked to in a couple of years who didn't know. For two years, I haven't so much as gone to the grocery store for a loaf of bread without people dripping sympathy all over me. I don't know where to put all that sympathy. It's horrendous. I miss these two so much. Over and over again, my mind repeats Connie and William, William and Connie. If I say their names often enough, maybe they'll wake me up from my nightmare."

He leans down to pick up a small leaf that's floated onto his son's grave. "This week, for the first time in two years, I managed to have a personal conversation with someone who just wanted to know me. Who didn't see me as the wounded, broken-hearted, miserable man that I am."

"How?" I ask.

"Car accident. Drunk driver."

We stand in silence, listening to the cicadas, until both of us start swatting bugs.

As we walk back to the church, it's clear Brett wants to change the subject. "There's a Carnegie library over in Dodge; it's round, very different from the rest. I could take you there, Saturday," he offers.

"That'd be great," I say. "Maybe I can buy you lunch afterwards?"

"I'll be pretty jammed until then," he says. "The former governor is coming out to make a speech on Thursday, to talk to whomever from Prairie Hill, to try to buck up morale."

"You know him?"

"Sure. John Carlin's always been good at buddying up to the press. Which is why he was the first governor in the state to get a second four-year term, beating a Republican incumbent the first time. He's pretty popular. Even with me, but that won't keep me from teasing him about the time he stood up my father for a Rotary speech because he had to officiate at a ceremony in Caldwell naming the Ornate Box Turtle the 'State Reptile.'"

TRACI

The Walmart incident is all over town. By the time I unlock the doors to let in the Quilters, everyone already knows my business. Everyone knows an off-duty security guard brought me home, thanks to Mr. Jack, who witnessed my arrival at 5 a.m. They don't know absolutely nothing happened, beyond listening to the guy brag about his grandkids who call him Poppa Pete.

"Heard you had a date last night," Rachel says when the Guilters gather.

"Not really," I shrug.

I could squeal on the teens, but don't. I'll figure it out myself. Luckily, Rachel doesn't push me for more information. I'm afraid she'll fire me, but she just shakes her head. Or maybe she'll write it down in that evaluation notebook she carries everywhere.

Angelina shows up, wondering if it's okay if she asks the Quilters about the library, if they know any stories about how Carnegie gave money. Sure. Why not? It will keep me from trying to teach I-don't-know-what when I'm so exhausted I could sleep on a bed of tumbleweeds. So far, the women seem happy enough, working on their potholders, but surely they expect something from me. They're chattering away about the latest episode of *One Life to Live* when Angelina interrupts, tells them what she wants, and turns on her tape recorder. Then, dead silence. Not one member of the No Guilt Quilt Guild has a single thing to say.

Angelina is nervous and starts prattling on about how Carnegie came from a textile family in Scotland. His hometown of Dunfermline was known for its fine weavings, which were exported to America. Tariffs were lifted on linens about the time Carnegie was born; and exports tripled in about three years, giving them a good life. Then came the Panic of 1837; when it got too bad, the Carnegies borrowed money to immigrate to America.

The women nod politely but I can't tell whether they're interested or bored. I do know Angelina is not getting what she came for. After a break, she starts jabbering some more, trying to show interest in what they're doing so they'll help her out. Reading from her laptop, she announces quilting is no longer for old people. "There are more than twenty-one million quilters who spend $3.6 billion annually on their hobby," she says.

"That's what we are," Rachel says. "Economic stimulators. Too bad we can't stimulate donations."

What they're not are women who want to tell old stories to Angelina. She's obviously disappointed as she packs up her laptop and stack of books.

The Troubled Teens show up right on time. I'm not sure what they're expecting from me, but I play it totally cool. They don't ask how I got back from Great Bend. Maybe they, like everyone else in town, already know.

They've each brought an egg, their "baby," which they're tending for a week as part of Life Skills class. Except Sylvia who has brought two. "Twins," she tells me. Defiant as always.

"They're boiled?" I ask. She rolls her eyes and doesn't answer.

Since I struck out with potato printing, I suggest a mural, figuring it can also serve as the "exhibit" we're supposed to have at the end of the summer. I show them postcards of graffiti works by Keith Haring, hoping they'll be inspired by his activism. They whine and groan, but I get them to look at the odds and ends of paint in the storage room and suggest they concoct a color to cover the one wall we'll use in the gallery space.

It takes only a matter of minutes for them to dump all the paint together, ending up with a dark mud brown. When I ask them to name their color, they call it "diarrhea." Appropriate. About the ugliest color you could ever imagine and with little lumps that could be partially digested food.

Heeding my orders, they put down newspaper before they start painting; it takes them even less time to spread their concoction all over the wall, using big fat brushes and paying no attention to evenness. Although it might look like creativity, Rachel will see it as pure sloppiness. Or worse. I should have cleared it with her before I gave them the mural assignment, even though she'd encouraged me to use the gallery as my own.

Suddenly desperate, not sure what to do next, I head to the toilet. When I get back, the Teens are standing in a row, hands on their hips, defying me to what? And then I get it. The mural is covered with slimy yellow eggs and cracked shells. Their "babies." Not hard-boiled at all.

They want me to be mad, to rage indignantly, to tell them they're threatening my job, and I'm tempted. But it's actually a brilliant idea. They look confused when I congratulate them, so I bring out my own quilts from the artZee Gallery. "Great minds think alike," I say, pointing out the ketchup and bubble gum. "Food can be an awesome artistic medium. A great way to make a statement."

Sylvia's gone for such a short time, I hardly miss her, but when she gets back she's got mustard, salt, and chewing gum. She hands everyone their own pack of gum and they each put five whole sticks in their mouths at once, chewing with as much noise as is humanly possible. Juicy Fruit smells up the building. Then she takes the lead in sticking the gum on top of the eggs, demonstrating how to smear the mustard, and finishing off by dabbing salt on top.

Copycats. But copying is the highest form of flattery, so I say, "It's derivative. That's when one artist takes an idea from another idea and makes it her own. Like some people thought I took this log cabin quilt idea from a famous artist named Robert Rauschenberg. Here, I'll show you."

The teens huddle close, even Sylvia, as they look at the examples.

"Once you get famous, everyone will want to know what your work means. You'd better be ready to tell them why you used eggs, gum, mustard, and salt." Remembering how the critic screwed me with his own descriptions of my motives, I tell the Teens, "Like one critic thought the ketchup here represented blood."

"Gross," Sylvia says, wrinkling up her nose. "How disgusting."

But she grins as she says it, like she's kind of impressed. For once.

GAYLE

Today I had it out with our fifth insurance claims adjuster in as many weeks. He asked for the deed to the house. Again. I pretty much yelled at him, "How do you expect us to find a piece of paper when we haven't been able to find the refrigerator, the stove, or the dishwasher?" He asked if we hadn't put the deed in the safe deposit box at the bank and if not, why not. I suggested he go by the bank himself to see if he could find it. In the midst of the rubble that's there.

I thought Mark would scold me for being impolite, but he gave me a thumbs up and the biggest grin I've seen since before the tornado. "You were *good*," he pronounced. "That guy deserved an earful and a half. My wife gave it to him; she ain't no mouse."

Tornadoes should have names like hurricanes do. We refer to BT, Before Tornado, but it's too generic, not separating it from all the other tornadoes that aren't ours. "Satan," is what I would name it.

ANGELINA

After getting absolutely nowhere with the Quilters, I decide it's time to find my grandmother's house, with or without Jennifer. I've been here ten days, and I should've done it nine days ago. We used to walk into town so I know it can't be far. Every day, my father would drop me off at the library where I would fill my arms with books before walking back to the farm—to the end of Main Street, then toward the trees Grandma told me were planted as a windbreak during the Depression.

But in a matter of minutes I don't recognize anything. There are no signposts, not even the creek where boys used to splash for entire afternoons. Disoriented, considering the road not taken, seeing my confusion as a metaphor for my life, I head back to Elena's.

My bedroom is almost cool, thanks to the world's largest ceiling fan, but the soft white noise deepens my sense of doom. Questions keep pricking me like mosquito bites. Was my mother right? Was I wrong to close Sprint Print? Could another person have made a go of it? Should I have worked harder, been smarter, put my heart and soul into it? What will happen to me if I don't nail this PhD? Is there anything else I can do? Any other contribution I can make and still earn a living?

As I lie across the bed, the quilt carefully turned down so I won't muss it, I reach for my diary of books. Why can I no longer concentrate enough to read? Has obsession with my goal robbed me of my biggest delight? It's been a month since I've made an entry, a month since I sunk into the delight of a new book. Opening the diary at random, I spot Nancy Drew and remember how she could figure out anything, thanks to the dark blue convertible her father delivered on her sixteenth birthday. How do I channel Nancy Drew? Where is my father when I need him?

With a tap on the door first, Elena pops in with a cheese plate. "I brought you something else," she says, as she hands me a book. "I know it's none of my business but we were putting together an Oz display at the library."

The book is *The Wizard of Oz and Other Narcissists* by Eleanor D. Payson. Before Elena has even shut the door behind her, I start reading about how to cope with one-way relationships. In a couple of hours, I devour a description of my mother. It's a book I should've read a decade ago. Here is someone who understands my depression and low self-esteem, my feelings of helplessness. It's only a book. It *is* a book. Books have answers. And librarians are masterful at handing out answers just when you need them most. That's why libraries are so essential, why my dissertation is so important. If only I could find my way in. Find a way to add to our understanding of how and why they were built, who made them happen.

That night, I dream of my grandmother wagging her finger at me, her gingham dress covered with a floral, rick-racked apron. "You know you're trying to tell the wrong story, don't you? It wasn't Carnegie who made the libraries happen. He was a funny little man who wore high-heeled shoes and a top hat so no one would know he was short. He made lots of money, but the women built the libraries. No one gives them enough credit."

"How can I find out?" I ask her. My voice is the voice of the child she knew.

"Start with the journals. I hid my secrets so no one from New Hope would see. But it's been a century since that library was built. Guess it's time the truth came out. No matter about my reputation now. If it'll help you reach your dreams, dear."

TRACI

Rachel decides it's time for a "check-in," to assess how things are going. It's been less than two weeks and it doesn't seem fair to evaluate me already, to figure out whether they should let me stay. She arrives with a loaf of zucchini bread and a forced smile, deciding not to comment on the egg wall after taking a quick look. We sit at the big oak table, and when she takes out her notebook, I know I'm in trouble. There's the issue of the Walmart trip, and I still haven't given her a "syllabus," instead playing each day by the seat of my tattered jeans. I've managed to get through a few lessons but there are almost fifty more weeks in the year and I'm way short of inspiration. That's if they let me stay. I haven't unpacked my bags, assuming they won't.

I force myself to stop biting my cuticles so she can't see how freaked I am, but I can't keep myself from sweating.

"Okay, I know you haven't been here long, but I don't want this assessment to sneak up on us," Rachel says, once she's settled, with her notebook opened to a clean page. "We've got some serious issues and better to face them head on, don't you think? At the end of your residency, we have to show both quantitative and qualitative measurements, so best to keep on top of things."

"Sure," I mumble, not having a clue what quantitative and qualitative measurements might mean. She might as well be speaking Greek.

"Let's start with the most positive factors," she says. "The Quilters loved your potato printing project. Jennifer called me this morning to say she got a commitment from them to make one hundred pot-holders to sell. At $5 apiece, that's $500. Everybody needs potholders, right? Of course, it's only a drop in the bucket toward what we need."

She takes time to write this in her notebook.

"The Teens keep coming back. That's no small feat. They may be grumbling all the way, but they show up." She scribbles that down too. "Would be great if they could help with the fundraising, so maybe you can figure that out too."

Right! That would be a challenge. Unless they want potholders covered with rotten eggs. Or pre-chewed gum.

"Now as far as numbers, we still need to be getting more people involved. I thought word would spread, and we'd soon have more teens and more quilters. But we need to be more proactive. What do you think?" she asks. "Any ideas?"

Totally stumped, I beg for a few days to make up a plan. Rachel likes plans. It'll give me time to Google "quantitative and qualitative measurements."

I'm hoping that might be enough to satisfy her, but she starts pat-ting her cheek, like she's stumped too. I wonder if she's going to bring up the diarrhea mural, but instead she says, "Traci, I know you need to get your own work done. That's part of the residency. But I have to ask you not to forage in people's garbage cans."

So that's what this is about. Jack must've seen me raiding his trash and tattled on me. Not that there was much there to raid. A few card-board boxes, to turn into canvases, but nothing else was the least bit helpful. Not worth smelling the rotten sardines or having to deal with his used dental floss, which was tangled through everything.

"You might ask Jo to save boxes for you," Rachel continues. "But I'd stay away from Jack."

She reaches for her purse and digs through it until she finds her billfold. As she hands me two ten dollar bills, she says, "I'm sorry we haven't been able to pay you. Our fundraising drive went from tough to impossible when the Methodists announced they're going to renovate their parsonage. But here's twenty dollars so you can go to the rummage sale this weekend at the Little Church of New Hope. Maybe you'll find something there. You're such a genius at making art out of castoffs."

I take her money, almost as humiliated as when I used to beg for subway fare. It's not like I need it right this minute. Plenty to eat is more than I'm used to.

"You need to make work, Traci," Ruth tells me in her sternest voice. "You have to have new things for the exhibit at the end of the summer, and you've got to plan for life after New Hope. Whether it's the end of the summer or the end of the year."

That's the first time she's said it out loud, that they might not be able to keep me here.

Later that night, I dream of my landlord, coming to exterminate me with a can of bug spray bigger than him. Then I dream of hitchhiking to Los Angeles, but once I get to the beach, I'm surrounded by pimps, selling me to greasy men who look like Jack. Some people worry about whether they dream in black and white or color, but I swear it's the smells that turn my dreams into nightmares. Gross and putrid rotten egg stink saturates my naked race from danger.

GAYLE

I ran into Sally today and felt thankful Vic is grown and living in Salina. What's left of my heart broke in half when Sally told me her four-year-old, Tiffany, who should be worrying about whether to dress her Barbie as a hippie or a model, now keeps 'playing tornado.' 'The tornado is a monster,' she tells her dolls. 'Get down on the floor, cover your heads, pray God will keep you safe.' She keeps asking Sally, 'Is a hurt-icane even worse than a tornado?' When she throws a tantrum, and she throws many, Tiffany beats her new teddy bear against the floor.

"The thing is, I get it," Sally tells me. "I'm so short-tempered myself, I absolutely blew up at that woman, Mrs. Gene Lubbers, the other day. She'd brought in about the thousandth used teddy bear, demanding we write thank you notes for each and every one of them. 'How the hell are teddy bears going to help the situation?' I asked her. 'Just what are we supposed to do with them?' All she wants is to see her photo on the front page of the *Gazette,* presenting them to us. Our kids never want to see another teddy bear. They associate teddy bears with the loss of their homes and their need to be grateful to some silly, self-promoting, egotistical woman when they've lost a whole room full of their own toys."

ANGELINA

Traci suggests the Quilters might open up more if I turn off the tape recorder and pick up my own needlework. "Pretend not to be listening, and see what they say," she says. "Don't ask them direct questions, just go 'I always wondered what it'd have been like if I was here when they built this library.'" A cop once told her the most effective part of the interrogation comes after he's closed his spiral notebook, when he pretends the interview is over. Then the truth comes pouring out.

The problem is I know nothing about sewing. I'm all thumbs, have no sense of design, and don't own a needle to say nothing of fabric. When I tell her this, she wrinkles up her nose, as if to tell me she doesn't believe me.

"We'll go to that rummage sale at the New Church of Little Hope tomorrow," she says, grinning at the sarcastic way she inverses the words of "little" and "hope. "They might have great vintage stuff. You can have first dibs." The girl sounds like she needs a friend, and when she tells me she can teach me how to scrounge, to find treasures that cost nothing, I realize I could probably use some company too.

We get there at the crack of dawn, but it's already crowded, mostly women bumping each other in the narrow aisles. I'm so overwhelmed I don't know where to start but it takes Traci about ninety seconds to find a stash of vintage handkerchiefs. Roses, violets, daisies, with scalloped and lacy edges. She pretends to be generous, but anyone can tell she wants the vintage handkerchiefs for herself. "They're so p-r-e-t-t-y," she says, with a certain amount of disdain.

"Think of all the tears they've wiped," I suggest. "How many widows, how many lost children, how many hard times."

She looks almost defiant, as if she's never cried a tear in her life. "Yeah, I can use Elmer's glue to make them snotty," she says, crunching up a crisp, perfectly starched lavender one, with crocheted borders. Was she always like this or are the Troubled Teens having their effect?

It takes only a little eavesdropping to ascertain most of the crowd are refugees from the Prairie Hill tornado. "Why would you want that?" one woman asks another who is holding up an old patchwork apron. "You can buy something better with your insurance money."

"You're right. I'm just so nostalgic. Sentimental. This reminds me of the quilts I lost." She starts sobbing. "What I'd do for my great grandmother's quilt. Her wedding quilt from 1911," she sniffs, hardly audible.

Traci immediately steps forward, offering her one of the vintage hankies with a generosity I wouldn't have attributed to her.

"You should make one," she says. "A wedding quilt. I mean, it's terrible, but can't you make one to replace it? Isn't that what your great grandmother would want? You should come to the No Guilt Quilt Guild. We'll get you started." With that, she starts pulling out frayed shirts and blouses, and her handkerchiefs, and folds them into little squares and arranges them into interesting patterns.

"We came for clothes," one of the women says. "We've got nothing."

"Yeah, well, I can tell you for sure, the best time to make art is when you don't have anything. Any artist will tell you that." Traci says, as she continues to play with fabric. "You've got to throw all your pain into your creativity. Believe me; it's the best therapy."

The women continue to look at Traci with blank faces. "Please help me," she pleads, changing her voice. "I've got to get more people involved in my quilt class or they're going to fire me. Come to the arts center Tuesday morning. Trust me. The best art comes from tragedy."

The woman who introduces herself as Gayle says she might drop by. "I don't know that I want to quilt, but I might knit, if that's alright," she says. Traci assures her it's fine, and shows her a cashmere sweater that can be unwound and knitted as part of a bigger shawl.

You can see Traci knows tragedy. Tough as nails on the outside, but her heart beats kindness.

GAYLE

I don't know why Donna and I agreed to go to the No Guilt Quilters Guild. Can't believe we'll have much in common with any of them. It's been years since I've sewn anything; I've preferred to pick up knitting needles when there's time. But Traci, their artist-in-residence, was so emphatic and nice about it all, acting like we'd be doing her a favor. She isn't from New Hope herself, so it seemed like the right thing to do. She might feel as outcast as we do.

I keep rearranging my fabric on Mary's dining room table, remembering how Traci magically made patterns out of castoffs. If only I could recollect anything from my home ec classes, I'd feel more confident about sewing.

The one thing I remember is how to sew on a button, through the four holes, which represent health, hope, heart, and home. You wind the thread around the button, under the button, to provide space so the button doesn't shred the fabric underneath with strain and stress. Maybe it was supposed to be a life lesson about providing space for those you love, even if you hold on tight to all four corners. The lesson didn't cover the force of a tornado, when hope and home and a lot of heart would be demolished in minutes. Health too, for that matter. I still have a pain under my shoulder blades that won't go away. The doctor says he'll give me an anxiety pill if it doesn't subside soon.

If only someone could stitch together the few remaining pieces of my tattered life into something whole and new and beautiful. That's what I'm thinking as I pick up Mary's knitting needles and cast on stitches from the deconstructed cashmere sweater. It's hypnotic, close to comforting, to move stitches from one needle to another.

TRACI

Inviting the Prairie Hill women wasn't exactly my most brilliant move. When they show up, they sit on one side of the room, and the New Hope Quilters do little to welcome them. Someone mumbles, "What are *they* doing here? We raise lots of money to pay her salary, and her services are meant for those of us who live here in New Hope."

I have my hands full helping the six new quilters pick out patterns from a catalog of Kansas quilts I found on the bookcase, and then there's Angelina to help as well. With all the tension in the room, I do exactly what Angie did. I start talking nervously, telling them everything I learned from that catalog. How quilting can be traced back to Egypt during the time of the pharaohs, but patchwork quilts are considered an American art form. I tell them pioneer women were expected to have a dozen quilts ready for a dowry before they were married, Amish mothers prepare four quilts for their daughters and three quilts for their sons. One would be an all-over quilt, another a quilt from the scrap bag, and the third and fourth from newly purchased fabrics. They all nod, but I can't tell how much they already know or whether they're the least bit interested.

Gayle, from Prairie Hill, speaks up and chooses a crazy quilt to do. "That's what my life feels like now," she says. "Chaotic. I want to gather every scrap of my old life I can and try to piece together some sort of new life. It won't be orderly, but it'll have the parts." She'd come with her knitting and I'm pleased she's willing to consider a quilt.

"What a beautiful metaphor," Jennifer says, breaking the wall of silence between the two groups of women. "And you can embellish it with silk embroidery and make it even more beautiful than before."

"Not me," the younger woman from Prairie Hill, Donna, says. "All I want is order." She chooses a geometric quilt called "Flying Geese," which means cutting out a million triangles and piecing them together. That should keep her mind off her troubles.

Angelina chooses a simple nine-patch, because it's easy and, according to the catalog, it would have been done around 1912, about the time the library was built. She acts really grateful when I put a square together, showing her light and dark can play off each other. Rachel shows her how she can make three little stitches instead of a knot and pin the point, sew toward it, and the fabric will fall into place as she stitches along the line. I didn't know that. I might be learning more from these women than I'm teaching, but I won't point that out. Rachel might use it in her "assessment" to make me look bad.

The Quilters stay through my lunch hour, snacking on Rachel's brownies, unable to tear themselves away, as they each decide to do just one more square. It's like they're addicted, and if I didn't know her better, I'd swear Rachel spiked those brownies. They're a whole lot friendlier, chatter about a million miles an hour, but disperse, and quickly, when the Troubled Teens arrive.

The Teens have come not with an atomic bomb, but with a reporter from the newspaper. He has come to interview them, and me, and I know it is not a good thing. I do not trust people who want to get into my business.

Sylvia, however, pumps herself up like a balloon, stretching her t-shirt reading "Will Work for Shoes," desperate for attention as always. She leans in to talk to the reporter. "You wanna know about our experiences with Traci, the artist?" she asks. "We call her Trash." She runs her hand through her hair, while she considers. "Well she helped us make this mural. I mean, like, she didn't really help, but she made us do it."

"Tell me about it," the reporter says.

"You sound like my first foster mother when I brought my paintings home from kindergarten," Zed pipes in. "Like when she couldn't tell if I'd drawn an elephant or a zebra, so instead of saying 'What the hell is this?' she said "Tell me about it."

The reporter blushes. Dressed in khakis and a white shirt, he looks like a student intern, and he's been caught. In truth, he doesn't have the slightest idea what he's looking at, and the kids have turned hostile. Serves him right.

"So your medium here is?" the reporter persists, as he punches his phone. "What did you use to paint this?"

"Eggs, Juicy Fruit gum, mustard, and salt," Sam offers. "Kind of like the hollandaise sauce my grandma makes, except for the gum." Apparently Sam comes from a family that not only takes in foster kids, but also dines on hollandaise sauce for dinner.

"The meaning being?" the reporter tries again.

Sylvia sees her advantage, and blurts out, "You don't get it? Eggs are eggs, not babies, and we should have the right to decide whether they grow into babies or get crushed before it's too late. We should decide if they are going to grow up in a world where they'll be stuck by bubble gum in a place that's hot as a hellhole and full of dust. 'Chewed gum' is what I am since I gave up my virginity, according to my father. The salt is dust, if you don't get it. Like the dust storm we had last year. Who wants to let an egg become a baby in this godforsaken place?"

The reporter punches his phone again; he's recorded every word they've said.

ANGELINA

It's true. When I sit down with the Quilters, they tell me their stories. They tell me their stories *if* I'm stitching too. The minute I take out a notebook, or God forbid, a tape recorder, they drop into silence. The day I recorded, I actually caught the sound of a pin dropping. I could make a child's game of it, if it weren't so important. Notebook out: Nothing. Back to quilting: Chatter at a hundred miles an hour. Now you hear us; now you don't. The opposite of what my father always taught me about making eye contact. Which means I have to remember everything, then rush to Jo's to get it all down.

I'm still not getting enough relevant information, so I decide to take a different approach, by asking why so many of the libraries were converted to arts centers in the 1970s. Why did they give up the original function? This time period is within memory for most, and maybe it'll help in my quest for details about the buildings. Maybe they'll remember bits of history they heard then.

After everyone's settled down and pulled out their plastic bags of quilt pieces, I ask the group at large, "What do you remember about the conversion of this building?"

"Meatloaf," Becky says with a grin.

"Meatloaf?" Jennifer asks.

"Yep, meatloaf. My father was not so keen on all the trips Mom made to Topeka trying to get grants for the renovation. Thought she should be at home ironing his shirts instead. So to butter him up before each trip, she'd make his favorite supper of meatloaf, baked potatoes, and blueberry cobbler. By the third dinner, we were onto her. She'd serve up the meatloaf and Dad would ask, 'While you're in Topeka, could you pick up some wine? That Chardonnay you got last time was pretty good.'"

"Must've been magical meatloaf. I need that recipe," Jennifer laughs. I guess she tries to please Frank, after all.

"Not sure I have it. She used saltines instead of bread or oatmeal, and took care not to overwork the meat, to handle it as little as possible." Becky looks frustrated that someone wants a recipe she can't provide.

"My mother didn't bother," Shari sighs. "She was out-and-out defiant about those trips, reminding us before each and every one of them that she'd have finished college if they hadn't gotten married, which made my father mad, which eventually led her into the arms of her grade school boyfriend from Rice Center."

"Whereas Suzanna Smith decided she'd had enough of this town and its lack of cultural opportunities and set out for Santa Fe, where ultimately she proclaimed her love for Lucy," says Jennifer. "Even I know that, and I didn't get here until twenty years later."

"Yep, women did find their 'liberation' with the renovation of the arts center," Rachel laughs.

I may be getting more information than I'd bargained for. These women seem to have developed entirely new lives with the transformation of the library. Once they drank the empowerment juice, they were off and running off.

"But what do you remember about the library building?" I ask, trying to steer the conversation back to topic.

"It was too small," Rachel answers. "We'd outgrown it and you could hardly turn around for the stacks of books. The wiring was mysterious and the plumbing temperamental. It was always either too hot or too cold. We'd already decided to build the new library attached to the consolidated school, and then Brett's mother went to Lawrence and saw how they'd converted their library into an arts center. One thing led to another. It became our bicentennial project."

Traci passes around a plate of oatmeal cookies, and no one refuses.

"Remember our slogan?" Rachel asks. "'Hope is a verb.' We wanted everyone to realize how proactive we could be in making the community better. The women made it happen, and they did it for the community, but they also did it for themselves. Even here in the boonies, women's liberation was beginning to have an impact. Your grandmother called the steering committee 'one big self-esteem factory.'"

"More details, please?" I ask, as I make a mental note of "self-esteem factory."

"When we got possession of the building, we spent every Tuesday and Thursday evening, and every Saturday and Sunday afternoon, cleaning and painting. Even so, it took six months. Everyone helped. We gave gloves to the toddlers, some of them just old enough to walk, who helped pick up the bugs; we carried out bugs by the bucketful. And seniors helped, some so old all they could do was polish the brass handles on the windows. It took twenty-eight gallons of paint for the building. We had more fundraisers than you can shake a stick at. Making potholders now seems easy in comparison."

"Any other challenges you remember?" I ask.

"Our biggest one was deciding what color paint to use. Finally, after way too many hours of discussion, we brought in an interior designer from Wichita who suggested a very dark green for the walls and ceiling. 'Derbyshire' was the paint color. I still remember because it was such an inappropriate name for a building in the middle of Kansas. We did it her way. And two years later repainted everything white."

That night, I can't get to sleep, fighting the notion that I'm too stupid to see something that should be clear. Why can't I pull myself away from here and get back to work on Andrew Carnegie? Finally falling into a fitful sleep, I dream of one big self-esteem factory with hospital-white walls. My grandmother appears again, this time in her orange and yellow plaid housedress, hands firmly on her hips. "Angie," she tells me, sounding exasperated. "I told you before. You're trying to tell the wrong story. It's the women who made the libraries happen. They were the ones with courage. Theirs is the story you need to tell."

When I wake up, I can't get the dream out of my head. Maybe Grandmother is right. The brave women who were resourceful enough to make the libraries happen on the Plains must've been like the women of the No Guilt Quilt Guild who patiently and persistently work to keep the arts center going—seeing their tasks as being as unremarkable as arguing over the price to charge for fudge at the Fourth of July parade or how many quilted potholders they can make, when they're changing lives, one after another, including, of course, their own.

TRACI

3 potholders X 13 women = 39 potholders X $5 = $195.

Hardly a drop in the bucket when it comes to supporting my salary. A whole morning's work for the No Guilt Quilt Guild. They're discouraged. They ought to be making their own quilts, not potholders to pay me. Will they even be able to sell them?

Rachel thought publicity would help the fundraising campaign, so I figure she'll be delighted when I hear the *New Hope Gazette* has run a feature story. Turns out a photo of us, the Troubled Teens and me, standing in front of the mural, is on the front page. Unfortunately, the mural doesn't show up well, and the kids have taken on their defiant pose, arms crossed across their chests, one leg in front of the other, feet firmly planted like they're waiting to be punched. The article's got the quote about babies and hellhole exactly as it was said. Another one from Rachel, about how important it is that the Teens have a place to express themselves, even their darker sides, sounds lame in comparison. Rachel won't do a happy dance after she sees the article.

When the Troubled Teens come in, they've each got a copy of the paper in hand.

"Can you believe it?" Zed asks, proudly opening his copy in front of his chest. "We're on the front page of the paper," he says, punching the paper with his forefinger. "Like the football team when they win a trophy."

"When we get famous, people all over the world will see that photo,"

Sylvia says, pouffing her hair like the most pompous of Hollywood stars. "You don't think I look fat?" she wonders, worried about her ultimate fame, her boobs about to bust out of her t-shirt she's so puffed up. Her t-shirt reading, "Keep Calm and Carry On."

"At least you don't have zits," Zed says. "But it won't matter when I'm the coolest guy in the universe."

They act like they've already won Grammys.

"We gotta link this to our Facebook pages," Sylvia says heading straight for the computer, not bothering to ask permission. Everyone follows her to my desk, and hangs over her shoulders while she enters her password. She's got the fastest fingers in the West; it takes her a nanosecond to pull up the article and link it to her Facebook page.

"You next," she says to Zed, and he does the same. Madonna, then Sam, take their turns, linking to the article, stopping long enough to laugh at a post of a dancing cat.

"Your turn," Sylvia says when everyone's made the link. "Your turn to link to your Facebook page," she insists.

"I'll do it later," I tell her.

"You'll do it now," she insists, typing in Traci Ashe, then just Trash, searching for my Facebook page. "Wait a minute. Don't tell me you don't even *have* a Facebook page. Hey guys, have you ever met *anyone* who didn't have a Facebook page?"

"Well my grandpa didn't have one, but we made him one." Sam says. "We'll figure out a photo later." It takes him about ninety seconds, and I see my name up there, real as life, like I exist and might have friends.

GAYLE

We went. I'll say that much. The Hopeless No Guilters didn't exactly throw down the welcome mat. Mrs. Gene Lubbers, the teddy bear witch, complained we were there, like we couldn't hear, and everyone else pretty much ignored us.

Donna argued when I pointed this out. "Traci was lovely," she said. "And Angelina, she's a brainiac for sure, but I liked her, felt like she could teach me a thing or two. Rachel was just trying to encourage us with her stories about renovating the library and turning it into an arts center."

Like that was a big thing. Not compared to what we'll have to do if we rebuild all of Prairie Hill.

"You're not being fair," Donna kept insisting. "They don't know what to say. Would *you* know what to say, if you were in their position?"

She's right. I decide to knit a potholder for the cause, using the bulky, orange rayon yarn Mary found on sale. It's ugly as sin, but gives me something to do.

ANGELINA

I could have found the Green Valley Carnegie library even without Jennifer, but she'd insisted we meet at Jo's so she could take me. She also offered to take me out to my grandmother's farm, but when I called, Thad Hopkins asked me to wait until next week. I'm desperate to see it, but he sounded even more desperate to put me off.

Green Valley is more forlorn than everyone told me. There's a barber shop next door to the library, right on Main Street, opposite the bank, the most prominent site on the block. The bank bears a sign "CLOSED, Back in an hour or so." Looks as if the hour's turned into a decade, maybe two. Is this what Prairie Hill looked like before the tornado? Everyone says it was a desolate, dying town.

A young girl bounds up the library steps, the steps of a simple limestone building with no columns or portico, and my spirits lift with her bounce. We follow her in, watching as she proudly announces to the librarian, "I'm five. I can have a library card now. Yesterday was my birthday, and now I can check out books all by myself. My mother says I can check out seven books every single week."

The librarian, Hilda Swenson, according to the placard on her desk, exchanges smiles with us, although hers turns from genuine delight at having captured a young reader to a forced welcome as she wonders what business we have. She attends to the girl but can't take her eyes off us as we survey the stacks and old card catalogues. I'm so worried about her stare that I almost miss the museum case with artifacts, including an iron railroad stake, a weathered copy of *Aesop's Fables*, and an old game of dominoes.

It's Jennifer who spots the piece of paper mounted at the end of the case—an invitation, engraved, yellowed with age, and in an old italic font I don't recognize. We lean in, our heads almost touching, in order to get a closer look at the antique print on the worn paper. Jennifer reads the paper out loud, in a hushed whisper:

The Library Board of Green Valley, Kansas begs to announce that its Carnegie library has now been completed and that its formal opening will be held next Thursday evening, May 1, 1912, at 7 o'clock.

Inasmuch as our new library must have more books than the ones the Board has already provided, and as much time is required to acquire such books in the ordinary way, it has been suggested that if everyone would donate one or more books from his private library this would give at the start a substantial nucleus for such a library as we hope to build. And so we trust that all who can will adopt this suggestion and bring a book on the opening night.

Your Library Board sincerely desires that everyone interested in the library be present at this opening whether he has any books to spare or not.

A short program has been arranged with remarks by Mayor Michael Seward and a vocal rendition by Violet Wray.

"So the Green Valley Carnegie library opened just before the one in New Hope. Without books. It must have been quite a contest to see who was up and running first," Jennifer says.

I spot more pages in another case, and when I go over to look, find journal entries done in what I'm sure is my own grandmother's hand, written on ecru paper as the earlier entry had been. I put my nose so close to the glass that I steam it up and am so engrossed that I jump when the librarian sneaks up behind me. "We'd like to take a closer look at this diary," Jennifer tells her. "Can we take it out of the case?" As always, Jennifer's tone is open and friendly. "We'll be careful."

"Sorry." Ms. Swenson doesn't look the least bit sorry. She answers nothing more as she takes a key from her pocket and locks the case. Surely she doesn't imagine we mean to steal it. This librarian is being stingy with her information and looks as if she might pick up the phone and call the police. I'm suddenly too conscious of my heart beating too fast.

"Do you have anything else? Any other records or documents that might be helpful to my friend who's writing her dissertation on Andrew Carnegie and how he built the libraries?" Jennifer persists.

"Maybe," she answers as if it's enough. "But she'll have to present credentials."

I start to tell her about my dissertation but reconsider as her sour face turns even more threatening. Does she worry I'm stealing her soul by telling the story of libraries the way some cultures, like Native Americans and the Amish, thought photographers stole their souls when they snapped images? Now that we know it's here, I can come back later and copy it. A strategy would be in order. My father would know how to charm her, how to compliment her or crack a joke, but I'm caught wordless.

Ms. Swenson is still staring at us with her arms resting across her chest. She's about five feet tall, but amazingly intimidating with piercing blue eyes and pure white hair pulled up in a bun at the very top of her head. She's not old, I realize; she's younger than my mother, and once seriously beautiful. Life has served her a lemon or two.

"Is there something else I can help you with?" she asks, not at all helpfully.

"We're interested in the old Carnegie libraries," I offer, wishing my voice sounded strong or at least confident. "I'm spending the summer in New Hope, doing some writing." Maybe repetition will get the point across.

"Hmmph," is her retort. "They don't even use their library. Built a *modern* one."

She makes a point of looking at her watch and announces, "I'm closing early today," nods to the door, and turns her back on us to end the conversation.

TRACI

Sarah, from Prairie Hill, can hardly contain herself. "They found my quilt. I can't believe they found my quilt. Fifty miles from here, over in Stafford, a guy found my quilt, stuck in a bale of hay. Someone told me to keep checking lostquilt.com and sure enough, six weeks after the tornado someone found it, and his wife was smart enough to post. I knew it was mine because it was embroidered 'Made Especially for You Grammie' and signed by all eleven of my grandgirls."

She starts sobbing, then everyone does; even I start leaking tears.

Through her sniffles, Gayle says, "I wish someone could find the quilt my grandmother made for me. Kansas Troubles. Had all the old quilt blocks like Windmill, Rail Fence, Kansas Dugout. I thought it was odd she gave me such a somber quilt, but I guess she knew what was coming. How tough I'd have to be."

"Me, I'd like to find the journals the library had. I can't believe such valuable information just blew away," Angelina says. "It looks like Green Valley has a few pages, but everyone says there were more in Prairie Hill."

No one can believe Angelina has managed to work her libraries into this conversation too. The woman is obsessed. Gayle and Donna exchange a look, like they're asking, "Can you believe it? Libraries again? When we've lost our homes?"

After everyone leaves, I decide to look for her journals.

I Google "Carnegie library journals," although she's probably already done that about a hundred times. I come across wonderful images, vintage postcards, of all the Carnegie libraries in the state. I bookmark them, wondering how I can make them into something. Maybe transfer them onto fabric, using them as blocks to make a quilt they can auction. That'd make me more popular, if I could raise some money. And the subject matter is safe enough that I won't piss anyone off.

When Sam comes in, he offers to help me at the computer, figuring I'm hopeless since I didn't have a Facebook page. I tell him we're looking for journals that might've blown away in the tornado. He leans over me like I can't read for myself. We find lots of touching posts, along the lines of "I know this is a long shot, but I'm looking for my grandmother's Wedgwood teapot." Sam is totally hooked by a signed soccer ball that was found a hundred miles away in Lindsborg. "'To Ronald,' it says. We should ask around to see if we can find a Ronald," he suggests.

When the other Teens arrive, Sylvia singsongs, "Sammie has a girlfriend," and I realize she means me.

"At least I'm not a lesbo," he taunts back.

"Am not. And you know it," she screams, coming close to claw him.

"Yeah, I know it," he says, and gets up and throws his arm around her. He really is a teddy bear. "You're not a whore, either, even though some people call you that."

Zed slips into his place while Sam is hugging Sylvia and quickly signs into my Facebook account. I'd meant to change the password but hadn't gotten it done.

"Wait a minute," Zed says. "You should have friends requests. Even Sam's grandpa had ninety-four friends requests when he signed up. Either you're not who you say you are, or you don't got no friends."

Sam pushes Zed off the seat in front of the computer, starts madly punching keys while Zed stares at me like I've got leprosy. I shrug and watch until Madonna gets bored enough to promise a round of malts at the soda fountain, at which point they all push and shove to get out the door at the same time. Forgetting the mystery of me. It's true, I have no friends. Sam "friended" me with the Troubled Teens, and put in requests to Jennifer, and Rachel, even his grandfather, but I honestly can't think of anyone else. Still, that doesn't keep me from checking about every two minutes to see if anyone has posted anything new. They say Facebook can be addictive, and I can see if you had a million friends it might be. But for me, seeing Grandpa's photo of the jigsaw puzzle of a tractor he finished last night, or knowing Zed's foster dog might have had a seizure, or getting Jennifer's recipe for her carrot cake, doesn't exactly give me goose bumps. More proof that no one loves me. No one loves me in the whole wide world and cyberspace too.

GAYLE

After I told Traci about my lost Kansas Troubles quilt, she came over, sat down beside me, and suggested I too might make a quilt about my experiences. "You could call it BT/AT, Before and After the Tornado." I wasn't buying it, so she told me she sometimes deals with her own fears through art, like she could see right through me, and understands how generally insane I am right now. When I tried to tell her I'm downright crazy, she shrugged and said, "Crazy makes great art. Provides awesome inspiration."

To demonstrate, she brought out the handkerchief coverlet she's whipped together since the rummage sale and showed me how she's embroidering black French knots to represent bedbugs, then adding small pieces of barbed wire. "You wouldn't believe how flipping freaked I am of bedbugs," she told me. "But somehow this makes me feel like I've got some control over the matter. I'm the master here."

While Angelina was babbling on and on about her libraries, Traci worked with me, helping to design three strips, to represent time before, during, and after the tornado. The "before" and "after" being bright and cheery, the tornado in the middle being dark and threatening. She made me start with the "after," which is so hard, because I have no idea what it'll be, but I started playing with bright pinks and blues because what I want more than anything is a grandbaby.

For twenty whole minutes I forgot about everything but the future, how great it would be to snuggle up to a baby, letting her or him, I don't care which, hold onto my pinky for dear life. Giggle when I make funny faces and animal sounds. I was doing fine until I started listing nursery rhymes I could recite. Which all involve falling: Jill falling down the hill, Humpty Dumpty falling off the wall, London Bridge falling down, cradle with baby falling down, Ring Around the Rosie, we all fall down. Falling down the tunnel of a tornado like I dream every night. Always falling into despair after I've dared to hope.

Twenty minutes I didn't think about the tornado. A record. My personal best. That's what I have to hold onto. Tomorrow I'm aiming for thirty.

ANGELINA

Brett's making good on his offer to take me to Dodge City, to see the round Carnegie library there. When I'm safely seat-belted into his car, and he's double-checked to make sure his own belt is secure, he tells me it'll be a couple of hours, and I wonder what I'll say to this suddenly wordless man. Is it because I'm attracted to him that I'm suddenly nervous? He quickly becomes the consummate interviewer. When he asks what Elena and I talk about, I tell him about the wedding plans. Wedding words out of my mouth before I realize this will make me look like a silly girl. I'm sure he can provide a fountain of information about the libraries if we can get past the small talk.

It's not hard to find other topics. Once we get started, we have no trouble filling the time. We have so much in common. He too has inherited his father's business, a business that involves paper, fonts, and ink. The difference is he'd expected to inherit it from the time he was a young boy and never dreamed of doing anything else.

"Went away to KU to study journalism, but always knew I was coming back here. My dad thought four years was enough time for me to let off a little steam and learn everything I needed to know about the outside world," he tells me.

A hawk circling off to the right keeps us mesmerized for a minute or two. It is both elegant and dangerous.

"Okay, really, what possessed you to decide to summer in Middle America?" Brett interrupts the silence. "Are you here to write your dissertation or does something else bring you?" He keeps his eyes on the road but his voice manages to make me feel as if he can see straight through me. "Nothing sinister. Like I told you, I'm trying to write about Andrew Carnegie and the libraries he built." Brett's jaw is set in the same way my father's was when he wanted to get to the truth. I couldn't keep a secret from him if I had one to keep.

He doesn't say anything, so I fill in the space. "Did you know Andrew Carnegie built fifty-nine libraries in different Kansas communities? Kansas ranked fifteenth out of forty-six states for the amount of money Carnegie contributed for buildings, thirteenth in the appropriation per population, eighth in the number of communities receiving public libraries, and eleventh in the number of libraries built." Maybe he'll be impressed at how much I know. "Now that I'm here, it seems even more amazing. Where are the towns?"

Brett looks offended at my question, and answers in a monotonic, authoritative voice. "There are over *five hundred* incorporated towns in Kansas with populations of under three thousand." He turns to glare at me. "Plenty of places to build libraries."

I've gone down another wrong road and made him defensive. That wasn't smart. Time to change the subject. I can't wait any longer, so I broach the subject of my grandmother. "Did you know her?" I ask. "It's obvious your grandmother detested her, but did you ever know her?"

"Sure I knew her. It's a *very* small town after all," he says, his voice dripping with sarcasm. He takes time to turn down the radio, which has been playing bluesy jazz, so I guess he's not too offended to talk to me. "The thing I remember most is her response to an editorial just before she died, in which I predicted people would be able to access full editions of *The New York Times* on their home computers. Maybe, someday, there would even be a time when computers would be small enough so you could take one to bed and read an entire novel. Your grandmother wrote a terse, two-sentence response, a letter to the editor: 'The only things a lady should take to bed are her man and a good book. No electronics allowed.'" He grins when he tells me, and I love it too, stashing the quote in my treasure chest of memories.

"She might have a point. Not a bad thing to remember about her. And Thad? What can you tell me about Thad Hopkins? How long have you known him?" I'm pleased how I easily insert my questions into the conversation, seeking information before I make my way to my grandmother's farm.

"Thad? I've known Thad for thirty years, six months, and … four days. No, make that three days."

"You're counting?"

"It's not hard. He was born the day my father died. In the same hospital. Up in Hays. Your grandmother apparently talked my father into driving her when Thelma was about to deliver. Dad died, right then and there. Even with an entire medical staff at his elbow, they couldn't save him. I never did figure out why Amanda Sprint asked him to drive her that day. Or what happened that made his heart fail. He was in perfect health, never missed a day of work. Happened thirty years ago, but seems like yesterday. At the ripe old age of twenty-one, I took over the paper with the very next edition."

A soap opera is unfolding. I have a few hundred questions but it's Thad who's gotten under my skin. When I tell Brett that Thad keeps putting me off in my request to visit my grandmother's place, he tells me, "That's not like Thad. He can be temperamental, especially since he got back from Iraq, but generally he's congenial enough, especially with women. He's always liked women. Young women, older women, plump women, skinny women. But something's not right lately. He's been turning into an eccentric bachelor farmer, but this is more." Brett stops talking long enough to crank up the car's air conditioner, as if the effort demands all of his attention. "I keep meaning to drive out to see if he's growing marijuana or making meth or something.

Everyone knows he's not pulling in the wheat crop he should be. He seems moody. Even angry."

We drive in silence for the next twenty minutes, my considering how this whole town is tightly knit together, like one of Traci's wall hangings. If you pulled out one string, would the whole place unravel?

I'm so deep in thought that I'm startled when we pull up in front of the arts center in Dodge City, which is, in fact, a splendid structure. I wish I knew more about architecture, because this is different from anything I've ever seen. Carnegie was particular about library design, usually insisting on selection from a few, efficient styles, and this doesn't fit one of those templates. The bulk of the building is round, red brick, but on both sides of the main entrance, there are shallow, house-shaped additions. Stained glass windows surround the top of the dome. The building is substantial, but there's a dollhouse feel to it, as if the designer had kept playing with concepts.

Brett has arranged for the arts center's president to show us around and she does so with utmost graciousness and pride. She tells us the building recently celebrated its hundredth birthday and has been used not only as a library and an arts center, but also, during hard times, as a disco club and train-themed family restaurant. "Can you believe this building faced a wrecking ball more than once, before we managed to get it on the list of historic places? Those early settlers must've been turning in their graves. They worked so hard to raise the money, even getting the city council to issue a license to allow a merry-go-round inside the city limits, with 25 percent of the receipts going to the library fund."

She leads us into her office, where she hands me a worn article from the *Dodge City Globe Republican*, dated February 1, 1907. "This is pretty funny and tells it all," she says. "How the men came around to supporting their wives."

I have to squint to read the yellowed clipping:

"When the word was given out 'they were going to have a library, whether any help was given them or not,' the men realized the library was practically a settled fact and they gracefully turned about and lent their assistance. Not that the men of Dodge City do not favor public libraries and everything in the educational line, but they believed other things should be looked after before a library proposition was taken up. The ladies had the matter taken up with Mr. Carnegie and happened to strike him on a dull day, when he had been able to give away only a few hundred libraries, and he readily took advantage of the opportunity to make it one more by giving one to Dodge City."

For lunch, Brett offers the Dodge City Country Club, but I choose the saloon on Boot Hill. It's touristy; I indulge in a sarsaparilla float and a big juicy hamburger with grilled onions, pickles, and fries. Full, I can only drool over the pies in the case—meringues and berries and a six-inch-high apple. It's not hard to imagine cattlemen stopping in before a drive, especially since the most authentic thing about the saloon is the smell of cow manure from the enormous feedlots down the street.

It's been a perfect day, beginning to feel very much like a date.

"So those guys in Dodge were smart to support the library efforts of their wives, weren't they?" I tease, once we're back in the car and on the road.

"Of course. But that's hardly news. A guy will do anything for a woman. Just look at what Frank does for Jennifer, just to make sure she'll be happy here."

"Would you do anything for me?" I can't believe I said it out loud. He'll think I'm flirting. A silly redhead.

"You betchya," he laughs. "Your wish is my command."

It's still mid-afternoon and I'm beginning to fantasize Brett will offer me iced tea at his place to end the day. Instead, he wonders if I want to stop at the barbed wire museum on the way home. "They have two thousand examples," he tells me, "of what they used to call Devil's Rope. Nothing civilized the prairie like barbed wire."

Soft snuggling is what I had in mind, and he's offering up barbed wire. Since I don't want the day to end, I pretend enthusiasm, but I'm far more excited by the hand he's put on my knee than his offer of another stop. Barbed wire reminds me of Hilda Swenson, and I mention the materials I want to examine at the Green Valley library.

"Hilda Swenson has materials you want to see?" He looks over at me, surprised.

"Maybe. She was totally noncommittal. I'm not sure what she has. We saw a few pages of a journal in the case, but she wouldn't let us look closely. The handwriting matched my grandmother's. I'm sure it was hers."

He glances at the clock on the dashboard, brakes in the middle of the two-lane road, does a hard a U-turn, then takes a left turn at the sign pointing to Green Valley. He doesn't say a word, but his mood has turned from maybe-interested-in-me to outrage. He's racing at about 90 mph, beating the steering wheel with his open palm, and determined in a way I haven't seen him before. No explanation. "You'll see when we get there," is as much as I can get out of him.

He's turned from sensitive to macho-bordering-on-scary in a few short miles. Although he is trying to give me the present I want more than anything, I'm not feeling the Christmas spirit.

When we get to Green Valley, he pulls into a diagonal parking spot on the empty street, bounds out of the car to open my door for me, grabs my hand, and drags me up the library steps. Inside, Hilda Swenson takes one look at the two of us and turns a ghastly white. She takes a few steps backwards, almost falling over, obviously upset by Brett. Her fear frightens me as well. The two of them look like cowboys ready to duel.

I walk over to the case where the journal was, thinking I can break the tension by showing it to Brett, only to see it's been removed. There is an empty hole where it was.

"My friend here would like to borrow materials you have. About the Carnegie library." Brett's voice is firm and confident, but his eyes have taken on the wild look of an animal about to pounce on its prey.

"Who is she? Your *friend*?" Hilda sputters in disdain.

"Don't know why her name matters. No one deserves such rudeness from you. But for the record, her name is Angie Sprint."

"Sprint? Ohmigod. You're Amanda's granddaughter?" She takes a step back like a bomb's exploded.

"Yes ma'am," I say, totally confused. Why does this make me so terrifying?

"The materials. Are. Mine," Hilda says to Brett, ignoring me, as if I weren't there.

"Hilda, don't make me ..." he says, stepping toward her.

"No, of course." She considers the unspoken threat. "You can borrow what I have for a week. But be careful with them. Brett, you can't ..." as she carefully opens her desk drawer and hands him a worn manila envelope.

"You owe me this, Hilda." He drops his voice to a whisper, but it's still a threat.

"This is all I have. There are more pages someplace, you'll see that, but I'd swear on a stack of a hundred Bibles, this is all I have."

She looks like he's hit her.

As much as I appreciate the materials, I'm not sure I like this bully Brett's turned into, right before my eyes. What does she owe him? And why?

TRACI

Even Angelina has a boyfriend. She's out for the day with Brett, who is kind of cute if you like the wholesome look. Which I don't. Still, she has someone, even if she won't admit she's got the hots for him.

The only one I've ever known who kind of liked me is Freddy from artZee Gallery. Gay as a chorus girl, Freddy. I didn't even bother to tell Freddy I was splitting town, not wanting to confess to bedbugs. How could I, after he'd told me he's a certified neat freak who washes and irons his sheets and pillowcases each and every day? Starches them too. He'd think I was garbage myself, instead of just using it for artwork.

Since I never notified Mr. Freddy of my whereabouts, I'm surprised when I get a friend request and a private message. "Your landlord is looking for you," Freddy writes. "Does he owe you a refund on your deposit? Should I tell him how to get in touch?"

"NO! NO! NO!" I answer adamantly. "He wants to kill me," I explain. Then, just before hitting "Post," I add, "Don't ask."

"Your business is your business," Freddy shoots back. "But I hope you're well and safe and having a fantabulous time. And you know I want the right to sell any and all of your artwork. You promised. Send it on."

I leave it at that, wishing I had artwork to sell. No need to tell Freddy I mean to be underground, under the radar, out of the sight of

Mafia Man who'd like to put me underground for real. Just because a few little bugs took up residence in our beds. No need to tell Neatnic Freddy that I'm in trouble for not washing my linens.

As I start copying images of Carnegie libraries onto transfer fabric for the quilt, I get more and more paranoid. My landlord can't still be trying to track me down on the issue of bedbugs. If Freddy can find my Facebook page, anyone can.

The images of postcards for the Carnegie quilt come out well, but the art-making isn't enough to distract me, and I start making a getaway plan. I have about $500 left from the pieces Freddy sold, and I'll have another $500 from the arts center when they pay me. Hardly enough to start somewhere else.

I call Rachel's son and give him the go-ahead to sell my VW, which he'd offered to do when he couldn't fix it. It makes me sad because, after all, it was not just my first car, but my getaway car. Shouldn't have gotten attached, shouldn't have named her Ruby Slippers. Then I decide I'll sell the Carnegie libraries quilt for my own benefit, because I can see it's going to be pretty impressive. Angie would buy it if she weren't as poor as me. But as brilliant as she is, she might find a way. Or maybe I can sell it to Brett, and he can give it to her. Would make her happier than a diamond ring.

I need to be ready to leave if worse comes to worst. Maybe I can hitchhike to LA where they have both garbage bins and garage sales, and it's warm enough to sleep on the beach.

GAYLE

We keep going back to sit with the Quilters. I'm not sure why except it seems a safe enough place to pass time. All the women chattering, mostly about silly things, never including us but not excluding us either. Today one of them accidentally said, "We are truly blessed," and then looked embarrassed, like she was bragging, like those of us from Prairie Hill aren't blessed. We are. We know we are. We looked Satan in the eye and lived. I said as much, which stopped the conversation short.

We're blessed, but we're not lucky. Over a thousand homes exploded during the tornado; they've already removed over twenty thousand truckloads of debris. The single death was Caroline McGee who sent her kids to the basement for safety, then hid under her own bed, where a loaded shotgun put a bullet through her head when the winds hit.

Someone from Greensburg told Donna we're entering the worst time now. Psychologically, that is. Everything's gone, almost cleaned up, we haven't totally decided what to rebuild, and we're all antsy, wanting to know what to do next. Not like we've got energy to do anything. The adrenaline's totally gone. I want to curl up in a ball and hide.

"That's why the arts center is such a godsend," Donna insists. "To be able to come here and feel somewhat productive. To stitch hope into a quilt or knit our future into an afghan."

A lot of people are tempted to sell out, literally. There are a few megafarmers from Denver, corporate guys who don't care a hill of beans about farming or our communities. They're sniffing around, trying to see who might sell.

Donna thinks if we do rebuild, we should include a cultural center. A place to gather like the Guilty Quilters. Maybe a library too. Like our husbands will go for that. All they want is to plant some seed. Everything else is superfluous. 'Next year will be better,' they keep telling us. They did that during the Dust Bowl too. People call Kansans the 'tomorrow people' because we have to believe next year will be better. I don't know. Maybe I've lost hope in tomorrow.

ANGELINA

Needless to say, I won't sleep until I've read the journals. It's still unclear to me how Hilda Swenson got her hands on my grandmother's journals, but I can't let myself worry about that now. The inscription confirms their provenance. Unable to wait to devour what's inside, I wash my hands and climb into bed, taking care to lock the door behind me so Elena will think I'm asleep and won't pop in. I plump up the pillows, prop my back against them, and start reading.

May 14, 1909

Today is an exciting day for New Hope, Kansas. An important day. We have formed a literary committee.

We were quilting at Claire's this evening and got onto the topic of books. The conversation started when Claire bragged she'd received a copy of Edith Wharton's new book from her sister back east. I would love to read it; unfortunately, Claire refuses to share it with the rest of us! She held it up to show it but wouldn't even let us pass it around. She is one selfish woman, that's all I will say. I have heard Edith Wharton writes about women who are not unlike Claire in their self-absorption. Perhaps that's the reason she did not want to share. She knows we would see resemblances.

Because she angered me, I suggested we start a lending library among ourselves, to share the few books we have and to buy more. Anyone who lends can also borrow. I'm not sure how we'll do it, how we'll raise money to buy more books, for even among us we don't have many, or what our husbands will think, but I do believe we can do it.

You should have seen Claire's face when I made the suggestion. If we can all read the latest books, she won't be so high and mighty. Just because her husband Branford owns the newspaper, she thinks she's smarter than the rest of us. And entitled. Just because the speakers from Chautauqua always stay with her and she hears their learned conversations, she thinks she's learned too.

Ada said since it was my idea I should have the first pick of books. I thought Claire was going to stomp right out of her own house. Since Claire can afford to buy fabric and have her dresses copied out of Godey's Lady's Book, she thinks she's Queen of the Town. (While I feel lucky to get the magazine at all and divide it into 30 portions when it arrives, to have something to read throughout the month.) I don't care. Now I will have the first choice of books.

June 14, 1909

My head is spinning! We spent half the evening talking about what to call our new literary club. Names suggested were:

New Hope Library, Social, and Literary Club

Shakespeare Club

Home Culture Club

Entre Nous Club

Women's Mutual Benefit Club

and others I can't remember.

We decided to consider our options before christening our new effort. I hardly noticed that I'd pieced a dozen blocks before the evening was over, we were so busy coming up with wonderful ideas.

We spent the rest of the time talking about books we loved; I even admitted I'd read The Awakening *when I was still in Philadelphia. Hortense looked absolutely horrified—and then laughed and told me she'd read it too. I must admit I'm shocked she's read it; she's old enough to be my mother. The others hadn't even heard of it, but they somehow guessed at its naughtiness by the expressions on our faces.*

I brought home Ben Franklin's essays and I'm making Ned crazy by quoting Ben. "Don't cry over spilt milk; Waste not want not; A stitch in time saves nine; A fool and his money are soon parted; Don't put off till tomorrow what you can do today." I'll need to hold my tongue so as to not send Ned over the edge or make him jealous of a dead man. I have no intention of holding my tongue with Claire. I can't wait to drop into the conversation, "The greatest monarch on the proudest throne is obliged to sit upon his own arse."

The talk tonight was such a nice change from worrying about the weather. Everyone in town is uneasy. We had a dust storm last week, it was blowing so hard you couldn't see across the road and it seeped into every crook and cranny in the house. Every piece of fabric now has dust woven into it; if you sit on the rocking chair, you create your own flurry; when I make the beds in the morning the sheets throw up clouds of dust. There's a layer of dust on every piece of furniture as well as the bins in the kitchen. I don't know whether I'll ever have the house scrubbed clean again.

Every time I dare to complain, Ned reminds me his parents came here in a covered wagon, with no more than the promise of free land they read about in a full-page ad in The Philadelphia Inquirer, *looking for people to lay claim to land to make Kansas a Free State. His mother made her first home in a dugout and was delighted when they moved into a soddie. Ecstatic when they built a wooden house with both its sitting room and kitchen overlooking the prairie, because a woman spends all of her time in the kitchen and she wanted a view. "Our children will even have indoor plumbing," Ned promises, and points to the corner of the house where he'll someday build a bathroom.*

We never talk about the drought his parents lived through in 1859, the driest natural calamity recorded in the country's history, when there wasn't a single shower in sixteen months. Or about 1874, when grasshoppers rained from the sun.

I want to dream as big as he does, which is why our literary efforts are so important. Our children will have their choice of books.

June 21, 1909

We decided on the name: Ladies' Reading Room Society. It's not my favorite, but when Claire said she'd donate $35 if that were our choice, I agreed. There's no way Ned and I could give that much to have my favorite name, the Belle Lettres Club. Hortense suggested the Hayseed Club!

I shouldn't be surprised Claire insisted the new library be housed in her front parlor. She will keep it "open" three afternoons a week, from 2–5 pm. Everyone who wants to borrow books will have to become a "subscriber," or buy "stock," paying a fee of one dollar per year per family. We argued for over an hour as to whether it should be fifty cents or a dollar, my arguing for the fifty cents. I was pacified by the fact that all funds will be used to buy more books. Hopefully no one will be left out for lack of funds. Our first purchase will be an encyclopedia, which will be purchased for $30 (with additional funds raised at the ice cream social.) We talked about other books we might buy, and it was decided we would buy as many books by Kansas authors as is practical.

I'm more excited about the lending library than I've been about anything in a very long time. I must ask Emily what everyone is reading in Philadelphia. I managed to put up two dozen jars of peaches today, even though it was hotter than Hades, but was joyful in anticipating the reading ahead.

Thank heavens the wheat crop has survived the drought. As hard as we pray for rain, one good thunderstorm (or God forbid hailstorm) could ruin it all. We know this from last year.

June 28, 1909

Now starts the fun part of gathering books. We have decided to collect books at both churches on Sunday mornings in July, and those who live in town will go door-to-door soliciting donations. We've also decided to host a box supper auction for the 4th of July picnic, believing there will be enough bachelors to bid up prices for our special treats. Hortense told us the Women's Mutual Benefit Club in Herington played a benefit baseball game, which was very successful; all the town's businesses closed for the afternoon so men could watch their womenfolk running bases and chasing pop-ups in long skirts. Claire about fainted at the mere idea of it all.

Still no rain, and we're all going mad with worry. That's why we need the escape of books so desperately.

July 7, 1909

Green Valley is getting a library. A whole building devoted to books. Ada was so jealous that she took it upon herself to write to the Kansas Library Association in Topeka. Mrs. Wilma Collins responded and gave us lots of good advice. In addition to memberships, she cited the following fundraising possibilities:

El Dorado mounted a playlet, "Six Cups of Chocolate," and performed it in Ellet's Opera House, charging $1/admission.

Eureka hosted waffle suppers and one woman made a Battenberg lace handkerchief that was raffled. $35 was raised.

In Manhattan, William Jennings Bryan lectured on "The Value of the Ideal," and donated half of the receipts to the library funds. Half of the receipts amounted to $152.70! They then held a parade with 102 floats representing history from Spanish explorers to the present time.

Other ladies have held rummage sales and conducted minstrel shows to raise funds. As Hortense pointed out, "As usual, in most active historical and cultural events since the Garden of Eden, the women were the prime movers." As always, she is right.

Mrs. Collins also told us we can rent boxes of fifty books from the Traveling Library in Topeka. Cost would be $2 to cover transportation, and books can be kept for six months.

In addition to the encyclopedia we've ordered with funds raised during our most successful 4th of July ice cream social, we have now collected three dozen books for our lending library. Someone donated a biography of Abraham Lincoln, and Hortense shocked us all by telling us she'd heard him speak in Leavenworth, when she was a young girl. He'd come out to campaign and spoke about John Brown and slavery, subjects of utmost importance before Kansas became a state. All the talk in the town was about Brown's upcoming execution for his raid on Harper's Ferry, VA, since everyone had an opinion about the violent role he'd played in killing five pro-slavery Southerners. Lincoln said he didn't believe in violence but had to admire Brown for his convictions.

Imagine having heard Abraham Lincoln speak! Hortense told us she hadn't understood it all, but she knew she was hearing something very important. It lasted over two hours. Lincoln was tall and powerful, and even a known slave owner stood up *to compliment his oration. Hortense described the parade and seeing Lincoln in his carriage, wrapped in a buffalo blanket because it was bitterly cold. Hortense usually doesn't talk much about herself but since I asked so many questions, she told me she'd also seen John Wilkes Booth playing Richard III at the same Union Theatre.*

It must've been exciting to live in Leavenworth then; it was the biggest city between San Francisco and New York. They built a library in Leavenworth over thirty years ago. Hortense told me it has two Iconic columns on either side of the door with a portico and wide stairs. It stands on a little hill, so it dominates the entire town.

When Ned proposed to me and asked me to move to Kansas, I thought he meant Leavenworth, or even Lawrence, not way out here in New Hope. Would I have said yes had I known? Probably. He was so handsome and full of confidence and energy. All the girls wanted him. No one else could compare and I felt so lucky he chose me.

It's dawn and I haven't slept, at first engrossed in my new treasure and then wide awake as I consider the many questions it raises. How did they get from the idea of a literary society to building an actual Carnegie library? Did they simply write a letter to Mr. Carnegie and that was that? Did the town rally around them or put up resistance?

Finally falling asleep and not awakening until noon, I miss Elena when she comes in from church. There's a note on the counter saying she's gone to gather wheat, which guests will throw instead of rice at the bride and groom. She read that wheat symbolized fertility to the Jews in the Middle Ages. "We're not Jewish, but wheat is much more appropriate in Kansas than rice. Is there a better way to say 'Go forth and multiply?'"

I take my late breakfast of contraband chocolate chip cookies out to the front porch, enticed by the weather. Sheet lightning on the horizon and the rumble of distant thunder, but otherwise no sign of rain. Still it makes me nervous. After stashing the cookie evidence in the garbage pail next door, I settle in to read *In Cold Blood*, trying to distract myself from the journal long enough to get a fresh perspective. The wind provides a creepy soundtrack to accompany the murder of the Clutter family. Truman Capote captured the horror of this slaughter and showed how the town of Holcomb must have been shaken to its core when four innocent family members were killed by two strangers with no greater motivation than wanting a thousand dollars in cash. An incident like that in New Hope would traumatize the entire town for decades.

As I sit on the porch swing, contemplating the murders of the Clutters, the sky darkens to almost black, making me jump at the sound of a sharp snap of thunder before the wind picks up and rain comes down in torrents, with hail the size of nickels interspersed with the water. The thunder gets louder, and I start counting the distance, the way I did as a child—one mile for every second: *one Mississippi, two Mississippi, three Mississippi, four.* And then there's not time for even one. I'm terrified and search the horizon for signs of a tornado, trying to remember what corner of the basement I'm supposed to huddle in if I see a funnel cloud.

The wind changes, and hail pellets start hurting me, just as I spot a man running down the street, wrapped in a plastic garbage bag, with more plastic over his head. His umbrella has caught the wind so it's inside out, all the spokes pointed straight to the sky. He stops to try to put it down, fails, then frustrated, holds it out in front of him like a spear, and starts sprinting. I can only stare. Until he dashes up onto the front porch, lunging at me. The Clutter killers still fresh in my mind, I have an adrenaline rush of fear and push him away, using the full force of my biceps and letting out a scream. Before I realize it's Brett.

"I knew Elena was out gathering wheat and thought you might be frightened," he says, his hands held up in surrender. "I thought this might be your first all-out storm, and I'd impress you with my chivalry. Instead, I've frightened you to death."

He wraps me in his arms when he sees how terrified I am, hugging me long and hard, soaking me. I can feel his heart pounding through his shirt; my heart is pounding even harder. This I've always wanted, to be held tight by a strong man during a storm.

TRACI

I can't get myself comfortable on the concrete floor, and I can't bring myself to climb into the pristine princess bed. The crickets are louder than ever, and I'm sure it's a coyote howling, not the dog next door. The moon's full and has managed to position itself as a spotlight through the small open window, aimed straight onto my face. I fight with the sheets. I punch my pillow, then turn it over so the cool side's against my face, then repeat the process. Again and again. I'm still tense from this afternoon's storm and can't settle down.

Might as well get up and try to figure out another way to entertain the Teens. Nothing left to do on the mural, and I need to be ready. I'd like to take over that wall on Mr. Jack's Pharmacy, let them do a mural there, but I suspect Mr. Jack might have objections. If he gets willy-nilly about my going through his garbage, he'd probably shit in his filthy pants if the Teens dared paint on his dirty, whitewashed wall.

Maybe we could do some yarn bombing instead. It'd be like graffiti, but with yarn, and therefore temporary. Less offensive.

Thanks to the Internet, it's easy to find pictures of yarn caps on statues, yarn-wrapped sign posts, and even a fully covered yarn bus. The whole idea behind guerilla art is to do it in secret, and the Teens would love that, but I'm no idiot, so I shoot off an email to Rachel with some links, so she'll know what we're up to. If she doesn't go for it, I'll figure out something else, because it's not worth annoying her to make the Teens happy.

As I'm shutting down the computer, I see a list of new posts, all on the arts center's Facebook page. Sam has put up the photo from the *Gazette*, the photo of the mural, rotten eggs and all, and linked to the article. Rachel is the first to comment, *"Congratulations! Can't believe what our artist-in-residence has accomplished in a few weeks!"*

And then the posts get ugly.

"You call this art? Then you should come wallow in my pig sty."

"We don't need this highbrow, artistic snobbery. What's good enough is good enough here."

"That So-Called-Artist needs to go back to New York Citee. Shouldn't be messing with our kids heads."

"Do our taxes support this shit? And I do mean shit. A piece called Diarrhea is nothing but shit."

"What happened to Family Values?"

"Now maybe people will believe me. We need to close down the arts center."

GAYLE

Yesterday's storm made me jumpier than a kangaroo, as images of our tornado flashed through my brain. I'm still haunted by our first looks at the devastation, after we'd plowed our way up from the basement. Lightning flashed, then we'd catch a glimpse of debris, then total blackout until the next look. Over and over again, like we were caught in a horror movie—short shocking snapshots interspersed with total darkness. Smashed overturned vehicles, arcing power lines, and busted up trees.

When I tried to explain this to Angelina, she immediately suggested I'm suffering from PTSD, post-traumatic stress disorder. Got on the computer to see if there were books I could order from the library that might help. *Post-Traumatic Stress for Dummies*. I thanked her but passed, having never been a believer in navel-gazing therapy.

Traci, always sensitive to everyone's moods, came over to give me special attention, which I could see got Mrs. Gene Lubber's back up, but I didn't care. Traci showed me how to decorate my fabric with polka dots, using a pencil's eraser for a stamp to be dipped into tempera paint. Orange polka dots on the purple fabric seemed like it'd clash, but Traci insisted they're magically colorful. I was scared I'd ruin the fabric, but she reminded me it was salvaged curtains; someone had ironed a hole right through the material, and if our experiment didn't work, we'd use it for rags. "They don't call me Trash for nothing," she said too modestly. That girl's always putting herself down.

I took out all my frustration on that fabric, concentrating so hard on getting it right, and in the end, the polka dots almost made me happy. God might've invented polka dots as a mood elevator. His own cure for post-traumatic stress disorder.

ANGELINA

The lights of the Carnegie library are on, so I stop in, even though it's after ten o'clock. The atrium is full of women, women making potholders, some of them quilting, others knitting. They're determined in their sweatshop activity, absolutely committed to keeping the doors open. Jennifer is prodding them on. "Please, can we do another dozen tonight? We need to be ready for the Fourth of July." They look exhausted. Determined, but exhausted. Even Sylvia and Madonna have shown up.

Watching them work reminds me of Carnegie's father, a weaver. I break the silence by telling the women he convinced his fellow weavers in Scotland to pool their funds to buy books, so one man could read while the others slaved away at their looms.

"The cigar makers in Cuba do that, too, don't they?" Jennifer asks. "Hire a person to read aloud while they work?"

Before you know it, the women are discussing what books they would read to one another. Jennifer suggests *Chocolat*, suggesting Traci has arrived in town to sprinkle good will and happiness much as the chocolatier did in the small, complacent, old-fashioned village in France. *The Da Vinci Code* appears to be the top contender, until I mention an old favorite of mine, *A Tree Grows in Brooklyn*. From memory, I tell them how Francie discovered she would never be lonely again, once she found the world was hers for the reading.

"I loved that book," Jen says.

"It would be perfect," Rachel concurs, nodding over at Sylvia whose head is bowed in her stitching.

Sylvia raises her head long enough for Elena to explain the book is about an 11-year-old girl who escapes her dreary life of poverty by reading. I add that the book was the absolute favorite of soldiers during WW II, so Sylvia won't think it's all about her. Sylvia shrugs, and Elena promises to bring a copy from the library so we can all get started.

For the first time, the building Carnegie built seems as appropriate as an arts center as a library. It's clear how much this place still means to New Hope in its current reincarnation, yet the ghosts of my grandmother and her cronies are closer than ever. I know them better for knowing these women.

As I'm thinking about them, and carefully placing my grandmother's journal in my computer bag, a photo falls out from a secret library pocket in the back. An old fashioned tintype. The woman is my grandmother. The man I don't know. They are standing in front of the library. I retrieve it from the floor, quickly, before anyone can see, and tuck it safely back in the hidden pocket.

TRACI

When Rachel asks me to join her at Jo's on Saturday morning, I know the news is not good. Not that she isn't her usual sunny, cheerful self when she insists on buying me not just coffee, but a six-stack of butter pecan pancakes with corned beef hash. Still, something's bugging her. Finally, after she's taken yet another long hard look at the newspaper article she brought along, she asks if we can talk. "Sure," I say. "Why not?" Why else would she want to meet me here? It's not like I don't know that even 213 potholders will only raise about a thousand bucks.

"You need to know there are more ramifications to the mural," she tells me, as seriously as if someone had died. "I thought it would blow over, but Gene Lubber has rescinded his $5000 pledge. I'm sending Frank Chase over to reason with him, but if he doesn't come through, we could be in serious trouble. Don't panic. I'm sure we'll find a way to pay you. At least what we owe you to date. But I thought you should know."

"Who's Gene Lubber?" I ask. "I mean I figure he's the husband of Mrs. Gene Lubber, but who is he, anyway?"

"He owns the funeral home," Rachel says. "Part of an old-time, conservative family. Although his father was never as conservative as Gene Junior is. Gene the First was more of an old-time, Kansas Republican, like Ike, not like this current crop who want to cut our throats while they're pinching our pennies. Gene the First was a great supporter of

146

both the library and the arts center when it opened. We couldn't have done it without him." She stirs more cream and sugar into her coffee, so it's almost white. "I don't know what happened with Gene Junior. Maybe it all dates back to when he was ten and the FBI pushed him into a corner, took him by his shirt collar and demanded he tell them the truth. The Lubbers were running rum then, supplementing the funeral home business by moving moonshine in their oak coffins. The FBI were too cowardly to actually look inside a coffin, so they picked on Junior instead. Turned him into a bully, if you ask me."

That's Rachel Smythe. Always giving everyone the benefit of the doubt.

"What would we have to do to get his money back?" I'm overstuffed with pancakes, but finish the side of bacon, realizing I could soon be scavenging on the streets again and glad for the few extra pounds I've collected.

"Take the mural down and apologize," Rachel tells me. "For starters. Maybe even fire you and forbid the kids from coming back."

"Because he's God?"

"Because he thinks he is," she says. "Or at least God speaks to him directly. If he had his way, he'd close us down and take over the building. Don't you worry though," Rachel tells me, the picture of worry herself. "We'll figure it out."

When I get back to the arts center, toilet paper is strewn everywhere, proof of the disdain the Teens hold. A few thousand yards hanging here, there, and everywhere. No way can it be called art. They don't give a damn about me or anyone else.

And I don't give a damn about them. I'm furious when they come in, all "itching for fight," as the natives put it. When they pull out their cellphones, devices designed to help them ignore me, I lose my temper. I can't believe what they're putting Rachel through to defend them, when they're so completely rude. I can't believe they'd put my job at risk, the whole arts center at risk.

"So how come you look like an old hag?" Sylvia asks, looking up from her phone. "I mean you look more like a hag than usual."

"So who gave you the baby bump?" I ask, too angry to filter. "Don't tell me they're now making you haul a cantaloupe in your panties to demonstrate what it's like to be pregnant."

Her face falls to the floor, and I realize she has gotten herself into a heap of trouble.

"Who's the father?" I ask.

She starts to stomp out, but Sam catches her. As she mumbles, "dunno," Sam slings his arm around her. "She doesn't know," he says, as if he could answer. "Could be. Well, see it happened at the morp."

"The morp?" I ask.

"Yeah, that's what we call the prom. Prom spelled backwards. The anti-prom." He doesn't let go of Sylvia, but turns his face down so he doesn't have to look at me. "A bunch of guys were calling her a lesbo and she decided to prove she wasn't. She doesn't know which one took."

"Oh. My. God." Sylvia kneels down to tie her sneaker, so I can't see her face. "And you thought if all those boys were screwing you, they loved you." I know the truth of this. "So now they're calling you 'slut' instead of 'lesbo?'" The question hangs in the air. "Have you seen a doctor?"

"Like no offense, but it's not any of your beeswax, is it?" Sylvia says, more defiant than ever. "I don't want that bad energy around my baby, y'know?"

She backs up and puts her hands on her stomach as if she has ever cared about another human being.

"But you've got to get help," I insist.

"You can't tell," Sylvia screeches. "You can't tell a-n-y-o-n-e. Or else."

What can she do to me worse than stranding me at Walmart?

"You have to get to help." I can't believe how passionate I am about this fact. There is no way she can ignore the baby in her belly.

"You can't tell," Sylvia repeats her screech. "If you tell, we'll tell on you."

"Tell what?"

"Tell Rachel you lied. Tell her what we found online. *The Village Voice*. That you're a trash can baby, garbage, never studied art. She'll fire you for sure then. You'll be back on the streets."

GAYLE

Everyone had settled down to their needlework when Donna broke the news this morning. "I have an announcement to make," she said, waiting for everyone to look up. "We decided last night we'll rebuild in Prairie Hill. It won't be easy, and I'm still not sure it's the best decision. Me, I'm ready to move to Lawrence, where I might be able to get a job, and we'd have some cultural opportunities. Clyde wants to move back. He wants to stay on the land his great grandfather homesteaded over a hundred years ago, before Kansas was even a state.

"That's wonderful!" Rachel exclaimed. "You must be so excited!"

"I'm getting there. I was dead set against the whole idea. Thought the tornado was a sign from above that we could move to Lawrence, like I've always wanted. Prairie Hill was dying before the tornado. No jobs. The kids all escaping the minute they could."

I know why Donna made up her mind this weekend. We went over to Greensburg and got the tour. Saw what they've done in the few years since a tornado wiped that town off the face of the earth. We stayed in the Silo House, the concrete house you can see on YouTube, where they dropped a Ford Escort from sixty-five feet above to show what would happen in a tornado. Destroyed the car but not a dent in the building. Designed like a silo because the real silo was the only thing standing after their tornado hit.

It's amazing what they've done. New hospital. New museum. New senior center. Whole new downtown. Even a grocery store. The arts center was the first building to open and became the first certified LEED platinum building in the state. They've put up wind turbines and damned if they're not powering the whole town off the same energy that destroyed it. They, like us, were forced to rebuild brick by brick, to start from scratch, thanks to Mother Nature. But they made the best of their daunting predicament. Now all homes are 35 percent more efficient than Kansas code requires. The mayor told us the original green people were their ancestors, farmers who valued conservation, and they were determined to become an example of the resiliency of the human spirit.

Most impressive to me is the fact the grown kids are moving back. Having their own babies. The pre-school population is exploding. People are finding new ways of making a living. Tourism. Solar industry. One guy came back from Austin, where he was a chef, to help his folks, and ended up manufacturing his own spice blend right there.

We won't have the money Greensburg did, what with the whole world in a recession. And I don't know that we'll do it all green in Prairie Hill. Lots of people believe this environmental crusade is overblown and political hogwash. They don't buy global warming, although they can get conflicted when they talk about the Biblical commandments to act as stewards of the land.

If only we can bypass the CAVE men, we'll have ourselves a thriving little community, better than before. CAVE men being Citizens Against Virtually Everything.

ANGELINA

Rachel decides I should come along to persuade Brett to write an editorial in support of the arts center. Maybe she got wind of our day in Dodge City, which is probable since everyone knows everything here. Or maybe she's clairvoyant and saw the light bulb go off in my head the other night, acknowledging the arts center's importance. I meant to decline but a sudden image of my father calling me "Scout" appeared, a habit of his whenever he wants to play Atticus and remind me of the courage demonstrated in *To Kill A Mockingbird*.

Rachel, Elena, Jennifer, and I squeeze our way into Brett's office to beg for his help. Fitting four large, sturdy, masculine wooden chairs into his office is a challenge. Once we're seated and he's closed the door to indicate privacy, I'm claustrophobic, but my discomfort might be worth the price since I have the chance to watch Brett react to a roomful of concentrated estrogen. I've thought of him as a powerful man, but he looks intimidated by this envoy of women. He knows we want something before we even finish exchanging niceties about the sweltering weather. He wipes his brow with his handkerchief and cracks his knuckles and looks miserable.

He's gracious, though. "Elena, how are Paula's wedding plans coming?" he asks, as if he hadn't heard all the details from me. "Jennifer, is Frank out watering his crops with a garden hose at this point? Remind him the Boy Scouts did rain dances in Prairie Hill before the tornado hit. Tell him to be careful." "Angie, how's the dissertation coming?" as if we hadn't spent Saturday together. How I'd like to tell him the truth, about what I found in the journal. Later.

Finally, he gets to Rachel, as if he knows Rachel holds the agenda. "Let me guess. You're here to talk about the arts center. How's it going?"

"Not going so well, despite the impressive work Traci Ashe is doing with our Quilters and Teens. She's even brought together the women of Prairie Hill and New Hope," Rachel tells him. "But to get right to the point: We're about fifty thousand dollars short of our fundraising goal and we'll need to close if we can't turn things around. We don't even have money in the bank to pay Traci for this first month. We've lost our Kansas Arts Commission funding thanks to the politicians, and memberships are down because of the recession. Gene Lubbers has threatened to rescind his contribution. We're still having our weekly potlucks and we're making potholders like crazy, but there's just not the money there once was. This drought isn't helping, some are supporting relatives in Prairie Hill, and a lot of people gave what they could to redecorate the Methodist parsonage. Not much left over, no matter how good the cause."

She stops to take a breath.

"And, by the way, your coverage of the mural didn't help any," Elena points out. "Could you not have finessed that just a bit?"

Brett looks stricken. "We tried to tell the truth, as we saw it. We went over there to do you a favor, to show what you're up to. Had no idea it would all turn so sour."

"You need to do an editorial," Jen says. "Be a leader in this fight to save the arts center. Show some balls."

Rachel winces at Jen's language. Brett turns strawberry red. "We've got a lot on our plate right now," he says, avoiding eye contact with any of us. "We're still trying to cover what's happening in Prairie Hill, their decisions about rebuilding. And there's the drought, may turn out to be the worst corn yield in seventeen years." He stops and makes a note.

"I don't know. I love you ladies, but I'm not sure your arts center is a priority."

"You're not serious, are you?" Rachel asks.

"Actually, I am," Brett says. "This isn't my cause. On top of which, I can't afford to piss off my advertisers. Lubbers was in, threatening to suspend advertising. 'Everybody knows us, there's no real reason to promote the funeral home in your paper,' he told me. 'Don't get it into your head to start defending the arts center. If you're going to go off on your liberal agenda, maybe it's time we part ways. Do our marketing on the Internet.'"

Brett gets up and stands behind his chair, putting both hands on the back, and leans forward. "Do you realize how long the Lubbers have advertised with us? Every single week they take out a quarter-page ad with a Bible verse. They haven't missed a week since before the Depression. The Great Depression."

The room is suddenly quiet, so quiet the hum of the air conditioner takes over, and I wonder if anyone will respond. Brett has turned his back on us to look at his bulletin board, where he moves an announcement of Saturday's livestock auction to front and center. Rachel rustles in her purse for a handkerchief, and Jennifer stretches, her hands linked together and arms lifted over her head in a yoga pose.

"What would your parents say?" Rachel asks, in the softest of voices. "After what the arts center did for you when it opened. You're better than this, Brett."

When Brett turns around, I get a glimpse of the six-year-old Brett and realize he'd been a pouter. He knows how to sulk.

"All I remember is my mother got it into her head to make the library into an arts center as a bicentennial project. It was 1976. I was home from college, and I spent the entire summer scooping up bird shit and bat poop and cleaning the place. A buck an hour. All so I could buy a used Ford Falcon."

Is he seriously resentful or just trying to deflect the question? Is he really unwilling to take a stand for the loss of a funeral ad?

"Let me refresh your memory," Rachel says. "A few years later, when you came home to stay, you broke your leg playing baseball, and you were devastated. Didn't know what to do with yourself and thought your whole life had come to an end. Willy Wilson, the drama coach, helped produce *West Side Story* that summer, and you put shoe polish in your hair to play Tony. Remember how all the girls went gaga for you? It was like the whole town had piped-in music. Everywhere you went you'd hear "I've Just Met a Girl Named Maria." Oh yes, and there was controversy about that. Willy Wilson had wanted to do *Romeo and Juliet* but you demanded something more 'relevant.' Not everyone in town thought it was the wiser choice."

"I don't need to worry you're losing your memory, do I?" Brett tries to make light of Rachel's comments with a brittle laugh. He looks uncomfortable, but she's not dissuaded.

"This whole town watched a broken-legged, broken-down young man turn into a strong, compassionate, and accomplished adult. All I'm asking is that you help give the kids similar opportunities now. You can do that, can't you?"

Brett puts his hands up in the air, surrendering, to stop Rachel's tirade. "Don't I even get a meatloaf dinner?" he asks, dead serious.

"Meatloaf's on me," Jennifer says. "Frank slaughtered Monday. I'll try to get my hands on the famous recipe. But remember this is the twenty-first century, and we have more power than meatloaf."

"I'll see what I can do," Brett concedes. "But you women better start writing letters to the editor too. Use that power."

These women are smart. Maybe not smart as in academic smart, or even street smart like Traci, but smart as in strategic, sensible, and savvy.

On the sidewalk outside after we've said goodbye to the others, I ask Rachel, "Will you really be able to save the arts center? Both raise the money and fight off Lubbers and his ilk?"

"Don't know," she answers with a sigh. "But I do know we've got to keep doing the work, putting one foot in front of the other. God helps those who help themselves, and it might take a miracle or two, but we've got to keep doing the work. That's what you learn in a farming community. If you don't seed, if you don't tend the crop, nothing else matters."

TRACI

The Quilters have turned into an army in their mission to save the arts center. All they can talk about is how to raise enough money to keep me here and keep it going. They got Brett to write an editorial in the *Gazette*, and it was pretty damn impressive. He wrote about how people wanted to live in a place that's vibrant and thriving. About how the arts center helped change New Hope from nowhere into somewhere. How even Brigham Young built an arts center before he built a church when he got to Salt Lake City. The historical reference impressed Angie for sure, as if she weren't already crazy for the guy. He wrote how "hope" is both a noun and a verb, and it's time we put some muscle behind the verb. He wrote about how he'd once had a son and dreamed his son would find his own voice here.

The women wrote their own letters to the editor too. Jennifer wrote the arts are the soul of a community, whether it's a big city like Washington, DC, or a small town like New Hope. Rachel bragged about me, how important I've become to both the Guilters and the Teens, what a difference I've made. Even Gayle, from Prairie Hill, wrote saying how jealous they are of our arts center. The *Gazette* published them all.

None of it is making much difference though. The Wednesday night potlucks have dropped off, and tonight raised twenty dollars. Rachel didn't want me to notice when she counted the money, but I can see there are just a few bills, most of them single dollars. Some families have stopped coming altogether, scared of the Lubbers and their pals. The contributions are down (as is the quality of food, to be honest. Lots of chicken, some of it leftover, more Jell-O than ever). Rachel said not to take it personally, that people are feeling both hot and poor, but she has a crease in her forehead that usually isn't there, so I can tell how worried she is.

When I turn on the computer, there are responses to the editorial on the art center's website. Really mean responses. Anonymous and mean.

"If we wanted to live in a city of depravity, we would live in a city of depravity," Citizen for a Clean America writes.

"Junk is junk is junk is junk," and *"Junk is NOT art,"* writes Patriot.

"Frivolous at best," says letsgetserious.

"Send 'the artist' home," writes Watchdog.

As if I have a home.

The decent thing would be for me to quit, pack up my supplies, hitchhike out of town, end the controversy, and let the Quilters hang their ordinary, well-made quilts. At least those quilts are getting more impressive every day as the No Guilters are learning to play with color and embellishments. At least I can be proud of that. If I left town, maybe everyone would settle down and they could keep the arts center.

It would break my heart to leave now. This comes to me with the force of a Grade Five tornado. As hard as it's been, I like it here, like having such a great space, like being part of a bunch of women, whether or not they give a damn about me. But if things don't get better, I should definitely move on. It's the best for everyone. Hell, if I'm not going to be here anyway, I might as well tell the truth about Sylvia and get her some help. That's it. I'll do that much. Keep a baby from being left in a dumpster, even if I do nothing else.

GAYLE

Honestly, I don't know what got into me. How I decided I should write a letter to the *Gazette*, blasting those idiots who want to close down the arts center. Those holier-than-thou folks have certainly never met Traci and Rachel nor seen the miracles they're performing with Sylvia and her teen gang. They haven't seen how the place is like church in the way it pulls people together and gives them reasons to get up in the morning.

I don't know why I decided I had to put my nose in New Hope business. Tell them the arts center was the best thing that ever happened to their smug little town. But I did and before I could change my mind, I took my letter down to the *Gazette* office and slipped it under the door. My heart was pounding about a million times a minute. I didn't think they'd print it, but I still felt kind of proud of myself for standing up to the bullies.

Something changed inside of me. When I got home, I told Mark we could take one of the FEMA trailers and move back to Prairie Hill. Yes, it's the first step in conceding we'll probably rebuild there. Mark was overjoyed when I told him, reminded me of Vic when he got his first toy train. He smothered me with hugs and kisses, out of character for my most un-demonstrative husband, and said, "That's the girl I married."

I've been selfish. Prairie Hill means the world to him, Prairie Hill *is* his world, and I shouldn't have procrastinated just because

I'm now afraid of my own shadow and every other shadow too. We need to get back to Prairie Hill and make some buildings that cast some shadows.

ANGELINA

Jennifer is taking me out to Grandmother's. Finally. I can't believe I've been here so long and haven't been able to see it. Thad Hopkins made it clear he didn't want me to come out, and my geographical sense has been off, and I can't picture what direction to go. And let's face it. I've been a coward about going alone, afraid of what I'll find, and how I'll feel, after the vehemence from Brett's grandmother and Hilda.

"You know, maybe your sense of direction is off because they put in a new road," Jennifer says, once we've started out. "We haven't had rain in so long, I'll bet the creek's dry. Let's try to go the old way."

Sure enough, it all begins to come back, just after we leave the city limits. There's an old farm stand, a windmill, and a country church with its own cemetery. When we get to the dry creek, I remember the day we waded in it; several boys had already arrived, were soaking wet, and showed me how to catch tadpoles and the small toads that were hatching. There had been so much water in the creek my father had cautioned me to be careful so I wouldn't be swept away. The creek doesn't look as if it's had a drop of rain in the thirty years since. More threat of drought than floods.

Pulling up to the old farmstead, I'm overcome with a sense of doom. The house is decrepit, as if the slightest wind could blow it down. So small, it's a miniature of what I remember. The rosebushes my grandmother tended with such pride are withered. The greenery that lived around the house is now vine-y and eerie. I can identify the old tree from which my tire swing hung, but it's stripped of its leaves and looks like it was hit by lightning. Over to one side is a huge heap of metal, a junkyard, where tomatoes and cucumbers once grew. When we get out of the car, we're rushed by a swarm of grasshoppers. I suddenly understand my mother's perspective on Kansas but try to focus clearly on my memory of a more charming place. The whole place looks downright spooky.

I'm just about to tell Jennifer we can turn around and go back when she pushes me forward, pointing to a man standing in front of a trailer. Once he sees us, she turns tail and goes back to the truck, leaving me to face him alone.

Thad Hopkins is expecting me but he hasn't baked cookies. From what I can see, he's well built, but he takes the power position with his back to the sun, so his body is silhouetted. He has a crew cut and is clean shaven, about 6'2", but it's hard to make out his features, and he doesn't take off his reflective sunglasses, so it's impossible to make eye contact. He's not the least bit interested in meeting me, and now that I've seen how little care he's given to a place I cared so much for, I'm equally as disenchanted.

"Shi-i-i-t," is his first and only word of welcome. He's carrying a spatula in one hand and slaps it against the palm of his other hand to emphasize his point.

"Thanks for letting me come for a visit," I offer.

"Whadya want?" He backs off slightly, putting the spatula in his back pocket and then clenching both hands into fists, which he thrusts into his pockets.

"You knew my grandmother, right?" My voice quavers at this innocent question.

"Yep."

"You probably knew her better than I did."

"Undoubtedly."

"I'm trying to write about the Carnegie library that was built in 1912. Thought maybe I could get some insight into her efforts."

"Wasn't around then," he tells me.

"Well, that's obvious. You're not as old as I am. But maybe if I have questions …

Before I can finish my sentence, he snarls, "Maybe. Call first."

Dogs barking threateningly not so far away underline the sentiment.

I want to at least walk around the house, but I'm not welcome, so I thank him and say goodbye. I'll have to figure out another way in. The entire conversation has lasted less than two minutes. My father would have said he needs charm school. My mother would call him trailer trash. He looks familiar but I can't place him, and I'd definitely remember the attitude.

When he raises his sunglasses, it hits me. He used to be the pony-tailed hippie guy sitting around the table at Jo's, the one with a quick sense of humor. More has changed than his haircut.

By the time I get back to Jennifer's car, I'm shaking. And sobbing. Confused and, ultimately, defeated.

TRACI

I don't tell anyone about my plans to leave. I let Rachel hug me when she comes in, and I clear a space on my desk so Angie can set up her laptop. She still likes hanging out here, sometimes working, sometimes pretending to work. She was going to stay in New Hope for a couple of weeks but she can't tear herself away. I totally get it. This place has a way of making itself feel like home.

Rachel was less averse to the idea of yarn bombing than I thought she might be, but she's got her own take on the matter. "Needs to be done within the walls of the arts center, so we don't antagonize anyone," she tells me. "And something positive. What about little red hearts?" She'll come by to help. Like that will go over with the Teens. Crocheting little red hearts with Granny.

The Teens surprise me. They're in a strange mood, kind of somber, and so quiet Angelina keeps writing. At least Sylvia is somber and as Sylvia goes, so go the Teens. When I tell them Rachel will help us crochet yarn hearts, Sylvia rolls her eyes and says "What … e … ver," but her level of defiance is way low. Not normal. Sam's eager to participate, and Madonna announces she'll make some too, not to hang but to give to Rodney, her boyfriend. Even Madonna has someone to love her. "Madonna and Rodney, sittin' in a tree, k-i-s-s-i-n-g, first comes love, then comes marriage, then comes Madonna with a baby carriage," Zed chants. Both Madonna and Sylvia shoot him The Look.

Out of nowhere Angelina asks, "Did you know Andrew Carnegie started working when he was thirteen? Younger than you guys. Twelve-hour days. Winding bobbins. Then he got so rich he built over sixteen hundred libraries across the country."

"That's stupid," Sylvia says. "If I get rich, I sure as hell won't build libraries."

"What will you do?" Rachel asks, always interested in the other person.

"Buy shoes. Jimmy Choo shoes. A car. And guitars, so we can have a real band. I'm gonna be like Madonna. The *real* Madonna, not her," she says, pointing to her pal. Pregnant Madonna not Madonna the Virgin. No sign Sylvia's made good on her promise to see a doctor. As soon as Rachel hands me my paycheck, I'll tell on her. Before they throw me out of town.

We've finished our first fifty hearts and started hanging them from thumb pins around the gallery, when Sylvia announces, "This is crap. Making kids no one wants make red hearts. Like if we make a million hearts, someone might like us. Do you even know what it's like, to be so ugly your parents throw you out? Can you even imagine?"

Her boobs are about to pop out of her too-tight jersey top, as she stares me down.

"Yep, I do know, and you know I do," I think. But I still can't say the words out loud. Not with Rachel right there, taking up at least half the love available in the world.

As if reading my mind, Sylvia gets bold, hurls accusations at Rachel. "You don't know. You don't know what it's like to be passed around like you're crap. To be throwaway kid. To have your parents hate you so much they toss you out like garbage."

I glare at her, to make sure she doesn't spill the beans. I'm not ready. I want to sleep here tonight, maybe even buy enough to time to hang the quilt show, before they run me out of town for lying about my experience.

Rachel looks startled but only momentarily. She finishes yet one more red heart while she considers what to say.

"There's something you need to know about me," she whispers, her voice so quiet we all have to stop hanging hearts to hear. "Something no one else in town knows. Or at least talks about." She stops to pull another spool of crochet thread out of her bag and all of us stop to look at her. "My father was an orphan. Came on one of the orphan trains."

"What's that?" Sylvia asks, daring Rachel to interest her. "Never heard of them."

"I haven't heard of them either," Angelina says, which is much more surprising.

"Back in the olden days," Rachel tells us, "they sent orphans from New York City out here, to be adopted. Cleaned them all up, dressed them in decent clothes, taught them a few manners and prayers. In fact, they weren't all orphans. Some of them were neglected or their parents couldn't or wouldn't take care of them. My father was one of them. His mother got tuberculosis and died, and his father couldn't take care of eight kids, so he dumped them on the streets and took off. They found their way to the Foundling, and then they were boarded on a train out here. His brother got adopted in Ohio somewhere and had a hard time of it. He told us he was taken in by four different families, each more abusive than the one before. At one place, the whores at the brothel took pity on him and fed him breakfast every morning because he was so hungry."

It hurts me to hear Rachel tell the story. I hand her a glass of water and she smiles a thank you. Angelina is madly taking notes at my worktable.

"My father was luckier, although he sure didn't think so when he was alone on that train from Ohio to Kansas. Scared out of his wits. When they got here, they lined the kids up on the platform, and Mr. Smythe, as we always called him, went straight to my father and shook his hand. He had the farm and the bank and actually wanted a son, not a servant, like lots of people who adopted did. Love at first sight, no matter how ornery my father was. They brought him home, fed him a full farm dinner, more than he'd usually eat in a week, and his whole life changed."

"I've never heard of the orphan trains," Angelina says again.

"It's not happy history, the only kind we like to tell," Rachel tells her. "But something like two hundred thousand kids were shipped out West between 1870 and 1930. We never learned about it in school. I didn't even know about my father until he was ninety years old. His brother contacted him weeks before he died and that's when we learned everything. They hadn't seen each other in over eighty years."

"That is so sad," Sam says.

When I hear Angelina sniffling, my eyes get wet too.

"Sad, indeed," Rachel says. "But with a happy ending. At least in my father's case. The Smythes, and this library here, changed my father's life."

"How did it change his life?" Angelina asks, turning a page in her notebook.

"Well see, everyone made fun of him when he got here, played tricks on him. When he was dying, he told me how the first Halloween, the librarian overheard the boys in town talking about rolling over out-houses, like they always did. 'We'll blame it on the bastard Smythy.' was their plan. Well, that librarian asked my father to come here and tell ghost stories to the young'uns on Halloween night, and he did, and he did it splendidly. He had his alibi. People talked about what a fine actor he was, after he got involved in reading ghost stories. He always told me the library saved his life, but I never knew about the orphan train. It was Mr. and Mrs. Smythe who gave him eighty happy years. And the library. Actually gave me my life too, when you think about it."

No wonder Rachel has such a soft spot for the Teens. She might not even hate me for my beginnings. It kind of explains a lot about her.

"Wish someone would've adopted me," Sylvia says.

"Oh we have," Rachel assures us. "We have definitely adopted you."
She looks at them, and then me, as she says it.

If only.

GAYLE

Here we are. Home. In a trailer. When you have absolutely nothing, it takes no time to move. Turns out our name was already on the list, and it took just a phone call to get us in. Two months ago, I would've turned up my nose at this place, but now it feels like our own McMansion. And it comes furnished, complete with refrigerator, stove, microwave, coffeepot, dishes and silverware, sofa, rocking chair, coffee and end tables, and a dining room table and chairs. Even linens and dishes. Brand spanking new. It smells like plastic, but hopefully the smell will go away.

There are about three hundred trailers in this park on the edge of town. The streets are already paved and we have electricity and plumbing. Telephone and cable lines will go in next week. They say it makes more sense for us to be here together in this section of town, rather than on our own lots, because we'll soon be building there.

The neighbors are way too close. Luckily, it's Donna's family next door because we can almost touch each other through our kitchen windows. She threw me a package of Oreos as her housewarming gift, reminding me of the hot apple pie I'd delivered to her so many years ago. Later, she was close enough to poke her head out and ask if we were okay when she heard the smoke alarm go off when I was frying bacon. We're living in a box surrounded by other boxes, but I still prefer it to imposing on Mary.

It's a start. Fifty years old and we're starting from scratch. I may never drive through this town again without sobbing, remembering that most awful day of my life that was fifteen minutes or less. But we're starting.

ANGELINA

Elena hands me a letter as soon as I walk into her house. The letter has been forwarded from my mother, which means it's undoubtedly been steamed open and re-sealed. I handle it gingerly, noting the stamp is a Kansas windmill, celebrating the state's 150th birthday. My favorite secretary, eighty-year-old Bertha Jackson, must've chosen to stamp rather than meter it. She's a philatelist herself and laments her job offers fewer and fewer treasures in the form of commemorative stamps.

I slit it open and squint to read:

Dear Ms. Sprint,

I regret to inform you Dr. William Belvin had a stroke two weeks ago and will no longer be able to serve as your dissertation advisor. Due to your upcoming and imminent deadline, the Department has taken the initiative of assigning me to be your advisor. I agreed, somewhat reluctantly, as I'm not sure I see the point of your dissertation on Carnegie libraries. I don't get it. Hasn't this history already been written? Will people even be reading books ten years from now? There's a reason we'll be changing the degree to Doctor of Information Services rather than Doctor of Library Sciences. Wouldn't it be more relevant to see what Bill Gates might be undertaking? The leading philanthropist of our time? Andrew Carnegie's been dead for a very long time.

*Please email me and let me know what you're thinking. I'll be
in The Hague for much of the month, looking at digitalization of
libraries. (You should check out europeana.eu, now hosting over
ten million digital objects from 1500 European institutions ...
books, paintings, films, museum objects, archival materials. A far
cry from your little old libraries.)*
Sincerely,
Dr. Jason Young

My LITTLE OLD libraries? My LITTLE OLD libraries? How dare
he!

I stomp right upstairs to my laptop to email jyoung.

*Hi Jason, Sorry you're stuck with me but you'll love my dis-
sertation. Have found exciting new primary source material.
Provides historical evidence of how a few good women can
make the case for cultural institutions in their communities.
Totally relevant in this time of library closures and shortened
hours. Enjoy Holland. Don't forget to take time to smell the
tulips.*

Doesn't he get the fact libraries house treasures we pass on from
one generation to the next? How they organize, preserve, and provide
access to all that we know and have ever known about human existence? Can't he see that depending on Google is like opting for vend-
ing machine food, heated in a microwave, over fresh, organic veg-
etables straight from the fields? That no matter how much technology
advances, a librarian who puts a book in a person's hand empowers
that person forever?

I hit send before I can digest the fact I'm telling one gigantic lie as
well as pissing off the man who holds my PhD in his hands. Primary
source material? Primary source material with unknown content?

Primary source material I've searched for all month and have lost hope of finding?

I spend the rest of the afternoon in my room, deflated, seriously depressed about turning forty in two weeks. Empty. I am *little* and I am *old*. No job. Maybe no way to even make a living since Sprint Print is gone and, thanks to the economy, even small libraries can now find degreed librarians to shelve their books. I can't even read any more; all the print has suddenly turned fuzzy, and my arms don't stretch far enough to compensate for the blur.

Elena taps on the door and then hands me one more postcard. "Missed this one," she says, her eyebrows drawn together in a question mark. The postcard says quite simply, "I told you so."

"No need to have signed it 'Mom,'" I tell Elena, tearing it into shreds. For the first time ever, I say it out loud. "My mother is a witch."

TRACI

I roll the word "foundling" over and over in my mouth. Foundling. That's what Rachel called the orphans. A very strange term. Lostling would be more like it. Garbage. Trash. I try to think what it would've been like if someone like Rachel had adopted me. Would I have felt "found"?

It's hard not to be lonely, even here. Even though everyone is so *nice*. They don't realize it, but all they ever talk about is how much other people love them. *'Oh my Kevin, he can be such a tease. Last night he told me he was going to give me a trip to Kansas City to see the new performing arts center.' 'Do you know I've got Johnny trained to make the coffee every morning and bring me a cup before I'm even out of bed.' 'Ginger brought the cutest heart home from kindergarten the other day, saying I love it when Grandma reads books to me.'* Even their pets. *'Smuggles loves nothing more than to curl up in my lap and purr. So hard to quilt when she does that.'* They pass their cellphones around, with photos of their kids and grandkids and pets, like being loved is an Olympic sport.

I know more people here than I ever did in New York, but I'm still lonely. No one cares about me. It's more obvious how I don't belong. Why did I think I might? I'm different. And different is different here.

Maybe I need to show them different is good. The No Guilters have asked me to design a baby quilt pattern for them. Seems like they're all suddenly expecting kids and grandkids. In about seven months. "The tornado did it," Rachel told me. "Everyone celebrated being alive after Prairie Hill got wiped out."

But good grief, they don't all want identical quilts, do they? I need to design something where each of them can choose what they want. Maybe a set of animals and they can all choose their favorites. An alphabet quilt of animals. If they each pick their own fabrics too, they'll each be unique. Art-like.

I get totally entranced in my armadillos and zebras and it's suddenly past 2 a.m. But I'm excited. These are going to be pretty great, maybe something the kids will hang onto forever. I love the idea of a little Linus with one thumb in her mouth and the other hand clinging to a creation inspired by me. Yes, my Linus is a girl. I baste a sample quilt square in chartreuse, purple, and flamingo pink to startle their creative juices.

By the time I'm done, I'm so keyed up, I start crocheting more hearts and hang another dozen before stretching out on the concrete floor. It's almost dawn, and I'm so tired I think I might try out the bed some night. As long as I'm leaving anyway.

GAYLE

Mark promised me a surprise and I thought I'd figured it out when I found the bottle of champagne behind the milk carton. I reckoned he wanted to toast our new home.

But that wasn't it. Vic is here with Jill. They're married! In one instant, I was delighted because they'd done it and totally put out because they hadn't even told me, let alone had a wedding the whole town would've celebrated.

"And exactly where would we have held this wedding?" Vic asked. Today was their first trip back, and you could tell they were shaken by the absence of everything they'd ever called home. "Besides I knew you'd want your grandbaby to have wedded parents," he told me, with that crooked grin that could always get him out of trouble. "We're pregnant. We figured we wouldn't make it easy for this town to count days, by having a memorable wedding."

Yes, they'd snuggled up the night after the tornado, scared to death the two of them, forgetting to take precautions. A baby was conceived. MY grandbaby. Funny how BT I'd have been upset at the order of events, but now I only care about that child. It's not as if Vic and Jill haven't loved each other since they were four years old, playing tag and chasing each other, always forgetting who was supposed to be chasing whom. They'll make good parents, the two of them.

When I asked Jill about names tonight, she told me they haven't decided on a boy's name yet, but Vic is insistent a girl be named after me. "Gayle, like Dorothy Gale in *The Wizard of Oz*, who survives gale-force winds and makes it back home. A tribute to you, the most courageous woman we know."

It's astounding they believe I'm courageous. They have no idea how jumpy I can be. But I'm flattered and mean to try harder. Bravery may not be my middle name, but I can try to bury my cowardice.

ANGELINA

Thanks to Jason Young, I spend an hour moping in bed after the bad news about my dissertation. Finish off a bowl of butter mints Elena was testing for Paula's wedding, providing the rush of a sugar high. Then, I get mad. Plan to get even. I will write one of the most important dissertations of the decade. Be invited to lecture at the American Library Association's annual meeting, maybe give the keynote speech. Librarians across the country, no make that around the world, will be inspired by the stories of the Carnegie library movement and will credit me for changing their perspectives. Other universities, Harvard and Yale, will give me honorary degrees to ensure I will speak to their students. I will have forgotten Jason Young when he makes his way through the crowds to congratulate me. "I'm Dr. Sprint," I will say, graciously reaching out my hand to the rumpled and disheartened man. Or maybe I will mention him by name in my speech, as the imbecile who tried to stop me, and then simply turn my back and walk away when he comes up to greet me afterwards. Mother will read about my speech in *The Inquirer*.

It's not as if there are options. A Plan B or PhD-less long-term strategy. Tomorrow I'll have to come up with a future—where to live, what to do if I can't persuade the Lord of the Library School that I'm doing legitimate research. But today, I'm determined to proceed as if Mr. Young's letter was a hoax, a nightmare, or a drunken mistake. Enough of this black cloud thinking.

I pull on a pair of tailored pants and my "smart" top, the linen jacket that's classic enough for a preppie, carefully placing my owl pin on my breast. Kansas map in hand, I determine I can make a trek to the Kingman, Great Bend, and Lincoln libraries all in one day. They are less than a couple of hours' drive from each other, sprinkled like pearls along the blue highways. I will not be daunted. Whether I get my PhD or not, I want to see these Carnegie libraries.

The drive is unbelievably beautiful. And easy. If the Eskimos have a hundred words for snow, there ought to be more words in the English language for the verb to drive. Gliding along the smooth rural back roads is nothing like the stop-and-go, pothole-dodging, maneuvering in traffic in Philadelphia. With cruise control set to three miles over the speed limit, I sail along. The few cars I encounter have done the same. No need to pass. My mood lifts as my speed accelerates and then takes hold.

Kingman's library is a red brick, imposing, two-story Classical building, at the corner of a red brick street and the major highway through town, catty-cornered from the school. Steep steps lead up to what was once the front entrance, but now an easier path provides a more accessible entrance through a small garden with a statue of a woman reading to her children.

Gracie Weland, the librarian, is most gracious, if a bit bewildered by my request. After assuring her of my seriousness, she goes to her file cabinet to identify documents that tell me the library was dedicated on June 23, 1914, and was built for a sum of $9500. Seeing how entranced I am, how I want to look at every document, she leads me to an oak table, pulls out an oak chair, assures me both are original furniture, tells me to make myself comfortable, and returns to the counter where she can still keep an eye on me as I look through the old folders.

The announcement of the library's opening in *The Leader-Courier* tells the story in one long run-on sentence:

"A fine crowd visited the library that evening and inspected the elegant building, and the universal comment and verdict was that it was an institution of great value and benefit to the city, from all view-points; architecturally, convenience of location and far and above all, it will be of untold benefit to the young and oncoming generations that may visit it and share in the privileges and benefits to be derived from such an institution; as it will contain hundreds and thousands of books, magazines and papers, covering every conceivable subject matter of interest: such data having passed the necessary censorship and scrutiny of a competent Board; so the knowledge may be of a clean, pure and elevating and helpful nature."

All these years later, the library is still of great value to the community. There are still the old wooden card catalogues, but computers too. Patrons wander through. One is a teacher, returning a wheelbarrow full of books she had borrowed for her students. Another is an elderly woman from Kansas City, researching her genealogy or maybe looking for her high school beau. A third woman brings back a dozen mysteries, which she says she has "devoured" while sitting at the bedside of her dying mother.

Inspired by what I've found in Kingman, I head to Great Bend, passing through desolate little towns that must be in their last days. Why do some small communities flourish while others threaten to curl up and die? The drab and dying ones don't have libraries, churches, railroad stations, or schools. Only overgrown crabgrass, weathered houses, rusty cars, and dusty streets. Why do some places have more energy and commitment to change? Is it in the water? In the genes? Or a matter of circumstances? Do people walk faster in one town than the next? Why does a place like New Hope thrive when one like Green Valley shrivels up?

The Great Bend Carnegie was razed when a new one was built and there don't seem to be many records left. But a generous Lillian Beatty, who has worked in the library for over thirty years, takes time to tell me how they used a book brigade to move the books from the old library to the new library. "Every single book was handed down a city block, one person to the next person to the next," she tells me. She also tells me Hays razed their library, built a new one, and then, in a third reincarnation, built a front to look like the original Carnegie library.

Lincoln is a tiny town, but it has its own art gallery, which I would take time to see if I weren't obsessed with my research. My heart's going pitter patter with the potential of more discoveries. I haven't thought of dear Jason in an hour, or Brett, or Thad, or anyone else. Only of my libraries.

The Lincoln library isn't on the main street, but a sign leads me straight to the building that must be a Carnegie. It strikes me every thriving town has a sign leading to the library, as if Kansans know the library is the most important place in the community. They have their priorities straight, unlike a certain "information specialist" I could name.

This library too has two entrances, a grand one with steps and a back basement entry. The No Guns Allowed sign—a silhouette of a gun with a red slash through the middle of it—puts me off the basement entrance so I head up the stairs. It would never occur to me guns might be allowed in a library.

The librarian is sitting behind her big desk, helping a girl place a star on her Frequent Reader Card. The girl stands taller for having finished her tenth book this summer and is allowed to pick a gift from a tub of small toys. Her choice is a small beaded bracelet. As if the joy of the books weren't enough.

When she's done with the young girl, Martha Mills, the librarian, hears my story and claps her hands in delight. Quite the contrast to Witch Hilda. She asks me to keep an eye on the desk while she goes to a vault and pulls out the original handwritten minutes from over a century ago. When she hands the binder to me, I see the journal itself needs preservation, pages literally falling out, and worry I should be wearing white gloves to handle it. With goose bumps at what I'm seeing, I open it gingerly, delighted the penmanship is excellent and so readable. Knowing it's pure treasure, I request permission to take it to the back of the library where I can examine it in solitude.

It takes me less than two minutes to get caught up in the life of Miss Janice Dearborn, the librarian paid one dollar a week for her services in 1910, which included collecting fines of two cents per day. For the next two hours, I'm living a century ago, wrapped up in the challenges of a small town library and the details that made it run. It's easy to hear them haggling over how much to charge for the ice cream social, which ultimately was declared a success and netted the library $11.25, or discussing the price of admission for an entertainment, where seats would cost forty cents, twenty cents for children, and ten cents extra for reserved.

My head spinning with details, I head back to New Hope, cruise control set at 68. I pass the wind farms and imagine the windmills are dancing in the sky for my benefit. Someone told me if you could catch a ride on one of the blades, you'd be flying 200 mph. As it is, I feel like I'm flying down the highway. I'm so inspired by my discoveries the hundred-mile drive takes about ten minutes. Even the sign "Jesus Heals and Restores, Pornography Destroys" doesn't set me off on a tirade, the way such an attack on freedom of speech might. My mind is ready to explode; I can't wait to do more research.

As I pull onto Main Street, Brett's car is outside the *Gazette* office, so I pop in. He is interested in my discoveries, asks questions about how the towns learned about the Carnegie grants in the first place, if they were competitive in getting their own buildings.

"Who got theirs first? Did we lead the way?" He's disappointed when I tell him Prairie Hill, Green Valley, and Kingman all had libraries before New Hope.

He treats me like I'm smart, like every word I have to say is important. When he leans in close to look at the photos on my cellphone, popping a breath mint into his mouth first, I don't pull away, feeling every cell of my body responding to his interest. I want him to touch me, touch me anyplace, but when he puts his hand on my elbow I get so flustered I drop my files, and the photo of my grandmother with the baby who is my father drops to the floor. Brett picks it up, looks at it, and suddenly pulls away, as if he's seen a ghost not a photo.

TRACI

The baby quilts are a phenomenal hit. The ladies have become more creative than I've ever seen them, daring to mix polka dots and stripes with a touch of paisley. They're totally inspired and hardly need my encouragement. It's awesome. They all start telling me how fabulous I am and how lucky they are to know me.

Everything is fine until Mrs. Gene Lubbers struts in with extravagantly expensive silks in purples and lavenders she ordered from China. "I want to make a quilt for the Governor's wife," she announces, sucking up all the attention in the room. "It must be stunning. I want her to put me on the Friends of Cedar Crest, so I can help decorate the governor's mansion. You need to help me."

I suggest we meet privately in the morning but she wants me now. NOW. Never mind there are a dozen other women in the room and she's going to need major, major help. Rachel insists she pay me for my extra work, $500.

"Okay," she says and almost throws the material at me as she stomps out, Rachel yelling after her, "You'll need to make a 50 percent deposit. In cash."

The door slams behind her.

"Has anyone read Edith Wharton?" Angie asks from behind the desk where she's working on her laptop. "Mrs. Lubbers is like Urdine in *The Custom of the Country*. Charming and generous when she wants something. Once she gets it, or if she doesn't, she turns mean and spiteful. It's all about her. Everything's always about her."

"My seven-year-old granddaughter has her pegged," Rachel says. She told me, "'Mrs. Lubbers tries really, really, hard to be nice. But her personality gets in the way.'"

The rest of the room laughs as they consider the wisdom of a child.

"Did you ever read *The Sociopath Next Door?*" Jennifer asks. "The author says a full 4 percent of the population don't have a conscience. They can be charming sometimes but they're ruthless always. Have absolutely no compassion for humans or animals. They can't help it. They're biologically deficient."

After everyone else leaves, Rachel hangs around, and I'm worried she's about to give me my marching orders, that Lubbers' finally got to her. Something is on her mind.

"Just spit it out," I say, because I can't take her discomfort another second.

"I'm so embarrassed we can't pay you," she says. "We never should have brought you out here if we couldn't honor our commitment, but it never crossed my mind the Prairie Hill tornado would play such havoc here too. Anyway, I *promise* we will give you your full month's pay when we've sold the potholders at the Fourth of July parade. In the meantime, my son is loaning you his camera. It's the least we can do. See, it's almost exactly the model you wanted. And you've got enough to eat, right?"

Now that I have a camera, I cannot wait. When Angie told me about her grandmother's dilapidated farm, I knew I wanted to capture it. Even though she told me in no uncertain terms that it'd be trespassing if I went there. Even though she warned me about the killer dogs she heard barking. Even though her descriptions of Thad Hopkins make him sound like a serial killer. Even though last night's supper seems not to have agreed with me and it's going to be another scorcher of an afternoon.

Angie's been nice to me, bringing me books about artists, and I figure the least I can do is get her some good photos of her grandmother's place, so I load up my backpack with ground chicken, microwaved because I'm not sure if dogs eat raw meat, and head out on foot. It's three o'clock, and there's at least five more hours of daylight.

The asphalt road is gooey. Sticky with every step. When the asphalt runs out, the dirt road is hard as concrete, but there's still dust in the air from the empty fields. The muscles in my calves complain about the exercise and my shoulders start aching as well. Within half an hour, I realize I haven't brought enough water. Would serve me right if I died in the middle of the road, not found until my body is picked bare by vultures and my skull left to rot like a Georgia O'Keeffe still life.

When I make it to the mailbox marked "Hopkins," I see Angie forgot one important detail. In addition to the "No Trespassing" sign, there's a barbed wire fence surrounding the property. Although Rachel showed me how to navigate one, I've never had to do it. Copying her method, I push the bottom fence down with my left foot while pulling the upper wire higher with my right hand, carefully placing my fingers between barbs. Head down, right leg through, body hunched over, then left leg. I sit where I've tumbled to catch my breath before proceeding, sucking my thumb that got barbed.

The house is in even worse shape than Angie led me to believe. Boards are loose, the windowpanes are all broken with glass missing, and it hasn't been painted in forever. Desolate. Perfect. Using the sepia setting to make it look like another century, I get some cool shots. After I've clicked about a hundred pics of weathered wood and decayed tools, I spot a path through the wheat fields and set out for more photos there.

Which is when I hear the dogs. Loud and threatening barking. Dogs that sound as if they could tear a person apart, devour her, and leave her bones for buzzards to pick clean. No wonder Angie freaked and hightailed it home. Adrenaline races through my body, and I realize how long it's been since I felt the drug, once so common on the streets of New York. Scared to death but totally alive. Thump, thump, thumpety-thump.

Digging the meat out of my backpack, I proceed forward carefully, cooing "Nice Doggies," as I go. My skin is drenched. Are there different kinds of sweat, depending on whether it comes from fear or heat? Does sweat all smell the same? I can hear the dogs jumping up against the fence, metal clanging together as they disturb what sounds like metal pipes. My heart might beat itself out of my chest.

The gate pushes open easily; it's not even locked; and when I hold out my meat, the dogs run over, jump on me, then pull away, coy, or even shy. They're not killer dogs; they're collies. Even I know. Lassie, come home. I throw the meat on the ground, but I'd be safe having them lick straight from my hands.

Now fed, the collies will have nothing to do with me, watch from a distance, as I survey the landscape of the wide, open field. Spatulas lay out on the ground everywhere. Could it really be a meth lab? The collection of used spatulas lined up in a row would indicate just that. There are also rusty old bedsprings, with small pots in them, herbs growing. Marijuana plants? Surely there aren't enough here to make a living. When I lean down to sniff, they smell more like pizza than pot.

Totally baffled, I'm determined to figure out what's going on. The doors on the barn are chain locked, so the only way to see is through the windows, which are at least seven feet off the ground. I look for something from the metal scrap heap so I can prop myself up to peer through the windows of the barn.

A metal oil drum is the answer. I roll it over to the lowest window, tip it up, and climb on top to see what's inside the barn, grabbing the windowsill to balance myself. It takes a split second to adjust my eyes and register what I'm seeing. A makeshift kitchen with a small fridge and toaster oven. A single bed, unmade, up against one window. The place could use a good cleaning but it's not a disaster. Not any worse than my old flat.

I get down and roll the barrel over a few feet so I can see the other side of a partition. Re-perched on top of the barrel, I encounter a different scene entirely. Junk heaped everywhere. Tables. A studio! In one corner are sculptures, made of found objects. Mammoth figures made from junk. An American Gothic couple—the head of the man is an oilcan and the head of the woman a pie plate, the man holding a pitchfork and the woman a broom. But the expressions on their faces aren't hard and cynical, like the ones Grant Wood painted. This couple seems to smile, share a joke, know something we'd like to know. Behind them is a stucco wall covered with broken plates. Some fine china, some Mexican pottery, a few cup handles still intact. Amazing art.

Through the opposite window I can see a car, a VW like Ruby Slippers, but painted black with chalkboard paint, with graffiti all over it. Fuchsia ribbons wave from the antenna. An electronic guitar lays across the hood and a microphone hangs from the rear view mirror. A microphone and tape recorder set up in front.

How come nobody told me this man is an artist? Maybe a musician. This guy has no time to make meth. He's too busy welding, carving, etching, and soldering pieces that would sell for tens of thousands of dollars in New York. He's too busy making music.

The dogs start yapping again and because I have no more meat and am pretty queasy, I make my way back through the wheat field, back to the clearing and the farmhouse. My heart's still racing with the adrenaline of discovery; I'm panting and need to seize some air before navigating the barbed wire fence. I stop for a breath.

That's when I spot the door in the ground. I thought I'd seen every detail through the lens of my camera, but beneath some gargantuan weeds with thistles the size of baseballs, there's a door, opening up to the center of the earth. A cellar, like Gayle was talking about. A root cellar. A storm cellar. The safest place to be in a tornado.

The hinges are rusty but with a lot of tugging I pull the door open, then wait for my eyes to adjust to the dark so I can see well enough to climb down the steps. It's dank and moldy, chilly compared to the hot summer air. Smells like wine or vinegar. Spider webs strung everywhere, which I swat away with my elbow. Jars of pickles line the shelves. Should I take a few? No one would miss them. Nah, even I don't need to eat food that's been sitting around for a century or two. I'm nauseous as it is.

I pull out a jar of cherries, to take up into the light to photograph, wiping away cobwebs from jars of peach jam. When I reach for another one, I brush against something with texture. Behind the jars are two notebooks, covered with dust, ancient, looking like they'll disintegrate in my hands. I pull them out and take them back up the steps where there's enough sunlight to see. It takes everything I've got to push the door back shut.

Sitting down cross-legged in the small patch of sunlight to have a good look, I see the first book is full of bad photos, of an infant. Some photos of her in a crib, some in the arms of a man or a woman, some in a kitchen sink. Dark and out of focus. Who'd even keep these? I thumb from back to front, then see a notation on the first page. "Angelina, this is your story. The story of the first nine months of your life. As you look through these photos you may think they are not very good—well downright poor really—but you must understand I could never throw away a picture of a grandchild. You are my first."

For some reason, I start crying. The kind of sobbing that starts before you know it, before you even have a thought. That gushes out before you can figure out how jealous you are that anyone could be loved so much.

I pull myself together but can't bear to look at the second book, just stuff both into my backpack, re-check the cellar door, make my way through the barbed wire, and head back down the road.

A hot breeze has picked up and I can hear a coyote in the distance. When a rattlesnake slithers across the road, my heart about explodes. The rattlesnake rears up and hisses at me, but I stay perfectly still and after about a week, it slithers back through the rocks.

It's hotter and hotter and then I smell skunk, potent eye-watering skunk stink, and throw up. Diarrhea, liquid mud, matched by stomach cramps. I sit for a minute after my dump but I can't stay. Somehow I have to put one foot in front of another to get home.

I walk another hundred steps, counting each one, then stop to rest, walk another hundred, rest some more. Throwing up again helps, but now I'm weak enough to lie down by the side of the road and nap. Except for the rattlesnake.

A cloud of dust appears on the horizon, then covers me, as a red truck gets closer. When it passes, the driver slows down, and reverses the truck to come back toward me, stirring up more dust. I can hardly see, the dust is so bad, and I can't help coughing.

"Are you okay?" the driver asks, when he's stopped "What the hell are you doing out here?"

He's kind of cute in his cowboy hat, but I'm too sick to care.

"Just taking a walk. Taking some photos," I nod toward the Nikon. "But now I'm sick," I say between coughs.

'Did you lose your cookies?" he asks.

"What?" He might be crazy.

"You smell like puke. Did you barf? Upchuck? Vomit? Throw up your lunch?"

"Yep. That and took a crap too."

"Let me take you home, kiddo. Get in."

When he sees how weak I am, he jumps out, puts my arm around his shoulder, opens the door for me, lifts me up, and hoists me into the cab. Only then do I catch sight of the rifle behind his seat, realize he could be kidnapping me, but I'm too weak to fight against rape.

This gun-toting truck driver might be like one of the killers in *In Cold Blood* that Angie was telling me about.

"Where do you live?" he asks.

Or maybe he looks like Angie. Angelina. Angel. The one to save me from Death or welcome me to the next life. I tell him I live at the arts center.

"No one lives at the arts center," he says, giving me the once over. "Wait, are you the artist?"

It's too hard to answer; I close my eyes instead.

GAYLE

The stories of rebuilding break your heart. As if we haven't endured enough, contractors are coming in and taking advantage of our tragic situation. Cecily Tilton put down a $50,000 deposit, with someone who came highly recommended, a member of her mother's church in Tulsa, who now cannot be found anywhere. Except in an obscure court document from a decade ago, when charges were dropped on another case of fraud. Hers is the worst case, but there are others. Charismatic men showing up as if they cared and then disappearing with hefty chunks of cash. Thinking we're a bunch of desperate hicks who don't know any better.

So now that I'm still an absolute basket case when it comes to decisions, I let Mark convince me to sign a contract on our new "premanufactured house." We'd have called them mobile homes in the olden days. But these weren't anything like our FEMA trailer, which rattles the minute the winds come up, stirring up wicked memories and giving me the jitters. We picked the Cottonwood model, not because cottonwood is the Kansas tree, or because we lost our three in the backyard, but because the house looks charming as well as sturdy and will give us four bedrooms and two baths. I will have my very own crafts room. A "studio," as Traci would say. And a nursery for those grandbabies. Mark will have his shop and we'll have a TV room as well as a more formal living room.

This factory, Wardcraft, is an expert in getting homes up after a disaster and even puts us newly homeless persons ahead of their other customers. Wandcraft I call it, because it's like they can wave a magic wand and give us a house in a matter of weeks. Mark was impressed with their enhanced insulation packages and fiberglass windows; I liked being able to choose everything from cabinets to flooring to bathroom fixtures. I felt like a little girl at Christmas going through the toy catalog. It used to take us longer to pick pizza toppings. We circled what we wanted and they gave us a price, which we'll pay with our subsidized loan.

The homes are luxurious, like five star hotels, and I caught myself wondering how our shabby furniture would look. Before remembering we don't have furniture. "Tornado brain" we call it. We think about nothing but the tornado and yet we forget.

If I had my way, would I choose this brand spanking new house for the home full of memories and its dirty grout? No way. But as Mark keeps reminding me, our pioneer ancestors started with so much less. We're hardly moving into a sod house.

TRACI

Shadows move around the walls as the light changes. Quiet, whispering, muffled voices fade in and out. What I remember is the cowboy carrying me downstairs, laying me on the bed, carefully, like I was a princess or something. He made a phone call, told someone he'd picked me up by the side of the road. "She looked green, said she'd been vomiting, then fainted. I told her I'd take her home, so ..."

Later, I don't know how much later, Doc Simmons comes and they talk about me after he's stuck a thermometer down my throat. Talk about me like I'm not even here.

"She's pretty sick, alright. Probably food poisoning," he proclaims once he's mumbled "One hundred and two, Fahrenheit."

"Sweetheart, can you wake up for a second?" he asks me, putting his hand behind my back and sitting me up, because I seem to be too weak to take this action on my own. "Can you tell me what you've eaten lately? Chicken maybe? Barbecued chicken? Leftover chicken? Chicken salad?"

"Yes," I nod my answer.

"Which?"

"All," I whisper. I brought several chicken dishes home from the potluck.

"That'd be my first guess then. Salmonella poisoning. You should probably go up to the hospital in Hays," Doc Simmons tells me.

"No!" My scream comes out a squeak. How can I have gotten food poisoning here when I've spent a lifetime of dumpster diving, starting long before the freegans put on rubber gloves for their discard diets of garbage. They decided to leave no footprint on the earth while I only wanted to survive. Getting sick now doesn't make sense. Even with my cotton brain, I know this.

"You'd like the hospital in Hays." Doc tries to sweet talk me into it. "They have the best art collection in the State. Beautiful paintings on every wall. Mobiles hanging from the ceilings."

"Shoot me instead." As I start to gag, Rachel holds out a barf bag so I can vomit. "Please, no hospital. I wasn't even born in one."

"Do you have health insurance?" Doc asks.

"She's an artist," the cowboy answers. He's still here and it turns out he's Thad.

Hearing my prince defend me, hearing Rachel promise Doc Simmons they'll provide 24/7 bedside service, I drift off to sleep, dreaming of making art with Thad, his arms wrapped around me as he shows me how to solder and weld metal scraps to make a small sculpture, maybe a fountain. Yes, I like the fountain, with soothing dripping water. Dreaming of corralling chickens, me in stiletto cowboy boots and a pink Stetson hat, my rope a very long strand of pearls. When the chickens scatter to freedom, I shake my finger like a scolding schoolmarm and say, "Okay then, I'll become a vegan." Dreaming of opening a hope chest and finding treasures everyone wants, but I own, including an exquisite, silk, basket quilt. I put on a tiara and one by one, Angie, Jennifer, Elena, and Sylvia drop to a curtsy and kiss my hand.

Someone is always in the room with me. Every once in a while someone moves me. Takes away a bedpan and brings me another. Puts a cool towel on my forehead. Or a piece of ice on my tongue, which tastes good because I'm so thirsty. My body feels awful but I also feel protected. They call me names, but not Trash. Honey, Baby, Dear, Sweetie.

While I drift off, they keep chatting, which is comforting, like a lullaby. Rachel and Jennifer whisper, wonder if there's really no one they should call to report my ill health. Jennifer asks if she should bring chicken soup and they decide, given the circumstances, the BRAT diet would be better. That's what Doc Simmons recommended: Bananas, Rice, Applesauce, and Toast. Rachel says everyone in her church is praying for me and takes my hand to say, "God bless you" over and over again. Even Sylvia and the Teens come down, Sylvia declaring, "Wow. She looks bad. She's not gonna die, right? It'd suck if she died."

ANGELINA

If I'd known how sick Traci was, I never would have left town for the day. As much as I want to work on my notes, I won't concentrate until I've seen her. That girl has gotten under my skin, needs me to defend her from the world. Even though I'm only ten years older, I feel the need to mother her or become a favorite aunt.

Thad is hanging around her bedside, and it's obvious he's got a major crush on this sick, helpless girl. He keeps fondling the quilts on her worktable, pointing out details such as fine stitching and choice of embellishment. "Do you see these peppermint hearts she's glued on?" he asks. "Valentine hearts with sayings like 'Be Mine,' and 'Crazy4U.' This girl pretends to be cynical about love, but has a heart the size of Planet Earth."

Traci seems to have softened him up, but I still don't appreciate the way he's treated me and I don't trust him to be left alone with her. I can't forgive him. Would it have killed him to invite me to spend time at Grandmother's place, to check out the house, roam the acreage, and dig up some memories? It's not until Rachel comes in and I know Traci is well-tended that I head to Jo's, to meet Brett for lunch.

"I have a proposition for you," Brett says, once we've ordered our tuna sandwiches. His voice is all business. It's not going to be the proposition I was hoping for when he had his hand on my thigh; that much is clear. Not the proposition I might have taken when he had his arms around me in the storm.

"Yes? I'm all ears." I try to appear open to whatever he has in mind.

"After I wrote the editorial, Rachel convinced me to run a feature story about the Carnegie libraries in the state. She thought it might help put the arts center into a historical context, explaining the efforts needed to bring culture to the Plains."

He stares at me with his deep, hazel eyes that give nothing away. "Problem is, I'm knee-deep in another feature. We're writing about the Iowa cornfields this month. How farms a hundred years ago used to produce forty bushels of corn to an acre and will soon be harvesting two hundred bushels on that same acre. That's over ten thousand pounds, five tons per acre. Just think of it, thirty-one thousand kernels planted on an acre of land."

"That can't be healthy." I feign interest, but want to get back to the libraries.

"Probably not. But farmers like Frank will tell you they have to get bigger and bigger or get out. So they're up to their eyeballs in debt buying equipment, irrigation systems, and hybrid seeds, and then buy more and more land to service the debt. Frank'll quote Earl Butts, the Secretary of Agriculture he interned with, who believes cheap food is what makes Americans rich. Gave me a statistic this morning, telling me we feed ourselves for 16–17 percent of our take-home pay, so we can spend our money on other things." He stops to slather ketchup on his fries. "Frank'll also tell you no one complains about a farmer with her mouth full," he says, stuffing his own.

The farm story is clearly a priority for Brett; he's told me more than I need to know about farming. I'm flattered when he asks, "So what do you think? Can you do a few interviews and develop a story on the libraries? Can't pay much, but it'd get your name in print."

I'm thrilled. It'll give me credibility. I'll be published. People will read my work. Any pay is gold. I can stay another week if I pay a few hundred dollars on my credit card.

TRACI

From my bed, I hear the Teens rehearsing upstairs. Singing tunes from old musicals, "Food, Glorious Food" from *Oliver* and "Tomorrow" from *Annie*. Orphan songs. With hip hop beats and percussion instruments, making them sound totally cool. As I drift in and out of dreamland, their voices turn into those of angels, the songs going on and on. They recycle old songs like I repurpose objects, making something new and relevant out of something the world has discarded. They really are musicians.

I'm determined to get up, knowing they won't keep me here, certainly won't pay me, if I'm not teaching. I'm in some crazy state, halfway between earth and somewhere else. Maybe hell.

"What time is it? How long have I been sleeping?" It takes everything to summon the energy to ask. Rachel tells me I've been out for three whole days, that everyone's worried about me. As I lie in bed, I try to remember how I got here, what I was doing. It comes back to me in blurry images. Thad's farm. The storm cellar. The photo album. Like a bolt of lightning it hits me the other album could be the journal Angie's so desperate to get her hands on. Her grandmother's journal. Suddenly I'm sure. If only I could get to my backpack to confirm.

I can't get out of bed on my own. It takes help to walk me to the bathroom, but I'm definitely conscious again. Conscious enough to remember my backpack and the treasure I found in Thad's storm cellar. I don't want Angie to know about it. It's mine; I found it. I'll give it to her. Eventually. But first I want to read it myself, pretend it was my grandmother who loved me so much she couldn't bear to throw away bad photos.

Pretty soon I'll be able to get up and they'll have to leave me alone. The focus of conversation seems to be shifting from me to Angie's fortieth birthday party. "She's so bummed about getting old," Rachel says. "About the whole dissertation thing, about losing her ability to read without spectacles, et cetera, et cetera, et cetera. The only positive thing she ever thinks about is those libraries. We want to do something to cheer her up. She thinks we've gotten so wrapped up in you that we've forgotten, and you know we wouldn't do anything if you couldn't join us, but now, well don't you think you might be up for a party next week? We thought we could do it right here, make it a slumber party, all show up in our jammies, so you'll hardly have to move. She'll always remember she had her fortieth birthday party in a Carnegie library. Won't it be fun?"

"I've never had a birthday party, so I wouldn't know," I tell her. Rachel looks positively stricken at this revelation. "When's your birthday?" she asks, and I can almost hear her brain spinning toward next February. Like I'll still be here.

After asking a hundred times if I'm sure I'll be okay, Rachel decides I'm well enough to be left alone for an hour while she runs home for crepe paper to try out a decorating idea. She asks me to think about making bookmarks for party favors.

Finally, I have the chance to look for my backpack. Can't afford to wait, even though I'm shaky.

Steadying myself as I get out of bed, I wait long enough to be sure of my footing, then ease across the room, stopping to balance on a chair. My backpack is not at the bottom of the steps where I usually drop it. It's not by the bed where it would have landed when Thad carried me there. Surely I didn't leave it in his truck? No, he dug out my keys while balancing me on his knee when he carried me in, commenting how he couldn't believe I locked the door, most people leave their keys in the ignition of their cars around here. Maybe he left it upstairs? Suddenly weak again, I wonder if I can climb the steps by myself. Resting on the bottom step to catch my breath, I consider my options. Which is a good move because I spot the backpack right to the side, under the coat rack. It's light, much lighter than it was when I was too sick to stand up, so, holding onto the staircase rail, I manage to pick it up and drag it to the kitchen counter to open.

The books aren't there. No wonder it's lighter. My backpack's virtually empty, except for a water bottle, wadded up Kleenex, and a tube of cherry lip gloss. The camera's there, so that's a relief. Why didn't the thief take the camera? Who could it be? Who's been in my space? Just about the entire world. While I thought everyone was being nice, someone was going through my things. Thad could've taken them, could claim they were his since they were found on his property. He's sure being nice to me though, if he believes I'm a thief. Angie wanted them so badly, even the Good Girl could've stolen them, building the case for her possession. Who's the crook? A minute ago, I was so grateful to the lot of them, feeling unbelievably loved and cared for. But I know better. No one should be trusted. Now I'm seriously pissed off. I'm the one who found the albums, who loves all things old. I'm the one who should get to decide.

Should I confront them together or one by one?

GAYLE

What's so disorienting about being back are the sounds. Or rather lack of them. I was dreaming chainsaw music for a while, just couldn't get it out of my head, but at night it's dead quiet. The birds are all gone, which makes sense. No trees to roost in. We're living in the middle of the Big Empty, and as much as I try to focus on the good energy of the Hopeful Quilters, I want more for myself. Here and now.

Angie and all her talk about the women a century ago makes me realize I'd not have made a good pioneer. I like my comforts and a sense of safety. Can't have one without the other and I don't suppose I'll ever feel truly safe again.

ANGELINA

Traci is still sick in bed. Her absence creates such a void; it's almost as if the whole place is grieving. Which is undoubtedly why the Quilters have jumped on my suggestion to read aloud while they're working. To fill the silence with words. In the end, they did choose *A Tree Grows in Brooklyn,* and it's truly gratifying to see how these twenty-first century Kansas women relate to a girl of a different time and place. An adolescent girl suffering from poverty and a parent's alcoholism.

It's even more touching when Sylvia arrives and insists she take a turn at reading. She does so in her most melodramatic style—standing as she reads and enunciating every syllable. She holds the book in one hand as she gestures with the other, her tattered jeans and peasant blouse the perfect costume. At first it's all about the theater, but then she begins to relate to the coming-of-age story of Francie, as she holds her head high and puts her hand on her breast, reading about Francie's loneliness, her sense of being different. Gayle wipes a tear away and I find myself swallowing hard to avoid sobbing too. It's the first time I've seen Sylvia not carrying cynicism on her hips.

By the end of the morning the Quilters have finished 475 potholders. If each and every one of them sells on the Fourth of July, it will add $2375 to the coffers. Almost enough to support Traci and operating expenses for another month. This fact is totally discouraging to me, but Rachel maintains her optimism. "We've just guaranteed we'll be open through July. It buys us time. We take this day by day," she says. "Keeping the doors open until the next miracle can occur."

If only her faith in miracles were contagious.

Elena arrives wearing a beautiful new scarf from her daughter, and that's when it hits me. Not a miracle, certainly, but an idea. Why are we not making designer scarves instead of potholders? The kind I've often drooled over in museum gift shops, like the Barnes, the Woodmere, and the Philadelphia Museum of Art. The kind that sell for $50–$150. Better fabric for sure—silk instead of cotton—but with the possibility of selling for fifty dollars instead of five. Ten times the price. Surely almost nine times the profit. If there's not enough of a market in New Hope, we could search for outlets elsewhere or try Etsy.

Rachel calls Traci upstairs to confirm scarves wouldn't be any harder to make than potholders. Traci offers to create a knitting pattern as well as one for fabric, so everyone can have her pick, using remnants for each to keep costs low. "Maybe I can make rectangles to look like a books stacked on a shelf. Or a simple triangle can become our trademark," she says.

"Genius," Rachel claps. "Pure genius."

The other women are excited too. Jen heads straight to the computer to search online for bundles of silk scraps, finding some from a necktie factory as well as vintage kimonos to cut up. She suggests the Salina garage sales held every weekend as another source for recyclable fabric and discarded yarn.

I'm still not trusting my own good idea until Elena promises to buy the first half dozen as bridesmaid's gifts for the wedding. "I'd like to commission them from Traci," Elena says. "I know hers should be more, at least $75 because she's a real artist, but they'll be splendid."

First $450 already raised! Rachel says she knows a source for old cashmere sweaters that can be upcyled, and I offer to design a card to be printed, in a clean, sans serif font like Arial or Helvetica. A name comes to me as well. "'ScARTlette' might be perfect, because they will truly be small works of art," I tell the group.

"You're a SmARTlette, yourself," Rachel laughs.

After the adrenaline rush of creativity, it's a challenge to settle down to work on Brett's assignment, but I find a quieter corner at the back of the gallery in which to consult my list of the Carnegie libraries that still exist in the state. Allen Gardiner's book, *Carnegie Libraries in Kansas* is filled with human stories that will add depth to my architectural descriptions. Chattering in the next room subsides as I immerse myself in the feud that broke out in Independence over the library. Mrs. Stich, wife of the mayor and undisputed social leader of the community, had a row with her former good friend Mrs. Guernsey. The source of the feud was a serious dispute over the use of the French article "*la*" while the two were on holiday together in Europe. Everyone in the community was forced to take sides, to support one or the other woman, long after the reason for the feud was forgotten. When all was said and done, the war between the two women lasted eighteen years during which time Mrs. Stich obtained Carnegie's pledge for a new building and Mrs. Guernsey retaliated by getting elected to the library board and requiring the Stich faction "to withdraw books from its own library under the patronage of the enemy." All over *la* and *le*.

Or take Pittsburg, Kansas. In the middle of coal mining country, in the southeast corner of the state, the feud went even deeper. There was violent opposition to accepting Carnegie's money after the coal strikes in Pennsylvania. The local paper wrote a scathing editorial declaring the library would be built in the blood and tears of the Homestead strike, "when children starved, women wept, and workmen were shot to death on the doorsteps of the shacks they had been driven from by Pinkerton's hired butchers. We are not in favor today, nor any other day, of holding out clamorous hands for any of this tear-rusted, blood stained gold for library buildings."

Thanks to a book by Theodore Jones, *Carnegie Libraries Across America*, I'm able to weave in other details about the movement. Many towns lied about their populations because Carnegie wanted to give $2-3 per person to a town. Over 175 Carnegie libraries across the country have addresses on Main Street, proving their important role to the community. During outbreaks of influenza, tuberculosis, and smallpox in the early part of the twentieth century, many libraries treated returned books in fumigation chambers where a specially formulated sulfur candle burned overnight.

I point out that library philanthropy made up only a small part of Carnegie's donations, although the libraries are what he's best known for. He spent 90 percent of his fortune, over $333 million, for "the improvement of mankind." According to one source, he funded everything from the Simplified Spelling Board, to more than 7000 church organs, to the Carnegie Endowment for International Peace.

I feel good about the article, am pleased with the richness of the history. I've gone into some depth, covering the architecture of the libraries, as well as the history and sociology. I've quoted an architect who noted the most impressive public buildings share one thing in common - the ability to deliver both a sense of occasion and a sense of intimacy simultaneously. He cited the great cathedrals and opera houses of Europe as examples, and that's what the Carnegie libraries do. Their formidable façades shout their importance, while often their entrances are at the top of steps. Once inside, the cozy rooms and oversized furniture whisper 'Welcome' and 'Make yourself at home.'

Will the people of New Hope enjoy reading my article? Will Brett be pleased? As satisfied as I am with what I've written, I keep wondering if there aren't more personal stories to be told. Why haven't I found other journals, if not my own grandmother's? Will more things come out once my stories are printed? This isn't academic research that will impress Dr. Jason Young, but I'm thrilled to be discovering the heart of the libraries.

TRACI

When Thad drops by to see how I'm doing, and sees I've managed to get dressed, he insists I go to Lucas with him. Tells me
he's been lurking around my space and noticed I like junk. What he
really says is he's impressed with my talent and knows a place that will
inspire me.

"What's so special about Lucas?" I ask. "You think I ride in trucks
with strange men?"

"Of course you do. We've established that. Can't you respond with
a little sugar when a guy asks you for a date?"

A date? A date! Who goes on "dates"? Still, it must mean he likes
me, if he's not going to rape me. And I do need to find out if he's the
one who stole my books.

I fill my water bottle, ask if he wants one too, and grab my backpack. When we get to the truck, he actually opens the door and offers
me a hand as I hoist myself up. I catch a glimpse of myself in the rear
view mirror and wish I'd taken time to brush my hair. I look pretty
sickly; and my hair is growing out with brown roots showing, standing out more conspicuously than the purple stripe I used to wear. I
sure don't look like a "date."

The trip is beautiful. So. Much. Sky. Cloud formations, like cotton
candy, changing every minute. The fields, just cut, are an awesome
shade of gold. Green pastures surround them. It's totally cool the way
the hay is stacked in so many different configurations. In rectangular

cubes, stacked like walls, almost two stories high. Round bales lined up along a barbed wire fence. Square bales scattered across the field. One farmer has positioned his in a perfect semicircle, and I mention it could be in MoMA.

"Probably better in an art museum than in that field," Thad says with a shrug. "Smart farmers know those hay bales run the risk of catching fire if they're stacked so close. One cigarette thrown from a car window and their entire harvest is gone faster than you can say Yankee Doodle. Their livestock would starve. As dry as it is, a prairie fire could take out a few hundred acres in a matter of minutes."

He's playing the tough guy, like he doesn't see the beauty all around him, but he's definitely taking it all in. "Your sculptures are cool," I say, trying to bring out the artist.

"How do you know about my sculptures?" he barks, his face turning purple. He slams on the brakes so he can stare at me like he could kill me on the spot. "Oh I get it. You were trespassing that day. You were trespassing, weren't you?"

"I guess. I was just taking a walk, getting some good shots of the countryside."

He counts to ten, out loud, slowly, "1.2.3.4.5.6.7.8.9.10," taking a loud breath between each number. He looks like he might explode. "You must never, ever, ever tell anyone what you saw," he says, working hard to keep his voice even. "Or else," he adds as if I don't get it. As if I've failed to see the rifle behind the seats.

"Is making art so terrible?" I ask, after very long minutes have passed. "Is it worse than manufacturing drugs, which is what everyone in town thinks you're doing?"

"Is that what they think?" He kind of snorts. "I have my reasons." He clenches the steering wheel, then turns to stare at me directly. "You must never tell," he says. "Please," he asks, putting his hand on my shoulder. "Promise?"

"Promise." I raise my right hand and solemnly swear. As if I have anyone to tell. Although suddenly I realize I do. Rachel would want to know. Jennifer and Elena.

We ride in complete silence for the next thirty minutes while I wonder what Thad's thinking, what he's hiding, and why he's hiding it. What's he up to? He wouldn't dump me in the middle of nowhere like the Teens did, would he? Stuff me in a garbage can like my mother did?

He slows for a tumbleweed, and I break the suffocating silence to tell him how I still regret not picking up one for an art project. How I thought it would be cool to weave cassette tapes through its branches and decorate it like a Christmas tree.

"You can always order some online," he says.

"You're bullshitting me, right?" I ask.

"Yes, and no." He looks over, stares at me, to judge me. "You could. There are tumbleweed farms on the Internet. But why would you? After the next big windstorm, come out to my farm. You can collect a lifetime's supply for free. But ask first, okay?"

After we've driven a couple of hours, straight north from what I can tell, we hit the Lucas city limits sign, and I get why Thad has chosen Lucas. The Grassroots Art Capital of Kansas. Population: 407.

"We will start with the Garden of Eden," my personal tour guide tells me, pulling up to a block's worth of concrete sculptures, seeming to have forgotten his anger, suddenly friendly again. This guy's got the moodiness of an artist, that part's for sure.

"Shall we take the tour or should I just tell you there are over a hundred and fifty pieces of sculpture here, some of them fifty feet high, representing the eccentric guy Samuel Dinsmoor's interpretation of the Biblical creation?" Thad asks, after we've both gotten out of the truck for a look. "His mausoleum is here too; he's encased in glass so you can see what he looks like about a hundred years after he died. He married a woman sixty years younger, who is said to have married him because he was so damn funny."

I believe the funny part. This place is capital C crazy. I would've fallen for Dinsmoor too. I love the concrete Eve with her apple, a serpent leaning down to grab a bite. And the concrete American flag. The guy worked on this installation for over twenty years, expressing his view of Bible stories and nineteenth century progressive political thought.

"But wait. There's more." Thad tells me, when we've finished and just as I'm feeling seriously wasted. "You've got to see this truck with the World's Largest Collection of the World's Smallest Version of the World's Largest Things," he says, as we drive a few more blocks. Turns out this woman photographs the "world's largest things" from all over the country, then comes back to make the world's smallest replicas. I totally want to meet her. Just then, she pops out to tell us about it, using the world's largest ball of sisal string in Cawker City as an example.

The woman's not a kook at all but a pretty smart cookie. She tells us Lucas decided "to engage in out-of-the-box-thinking," to emphasize what's special about the place. "That's the key to survival," she tells us. "This town would have shriveled up and disappeared if it hadn't claimed its place as the Grassroots Art Capital of Kansas. Now, people from all over the world come to visit. Eight thousand visitors a year."

Anyone worshipping grassroots art, outsider art, naïve, or visionary art, would want to make a pilgrimage to Lucas to pay their respects. It's a mecca, a vortex of unbelievable creative energy.

Thad is infatuated with her. She's pretty, in a clean cut kind of way, and totally fascinating. They're a perfect couple. Which means I'm jealous. Unbelievably jealous after just part of a "date." She probably minds her manners and doesn't trespass.

"I need to pee," I whisper to him when she turns her back for a second. I want to get him away. "Use the ladies' room," I correct myself, trying to sound more gracious.

We say quick goodbyes and then head for the truck. No sign of a filling station anywhere. Instead, he pulls up to the "Bowl Plaza," where I just about pee in my pants, giggling so hard. The City of Lucas has made its public toilets a tourist attraction. Embedded in the sidewalk is an amazing mosaic of an over-sized toilet bowl, made with objects that might be found there—keys, toothbrushes, a pocket watch, even an alligator —complete with a dog licking from the rim. The intricacies of the mosaic mural almost make me forget I came to do my business in the "Oval Office," the stool itself.

Business done, I meet Thad outside. He's grinning at my delight when he tells me they've just had the "Big Flush" installation of the plaza, and auctioned off the "first flush" on eBay as a fundraiser. A true community effort. On the big day, people lined up a parade, all of them holding toilet plungers, scrub brushes, and tissue rolls.

Checking to make sure no one is looking, Thad invites me into the men's toilet to see all the toy cars embedded in the mosaic. As I snap some photos of the mirror, I see Thad looking at me over my shoulder. Looking at me like he's really seeing me.

All the way home, Thad sings stupid country Western love songs, pausing long enough to tell me about the motel called "It's Not the Hilton, But It'll Do," in Atwood. "They call it the 'It'll Do,'" he tells me. "You'd like it. They put a stuffed concrete mixer, eight-wheel construction truck toy on the pillow to welcome you."

"It'll Do? What kind of weird name is that? Poor hotel. Must have an inferiority complex."

I want to do it at the It'll Do. Do it at the It'll Do with Thad.

GAYLE

It required less than three hours to haul off the debris of our lives, trucks and bulldozers filling the air with diesel as they crunched through what used to define us. A bicycle wheel, bedsprings, a rake without its handle. I bawled through every one of those one hundred fifty minutes.

Mark's right. There's not much that can't be replaced. Except the photographs, which I never found time to digitalize. Always too busy raising Vic, or delivering packages for Yesteryears or doing their bookkeeping. I'll never again see that photo of Vic eating an orange, the juice dripping down his chin. Or the one of him and Jill playing with Legos, building an entire town in an afternoon.

I couldn't have stood it if we hadn't chosen our new home. Tomorrow they'll start work on the foundation, at the same time our house is being built at the factory. I have to hold onto that and the grandbaby on the way. More photos to take and this time I *will* digitalize.

ANGELINA

Itruly do not mean to eavesdrop, but when I let myself into the arts center to take another look at the library scrapbook, I realize I should have knocked first. Traci and Thad are in deep conversation downstairs, somewhat flirtatious, but serious too. Their voices float upstairs, soft but audible. Before I can stop myself, I'm entrapped in their conversation. Standing perfectly still so the floors don't creak, hardly daring to shift my weight from one hip to the other, I can hear every word.

"Why is it a secret? I mean I have secrets too, but I'm proud of being an artist. As a matter of fact, sometimes it's the only thing I am proud of," Traci confides.

"Tell me your secrets," Thad says in his low, sexy voice.

"If I do, will you tell me yours?" She drops her voice to almost a whisper.

"Yep, I'll promise. That's how much I want to know you. But I hope you'll still like me afterwards. Promise we'll still be friends?" Thad sounds absolutely infatuated.

"As long as you're not an ax murderer. And you have to promise too." She lets out a big sigh. "I was found in a trash bin, right in Times Square, just a few hours after I was born. I have no idea who my parents are. A couple adopted me, hoping I'd save their marriage, but I made it worse. I left the day I turned sixteen and never looked back." She pauses for a second as if to let him absorb this story. Then I hear the dare in her voice. "Bet your secret isn't any bigger than that."

"That's a big one, alright. You seem normal, under the circumstances." His voice is affectionate and I wonder if he's hugging her. "You turned out okay, if you ask me."

"Tell me yours. Tell me why you don't want anyone to know you're an artist," she demands in a muffled voice.

"Okie dokie. Here goes." He clears his throat. "I was a bastard child, never knew my father, was called a sissy in school because I didn't know all those man things. To prove to the world, and to myself, that I wasn't really, a sissy that is, I enlisted. In the army. Was one of the first to go to Iraq. And one of the first out. The wound on my leg was hell to heal, took six months of serious physical therapy, but the disease in my head hurt even more. It was before everybody was talking about PTSD. I knew I was crazy. Luckily, while I was in rehab I met a guy, an artist who welded steel, and he took me under his wing. 'I rebuild my life every time I turn a piece of scrap into art,' he told me. He became like a father to me and showed me everything. Like you're doing with those teens upstairs. Do you have any idea how you're changing their lives? Anyway, this guy, Don Lion was his name, assured me I had talent and even got one of my pieces into the exhibit at Walter Reed Medical Center. I was hooked. I managed to wean myself off the morphine they gave me for pain but I could never in a billion years give up the art making. It's the only time I feel okay."

I get the impression Thad has given Traci more words than he's ever used in his whole life. He's delivered his speech in one long monologue; his long-withheld essence offered up in a paragraph.

"And how did you get from there to Angie's grandmother's farm?" Traci persists.

"My mother was living on the farm, and I came back to be with her. She'd been diagnosed with ovarian cancer and we knew she wouldn't live long. I wanted to be with her, after all she'd done for me." There is a pause, of respect perhaps.

"And she was living on Angie's grandmother's farm because …" Traci asks as if reading my mind.

"You don't give up, do you? Okay, she was living on Angie's grandmother's farm," Thad lowers his voice even more so I can hardly hear him. "She was living on the farm because she's my grandmother too. Turns out Angie's father is my father too. When Angie and her father came back one summer, things happened. Love at first sight, my mother said, but evidently he didn't feel the same, since he never came back."

Shock waves run down my spine. Thad and I are related. That's why he's been so temperamental, his mood so mercurial.

"Does everyone know that?" Traci asks. "Because I'm pretty sure Angie doesn't." There's another pause, as Traci considers what she's just heard. "And you don't want everyone to know you're an artist because …"

"Because everyone thinks I'm weird enough as it is. That's all I'm going to say. Time for a malt? Chocolate. My treat. We need to put meat on those skinny bones."

I bolt out the door before I can fully digest what Thad said. It can't be true. But instantaneously, it comes back to me, my recurring nightmare, of a thunderstorm that woke me up in the middle of the night, while we were visiting Grandmother. I ran to my father's room, to snuggle up with him under the covers. He wasn't there. My grandmother collected me and tucked me back in, and not another word was ever said. It explains everything though. Especially why my mother was so angry when we returned to Philadelphia. Did my father know he had a son? Did my mother? That makes Thad my half-brother. Does everyone know except me?

TRACI

A crowd shows up for the Troubled Teens class. At least two dozen loud adolescents fill up the room, with dares, double-dares, and foul language. Kind of scary, especially since I'm still weak from the food poisoning. My first class since I got sick and I'm paying for the trip to Lucas and the chocolate malt. I can take the kids one on one, but as a group they're a mob. The place smells like hormones—sex and sweat mingled together—with hair gel, suntan lotion, and bubble gum layered on top. Stinky enough to make a girl nauseous even if she's healthy. Which I'm not.

The newspaper article has brought them, and Sylvia wastes no time in showing off the mural to her paparazzi. Sylvia could face down the biggest head in NYC, with her pride in that mural. "This is our statement," she tells them. "How we view the world. As artists, we have that responsibility, to hold up a mirror to issues that face us. Some people believe art has to be 'pretty' but it's more important that it states what we're feeling. That it's an honest representation of the world as we see it."

Where in God's name did she hear that?

Luckily I convinced Thad to come by to help, insisting we could use some good male energy in the room. He objected, said he had no rapport with kids, but I told him all he needed was to pull out his military language. Swear like a soldier. Not sure that was the issue, though. He made me promise, again, not to let them know he was an artist and a musician. "Cross my heart and hope to die, stick a needle in my eye," I promised. Hadn't I already promised to keep his secrets? He pulls it off, for sure. Brings in a truckload of junk he hauled from Prairie Hill and sets to work making art. Even I don't have the imagination to use the unidentifiable pieces he's collected. Mangled, twisted metal. He's a genius at choosing the exact right placement of every piece of that junk. One minute it looks like a garbage heap and the next it's making a statement about debris that you'd look at and contemplate.

When Sylvia insists they're musicians, not artists, he pulls out steel pipes and shows the Teens how to beat them together to make a variety of sounds. Starts singing, "Five hundred twenty-five thousand six hundred minutes" and tells the kids it's from *Rent,* and the number of minutes in a year. "You're supposed to make every single one of them count," he says, pointing at his wristwatch.

Basically he's a natural with the kids and they like him as much as I do. He lets Sam know how strong he is when he helps lift a car hood onto the top of a wooden crate to make a drum. He demonstrates to Zed how different metals have different sounds and tells him to look up STOMP online. And when Sylvia tries to flirt with him, batting those long eyelashes big time, he treats her nicely, but calls her "sister," to reinforce there'll be no hanky panky. He also winks at me over her shoulder.

Anyone would be lucky to be his sister. I hope Angie thinks so when she finds out. I lost another night's sleep worrying about her, trying to figure out how she can find out without my telling her. This is new to me, being caught between two friends. I promised Thad, but Angie deserves to know the truth of her sibling.

After class, Thad seems to want to hang around, so I offer him the only lunch I have, a peanut butter and jelly sandwich. "Yummy," he announces when he's cleaned his plate. "PB&J is my favorite, and that was the best one I've ever eaten."

He might be making fun of me, or he might be appreciating the homemade plum jam Rachel brought by. Not sure which. But he seems pretty content, so I ask him again about the question that's been bugging me.

"Why can't anyone know you're an artist?" I ask, as I clear the table.

He shakes his head, determined not to say anything.

"If you'd admit it, you could have a show here," I argue. "You'd be famous around town, and everyone would know you aren't dealing drugs." He shrugs his disinterest, but I continue. "You don't want to earn some money?"

"Don't need it." His arms are folded across his chest, like he's protecting himself.

My face must show my hurt, because Thad stands up, puts both hands on my shoulders and says, "Look, I already have a gallery in Wichita, and am actually doing pretty well. Nobody here needs to know that."

"How do you keep it a secret?" I ask, staring into his intense brown eyes.

"Use a pseudonym. Trevor Sprint Quinn. After the father I never met."

"Do you know how long it'll take someone to figure it out?" I ask. "It took the Teens less than a day to track me down, and I was using only one name there. Trash. In New York City. Consider yourself discovered, mister. It's just a matter of minutes. Even if it's not me who tells, someone will find out."

GAYLE

Donna's got a hornet in her hat. She thinks we should be develop-ing our own library and cultural center for Prairie Hill. Angie convinced her there are more public libraries in this country than there are McDonalds, and we should have our own.

How on God's green earth are we supposed to do that? No one in town has any money, that's for sure. No one except Les Stites, the Chevy dealer. Every single person in Prairie Hill needed a new vehicle the day after the tornado, and Les made a killing. But ordinary people, people like Mark and me and the owners of Yesteryears, we don't have two pennies to rub together. The chance of funding such a project is slim to none by my calculations. It would be sheer insanity to even consider such a proposition.

ANGELINA

How can I let Thad know that I know we're related, without confessing to eavesdropping or implicating Traci? I still can't digest my new reality of having a brother. Of having a father who was a philanderer. It does explain why my mother was such a shrew. Or was it because she was such a shrew that Dad looked for love elsewhere? My mother was perpetually jealous, accusing him of falling for every blonde, brunette, and redhead within sight. And he did flirt. Always. His specialty was creating nicknames based on fonts. "Angie," he'd say, "do you mind if I call you Callie? For Caledonia. An old-fashioned typeface known for its stability, feet-on-the-ground quality, with a wisp of calligraphy to provide a touch of liveliness."

Maybe my father used the font-nicknames because he couldn't keep his women straight. He'd never confuse the attributes of a typeface, but perhaps the multitude of women's faces weren't so clear? How could I have missed the signs left by my font-loving, philandering father? And then there's another big question. Did he know about Thad? Thad would've been twenty years old when my father died, and yet I'm sure they never met. Did he know of his existence? He couldn't have known and done nothing about it. Or did my mother threaten to leave him if he supported his son?

And Thad? Surely he resented my having had my father all those years and his never being recognized. He's being civil enough now, although I can't forget how rude he was to me out at the farm. Is it because he feels fortunate to have gotten the farm? But why wouldn't he let me take a peek? Would it kill him for me to step inside the house that holds so many memories of one perfect month in my life?

Unable to concentrate on my research, I decide to join the No Guilt Quilters for some piecing and distraction. It's always comfortable to hang out there even if I don't quite belong. I like their company and respect the way they collaborate to get a job done.

After the short but sweltering stroll down Main Street, I join the Quilters who are in the thick of a discussion about the weather. How hot it is, how the corn is withering in the fields, how they're beginning to predict this will be the worst drought in fifty years. How they might have another dust bowl before the summer is over. One like the big one.

"Frank's mother talks about how she woke up one morning to an outline of where her head had been, the rest of the pillow covered with dust. She taped the doors and windows, but dust still got in, so she never set the table until just before it was time to eat and covered all the pots and pans, so soup wouldn't turn to mud," Jen tells us.

"I'm worried about cleaning up my stash, because it's already getting dusty," Rachel says after a few minutes. "Can't let Johnny know how much fabric I have hidden around the house. Under the bed, upstairs in the attic, some in the basement, and some in the garage. Not to mention what's still in the trunk of the car. I'd use the freezer too if he weren't in there all the time for ice cubes."

"It's a collection," Jen says. "That's what I tell Frank. Some people collect floral ashtrays, some porcelain Scottish terriers. We collect fabric. Our SABLE. 'Stash Acquisition Beyond Life Expectancy.' Big enough to be seen from outer space."

"Well, I admit I used to hide my yarn stash, divide it up and hide it, so Hubby wouldn't know how much there was," Donna says. "I was a bit of an addict. Every time I picked up a new skein, I got a rush, like I'd have a new life once I knitted it into something even more beautiful." She holds a lace scarf she's just finished. "Now my stash is scattered to hell and gone."

As they exchange stories, I wonder what happened to the library during the Dust Bowl. Who would know? Only Brett's grandmother who threw me out. Still, I haven't seen Brett in several days, so I head down to the *Gazette*, to beg for another attempt. I catch him just as he's gathering up papers to take home.

"No way," he says in no uncertain terms, when I ask politely if his grandmother might give me another chance. "She's not in good shape, probably won't last the week. I'm on my way over there now." He picks up his laptop and puts it in his old-fashioned leather briefcase. "Love your story, by the way. Exactly what we wanted. We'll run it next week."

I'm ecstatic at his praise, but devastated at the news there won't be another chance to pump his grandmother for information.

"You should talk to Joe James, he's back from his alumni board meeting in Lawrence and from visiting his grandkids in Atlanta," Brett tells me. "He's a bit of curmudgeon, but it's a ruse to cover up his soft heart. He loves talking the old times. You'll see the sign, Joseph James, Esquire, in gold leaf, on the other side of Jo's. Let me know if you come up with anything interesting. Maybe we can run another article."

He starts humming Marian the Librarian, as he leaves. "Gary, Indiana has a Carnegie library," I tell him.

TRACI

oc Simmons throws a hissy fit when I step on the scales. "One hundred pounds. This is absolutely unacceptable, missy," he tells me. "You must put that weight back on."

"Models are skinny," I tell him.

"You aren't a model and models aren't healthy," he argues.

No physician's confidentiality in these parts. Rachel hears within the hour and sets up a casserole brigade. My dinner is to be delivered every evening and I am to clean my plate. She'll be the first, bringing lasagna, garlic bread, and a tossed green salad, with plenty of leftovers for lunch the next day. Jennifer is in line for the next delivery.

After the Teens leave from an afternoon of tie-dying, I ask Thad if he wants to stay, since Rachel's lasagna is meant to serve ten. At first he declines, but when she walks through the door, it smells so delicious, you can see him salivate.

"You should keep her company," Rachel insists. "She'll eat more that way. Don't tell me you've got something better waiting at home. Sit here and make sure she eats."

She sets the table with bright yellow plastic plates from her picnic basket and makes a pitcher of lemonade. "Bon Appétit," she says, waving herself out the door. You'd think she'd be upset I'm not doing my job, but instead she's delivering meals.

"Eat! Eat! Eat!" Thad tells me, once we're seated across from each other at the dinner table. "Orders from the boss," he says waving his fork at me like it's a weapon.

It's weird to sit across from Thad at a dinner table. Like we're an old married couple with nothing to say. It makes me so nervous I've lost what appetite I had, until he starts telling me about how all the women in town brought him lasagna after he got back from Iraq. "Made with hamburger, made with squash, someone even decided I might want one made with tofu. Yum," he says, as he swallows a big mouthful. "Rachel's was always the best."

After he's sung its praises, I have to remember to slow down, not gobble, carefully put my fork down between bites, so I'm eating like a civilized person. As we eat, Thad talks about the artwork that's being created by the Teens and the exhibit we should hang. "What if we called it 'Re-Cyc-Lit'? You know. Double-entendre. Re-cycle but also acknowledging the library with 'lit.'"

"Angie will love it!" I eat my last bite of lasagna and regret the meal is over, but there's no way I can swallow one more bite. "Does that mean you'll participate? We can show your work too? Let the world of New Hope know you're an artist?"

"I'm considering it," he says. "I might do it just for you," he says, as he walks behind my chair and tousles my head.

I'm so excited, I get nauseous. He must see how sick I am, because he insists he'll do the dishes so I can go straight to bed. He walks me downstairs and brings my oversized nightshirt from the bathroom, giving me a long hug before he goes upstairs.

Doc Simmons was right. As much as I hate to admit it, the trip to Lucas might've been too much. I don't even have the energy to appreciate Thad's presence. My stomach is doing somersaults, and my head is pounding like a ten-piece percussion band, so I pop a few aspirins that Rachel left. I fall into the deepest of sleeps on my princess bed and dream of Thad. Instead of washing dishes, he's throwing them against a wall, breaking them, and then sinking the pieces in concrete to make a mosaic.

I sleep through the alarm clock and don't come to full consciousness until mid-morning, when I hear the Teens singing lullabies to the Guilters, which is truly bizarre. Does this mean Sylvia has come clean about her condition? I doubt it. Maybe she's just feeling maternal. I do need to tell Rachel, but I get a pain in my stomach realizing if I tell on Sylvia, she'll tell on me, and Rachel will send me packing. For lying to her about my extensive teaching experience, if nothing else.

Rachel comes to check on me and when assured I'm not going to die on her, suggests she take over the Teens for the afternoon. "I got excited about origami last night," she tells me. "Have you ever heard of the thousand cranes? If you make a thousand origami cranes, it'll bring you good luck. Knowing how you like to recycle, I thought we could make them out of old magazines. Hang them among the hearts. Bring you good luck. And good health."

Before she's finished, she's told me a story about a girl in Japan who was dying of leukemia and tried to make a thousand cranes before she died but didn't make it. Now kids from all over the world make cranes in her honor. Then Rachel tells me how another "origami activist" has Palestinians and Jews making cranes together. And how industrialists, scientists, and architects are using origami models to solve serious problems. She must've seen a PBS special, but I'm glad for her offer of help.

GAYLE

Traci's back in bed with food poisoning, and you can tell the Teens miss her even if they'd never say so. Sylvia lit up like a flashlight when Traci came upstairs to check out the ScARTlettes. When she left, I could see how devastated Sylvia was so I sat down with her and taught her some lullabies. That girl's going to have a baby too and she doesn't have the support Vic and Jill have. We sang "Hush, Little Baby," changing the lyrics to "Mama's gonna buy you" instead of "Papa" and then Sylvia changing the rhythm to a hip hop beat. Not my cup of tea, but I couldn't help but get caught up in her enthusiasm. That girl isn't as brave as she makes herself out to be, but she's gutsy, I'll give her that. Can't believe no one else has figured out she's pregnant.

Sylvia's baby, my grandbaby, and our new home will arrive in about six months. All just in time for the holidays. I can't remember the holidays without crying—the way Vic and I used to pop popcorn to string (what we didn't eat) with cranberries to deck the tree. Mark points out it's been a dozen years since we've done that, but it's still my favorite holiday memory. Hopefully, new babies will help build new ones in a new home.

Memories, and hope, are what the tornado couldn't take away.

The talk of the Dust Bowl made me feel wimpy, like a coward. Our tornado came and went in a matter of minutes. We didn't have months of darkness, of filth, of madness.

Donna told us her grandmother especially cried about her quilts during the Dust Bowl because there was dust in every seam. She washed them so carefully, and then hung them out overnight, so they wouldn't be bleached by the sun. All that care, and now they've been blown away by a tornado. God must've wanted those quilts for his angels.

ANGELINA

Joe James sounds as if he'll be a gold mine of information, so I'm up early, determined to catch him before his day gets busy. Brett assured me he'd be glad to see me, especially if I can manage to drop in before seven o'clock. "Yep, even lawyers work an early shift here, especially in the summer," he told me. "Way to avoid the heat."

But before I'm out the door Thad calls, telling me there's something we need to talk about. "Meet me at Jo's?" he asks. "In half an hour or so?" It makes me nervous, but at some point we do need to talk. That part is obvious. What do you say to a brother who shows up just as you're turning forty? A half-brother, but a brother nonetheless.

I stop at the counter to chat with Jo. "Soymilk with your coffee?" she asks. She laughs at my surprise and says, "We aim to please." She'd driven to Salina to get soymilk for me, and suddenly I flash back to my father's insistence we provide small town service even in the city. She blushes at my effusive thanks and changes the subject to complain about the weather. "You know, you can't really fry an egg on a sidewalk when it hits a hundred and ten degrees," Jo tells me. "My grandson dared me to try it; and the egg just sat there, all gooey. I made him clean it up," she laughs. She points to the table of men and says, "My grandson will be sitting there, telling that story, when he's ninety-five years old."

Thad is already seated at the same table with the same men as my first visit to Jo's. They're deep in conversation, and I step back to listen before interrupting, realizing they're talking about the arts center.

"The way I see it, this whole Freedom of Speech thing can go too far," one says. "We don't need to let kids mouth off and put it on display. Call it art. Bullshit is what it is." This is from the man I remember as the prankster who bragged about his high school triumphs over Prairie Hill.

"If we can't control what goes on display in our own public buildings, I say close 'em down," another one says, stabbing his knife on the table for emphasis.

"Thad, rumor has it you've been helping out over there. Are you out of your mind? What's gotten into you?" the prankster asks. "That Traci girl seems to be egging them on, excuse the pun, turning those brats into juvenile delinquents."

"What can I say? I like her. She's got gumption." I peek out from behind the partition to see he's grinning an adorable grin. Any fool can see the guy is smitten.

"Can't accuse you of being wimpy for lending a hand," the oldest one says, "you fighting in Desert Storm and all. But d'ya think we should support what they're doing?"

Thad scratches his head, considering his answer. "Yep, those American values, like Freedom of Speech, are what I went to war for. What that parade tomorrow is all about." He stops to wave Jo over for a refill of coffee. "See, I don't want anyone messing with what I say, like you don't want anyone messing with your right to bear arms. Every time there's a mass shooting, people say the Second Amendment goes too far. Every time someone suggests maybe we should change it just a little bit, you scream to high heavens." It's quiet as Thad gives the guys a minute to contemplate, then he continues. "Besides, remember those pranks you played when you were teenagers? Putting raw meat in lockers? Turning over outhouses? How's letting those teens let off a little steam by making 'diarrhea' art any worse? Nobody's getting hurt."

Thad notices me, picks up his coffee mug, tells the guys he's got an appointment, and motions me over to a booth, as far from the men as we can get. "Want more coffee?" he asks as he waves Jo over. She brings it and a pitcher of soymilk.

And then we sit. The man looks so uncomfortable, as if I've come to torture him. He starts playing with the sugar packages, lining them up in rows and then rearranging them, trying to make little pyramids. Not the confident debater I've just observed. It takes him a year and half to say he has something to tell me.

"Things I don't already know?" I ask, taking pity on the poor guy.

"You *do* know?" he asks. "Everything?" He seems totally stunned by this news. As I nod, he continues, "That we're related? How long have you known?"

"Forever," I shrug, determined not to implicate Traci by suggesting she told me or confess that I eavesdropped. Basically wanting him to think I'm smarter than I am.

"Did you know all along?" he asks. "Even before you got here, you knew?"

"Maybe." I will not have him suspect how stupid I've been. "I also knew you were an artist, which I figure is why you didn't want me to see the land. I don't get why it's a secret, or why I can't look at my grandmother's place, but it's not like I didn't know."

"And it's all okay with you?" he asks.

"Okay? Not really. My father committed adultery. You have to admit it's a little out of the ordinary, meeting you after all these years."

I'm desperate to find out if my father knew him, had contact with him, but there's no way I'll admit I don't know.

As if reading my mind, Thad offers, "For the first twenty years of my life, I didn't know who my father was. Mom and I moved to the farm to help take care of Grandma but I never knew why, or why we got to stay, until the week before Mom died. That's when she told me. By then, my father, *our* father, was dead too. He must've known about me, or he wouldn't have let us stay on the land, but he never once cared enough to meet me. Now you show up, after all this time. Did you expect me to roll out the red carpet?"

I can't squeeze back my tears, as I grapple with my father's cruelty.

"Ah, quit it," Thad says, upset at seeing me cry. "I had the greatest mother, who told me every day I was a 'special snowflake.' Called me 'sugarplum' until I went to kindergarten and then 'Prince Theodore.' She did alright by me and thanks to generosity, I've been able to set up a studio on the land our great grandfather homesteaded."

"It's kind of weird having a brother after all these years." I try to compose myself. "But we'll work it out, don't you think?"

"Of course. Well, I guess that's that," he says. "Back to work for me."

He looks relieved, puts five dollars on the table, like he can't get away fast enough. He doesn't ask how I found out or why I didn't mention our relationship when we first met. In fact, we've had only part of the conversation we need to have.

It's only eight o'clock, and my mind's digested enough for the day, but I head down the street to meet Joe James, determined to ask him about the library during the Dust Bowl. It's hotter than it was an hour ago and I can't imagine what it'll be like by noon.

The gold engraved name on the door is misleading. There's nothing fancy or elegant about the office. No receptionist. Joe James motions me into his office, as he clears a folding chair of a stack of papers. There are piles of books and documents everywhere and I wonder when he last had a client here. He starts to put his jacket on, but I shake my head, indicating it's not necessary, and he looks relieved.

"Young lady, I wondered when you'd drop by," he tells me after we're both seated. "So sorry, I've been out of town. But I'm always available to you."

"To ask you about the libraries?" I ask.

"To ask me about whatever you want," he answers. "After all, I'm your lawyer." He must see my confusion. "Since I was your father's lawyer, I assumed I'd be yours."

"Well, it's not legal services I'm after today," I assure him, hoping he doesn't expect me to pay for this consultation. I hurry to fill him in on my dissertation before he gets any ideas. "I've been hearing a lot about the Dust Bowl and wondered what happened to the library during those times. Brett thought you were the one to talk to."

"Ah, the Dust Bowl. Funny, I've been remembering it lately. What with the heat and a few of these little dusters that are coming up. People grouse when a little dust gets blown across the road, but the one we had in '35 was two hundred miles wide, like a tornado on its side. You'd touch anything and static electricity would fly. We lost my cousin then. He was playing in the fields when it came up, and he lost his way home. Found him suffocated in the fields, half mile from home."

He takes a handkerchief from his pocket to wipe his eyes, my image of him as a hard-nosed lawyer already shot. He pulls himself together and offers facts instead, as if he were prosecuting a case.

"We had forty-nine or fifty of those dust storms in the mid-thirties. Were like black blizzards, with drifts even. Some professor at K-State estimated it would take forty-six million truckloads to transport dirt that had blown from one side of Kansas to the other. An average of almost five tons of dust fell on every Kansas acre."

"What happened to the library?" I ask, horrified at his description.

"Oh, they closed it for a couple of weeks, but then the women got mad. Said books didn't cost anything and it was the one thing they could still have. Some days it was too dark to read, but that didn't matter. They wanted their books close at hand."

"Sounds pretty awful," I acknowledge. "It's amazing everyone didn't just leave."

"My father said he wouldn't leave, even if there was nothing to eat but rattlesnakes. He was that tied to the land. Mother said if he expected her to stay to cook, he'd better figure out how to keep the library open. Otherwise, he'd be eating those snakes raw."

I start to thank him for his information, but he stops me. "I'd do about anything for Amanda Sprint's granddaughter. That woman was special. She used to say there were two teams of people, the 'splitter-uppers' and the 'putters-together.' She was definitely a member of the putter-together team. I can tell already, Angie, you are too. She'd be proud."

TRACI

Too sick to get out of bed, I totally missed the Fourth of July parade. The Teens, apparently, were quite a hit. Rode on the back of a flatbed truck, singing their offbeat musicals. Thad came by to show me pictures of them and of the rollerblading drum corps, and then we watched the fireworks together from the front steps of the arts center, holding hands like some old-fashioned couple. The fireworks may have been wimpy by NYC standards, but they were my favorite sparklers ever. Still, I fell asleep about two minutes after the last boom.

No classes today, so I'm determined to finish the quilt. Those picture postcards I found online, of all the Carnegie libraries in the state from way back when, are pretty awesome. I've managed to transfer them onto fabric for patches, and would've already whipped them together if I could've stayed awake one night. The bed is way too comfy, and it's all I can do to haul myself out of it when the alarm goes off. But I must get an early start.

Before I've finished breakfast, Rachel comes by to pay me. Counting out bills from the potholder money they collected yesterday, I see the concern wrinkled in her forehead. She doesn't need to tell me how hard everyone worked for this. Again, it occurs to me I could sell the Carnegie quilt, but I want it to be my gift to Angelina—especially since the journals have disappeared. Is there anyone in the world who would appreciate this quilt as much? I want her to remember me, like

I'll always remember her. If they can't get it together to pay me next month, I'll figure something else out; but I don't want to sell her quilt.

Thad calls and insists he can help when I tell him how determined I am to finish piecing the quilt. This time I remember to brush my hair, and even throw on a floral dress I'd meant to cut up for quilt pieces, so I've just finished dressing when he arrives. He whistles when he sees me, teasing me as he kisses both cheeks, playing the French charmer. Turns out he can't help much beyond cutting a few fabric strips for binding, but he hangs around anyway, plucking out funny love songs on his guitar. The morning zips by.

"Ta-da!" I've finished the last stitch and snipped the thread between my teeth. It still needs to be quilted but the top is done.

"It is stunning," Thad tells me. "It should thrill even Ms. Angelina Academic." He runs his fingers around the outlines of the postcards, pretending to appreciate each stitch. "Hey! I've got a great idea," he says. "We should photograph you, transfer it to fabric, and sew it on the back of the quilt. Your 'signature.'" He's beside himself with excitement. I'm a reluctant subject, but Thad sweet-talks me and I agree, as long as I have the right to delete any of the photos I don't like.

The only person who ever photographed me was the reporter from *The Village Voice*, and we know how that turned out. The photo was of a crazed, skinny waif with haunted eyes, who looked like a beggar. You can tell how a photographer feels about his subject just by looking at the picture.

He lays me out on my bed, on top of a pastel nine-patch quilt, fluffing the pansy pillows behind my head, tucking my legs under my long skirt and wrapping another floral quilt across my shoulders, so it's just my face and florals that are within the frame. I see where he's going. It'll look like I'm lying in a field of flowers.

He steps back and starts snapping, talking to me quietly while he takes about a hundred pictures. "You're pretty. Radiant. You know that, right? Guys must fall for you all the time. I bet you left a string of heartbroken men when you left New York." His voice is soft, almost a whisper.

Finally, he comes to sit by me and hands me the camera so I can examine his work. I'm stunned. Not that I'm pretty, but I do look soft, cuddly, girly, and, yes, even sexy. So sexy I'm not surprised when he takes the camera back, lays it on the nightstand, and leans down to kiss me. So sexy that I'm kind of shocked when he pulls back suddenly, like he's kissed a frog.

"You're burning up," he says.

"Hot for you," I mumble, although I'm freezing, shivering with cold.

"Nope, that's a fever," he tells me. "You're still sick." He grabs the bottle of aspirin on my bookshelf and hands it to me with a glass of water. "Take your clothes off. Except for your underwear," he orders, as he unzips his jeans.

He wants to make love to a sick person?

"Mom's remedy," he tells me. "She didn't do it after I was five years old," he assures. Crawling in beside me, he explains, "The well person helps bring down the temperature of the sick one by lying together skin to skin."

I curl up inside the big cup he's made with his body, savoring his cool skin against mine. He tells me to breathe in with him, and then out, and I do so until he starts cooing a lullaby to me.

When I wake up from my nap, he's gone. No trace of his having been here, except for a note on the table. "I'd be honored to work as your unofficial assistant Artist-in Residence. No pay, though. And let's figure out how to tell everybody."

ANGELINA

I'm pulling out gray hairs on the eve of my fortieth birthday when Elena knocks, delivering the letter for which I've been waiting for three weeks because the new Chairman of the Library Sciences Department refuses to do official business by either phone or email. It takes me about two minutes to slit it open, read every word, crunch it up into a ball, and throw it into the trash. Unbelievable. My PhD committee, newly reconstituted under the chairmanship of Dr. Jason Young, has determined they no longer consider my revised topic to be academically acceptable. Can't see the scholarship that relates to librarianship. Well and good to document how pioneer women came together to raise funds, but wasn't it Andrew Carnegie who made it all happen and hadn't that history been told? As a department, they need to look forward, take on students who can predict what libraries will look like without books and how to adapt to the digital age. Too bad I didn't keep in touch with the field. They wish me well wherever I end up.

How can I go on, when the thing I've wanted more than anything is impossible? An English lit professor once told me the definition of tragedy is when options disappear, and they're definitely disappearing. Nothing for me in Philly. Nothing here. So what if I wrote a good article for Brett? Three hundred dollars will hardly sustain me. If I'd found the journals, first-hand documentation of the library efforts, would it have helped? Probably not. I sit on the bathroom stool and cry the way I used to cry as a teenager.

Elena's knock on the door forces me to pull myself together. She's got a bee in her bonnet, and one thing I've learned is not to mess with her bees. She's decided we should have our very own private film festival on the eve of my fortieth birthday. A Festival of Forty-Year-Old Films watched in the air-conditioned luxury of her living room. We should get ready for bed, make a huge bowl of buttered popcorn, and settle in to watch the best movies produced in 1971. She's got five pints of ice cream in the freezer. Two pints of homemade strawberry just for me.

Luckily, 1971 was a very good year in Hollywood. *Fiddler on the Roof, A Clockwork Orange, Klute, Dirty Harry,* and *Willy Wonka and the Chocolate Factory.* The choices will last us all weekend. After too much discussion, we decide to start with *The Last Picture Show.* Just as I've settled myself into her overstuffed sofa, Elena looks at me and says, "You don't want to wake up on your fortieth birthday wearing those torn sweat pants and that old t-shirt, do you? When you look in the mirror tomorrow, don't you want to meet your new life in your pretty, lacy white nightgown?"

She is like my mother. Micromanaging my lingerie. When I come back downstairs, wearing nothing but my peach polka dot terry cloth robe as an act of defiance, even though it's way too hot, we settle in.

"*The Last Picture Show* it will be then," she says, as she inserts the video.

Anarene, Texas takes on a whole new meaning when watched in a living room in the middle of nowhere. How easily New Hope could've atrophied into a bleak, isolated, culturally deprived town. Is this what Prairie Hill was before it got wiped off the map by the tornado? Had I lived there, would I have been Jacey, starved for more options? Would New Hope have suffered a similar fate if it weren't for my grandmother and her friends who made the library happen? Frankly, I'm not sure this distraction is cheering me up. Cybill Shepherd, Cloris Leachman, and Ellen Burstyn look so young.

First movie down, we try to decide between *A Clockwork Orange* and *Willy Wonka*, with Elena constantly looking at her watch. "Do you have a date?" I ask. "Or are you trying to make a statement about how fast time flies? I get that already."

Before she can answer, the doorbell rings, and Jennifer lets herself in. She's dressed in a killer nightgown, blue sapphire, slit up the sides. "It's a Come as You Are Party," she says as she pulls me up and out the door. "Friends await at the arts center."

She pushes me into her pickup, Elena squeezing in beside me, so close I can smell her expensive gardenia perfume. I pull my robe around me, breaking out in perspiration, maybe even a rash, from the sweat.

They haven't blindfolded me but they might as well have. When we get to the arts center, it's pitch black. Elena and Jennifer each take one of my hands to lead me into the atrium toward a gaggle of giggling women. Finally, light. Or to be more accurate, light in the midst of darkness. Dozens of lighted reading glasses are all I can see. Spectacles framing eyes like some bizarre puppet show. The women break out singing "Happy Birthday," each clicking the left light on her glasses for the "Happy Birthday" and the right light for "to you." Like synchronized lightning bugs.

Although Jennifer had said a friend or two was waiting, in fact the entire female population of two towns have gathered. The No Guilt Quilters from both New Hope and Prairie Hill. Even Sylvia and Madonna. All in their bedclothes. A few even in hair rollers. Donna has pin curls. Pretty proud of themselves for coming up with a slumber party to celebrate my fortieth birthday. Smug as can be.

When they do turn on the lights, the entire room is decorated in red. "Ruby red," Elena tells me. Red hearts the Teens have made, red origami birds, red crepe paper, and a few stray sheets of toilet paper.

"Ruby. For Dorothy's slippers?" I ask. "Because I've found my way back home?"

"Well that too," Elena says. "But also because ruby red is the traditional fortieth birthday color, the color that comes from the inner fire of the ruby stone."

"Librarians do know everything," Rachel says. "They're so smart."

Even the cupcakes are ruby red. And Elena, putting on her librarian's hat, lectures even on those. "They're known as Waldorf Astoria cakes, because there's an old urban legend, going back to the fifties, about a woman who dined there, asked for the recipe, then found a charge on her credit card for anywhere from a hundred to a million dollars depending on who's telling the story. Angry at having been duped into paying for a recipe she thought she was getting for free, the woman gave out the recipe to everyone to get her money's worth. It's been making the rounds since before you were born, Angie."

Jennifer chimes in, "Some people say it was a chemical reaction of the buttermilk to a lighter cocoa that made it red, but I think it's the food coloring. Loads and loads of food coloring. I use beet juice because it's healthier."

The gifts are tasteful. Handmade soaps, bath salts, candles, and sachets. "We resisted giving you a bottle of Geritol or a package of Depends," Elena says. "Not very funny. But I've noticed you're having trouble reading, and these are the cat's meow. Can't have you giving up reading." She hands me my own pair of battery-operated, lighted, reading glasses.

Traci presents her gift last, an exquisite quilt top made with postcards of Carnegie libraries magically transferred onto fabric squares. I easily recognize the Dodge City round library and the two towers of the Yates Center. It has to be the most meaningful gift I've ever received. She apologizes profusely because it still needs to be quilted, which she hadn't been able to do while bedridden. The Quilters promise to help out, but Traci still seems agitated. How can she not know she's just given me a gift I'll treasure forever? The first thing I'd grab if a tornado were coming. I request a clean sheet so I can lay my quilt on the floor and admire it all night.

Now that the gifts are open, we all look around at each other as if to ask what happens next. Are we really going to stay up all night? This group never runs out of things to talk about, but we've been talking for weeks now. I hope it doesn't turn awkward. Traci should be sleeping. I should be sleeping. I'm surprised they're not sewing and knitting if nothing else. I've never seen these ladies without needles in hand.

Just when I'm ready to thank them again, mostly to break the silence, Sylvia steps forward. Defiant, sharp-edged Sylvia who is friendlier every day. "Angie, we have one more birthday present for you. A *huge* birthday present. A birthday present better than any of you could've expected."

This doesn't seem fair to Traci, but Sylvia's a teenager, so I let it pass.

And then she pulls out the journal, tied with a single strand of twine. I know instantly what it is, but before I can even untie the knot to see my grandmother's handwriting, Sylvia grabs it back. Traci rushes forward and tries to grab it too, yelling, "You thief, it's mine," but she's still weak, and Sylvia wins the tug of war. I want to grab it myself, but Sylvia's holding my journal close to her chest, her arms crossed over it. To wrestle it from her might mean harming my journal.

"We should vote, don't you think?" Traci asks, trying to capitalize on the way everyone loves her. A vote can't supersede ownership by law—although she'll question who actually owns it.

"Maybe the best thing is for all of us to read it together?" Rachel asks in her best Mommy negotiating voice, aimed toward Traci. Rachel takes on an authoritative tone when she looks directly at me. "We'll get to the bottom of this, but don't you want to hear what it says right now? Sylvia's planned to read it to you tonight. As your birthday present. She wanted it to be like when Carnegie's father read at the mill. Figured we could work on scarves while she read. She and the band even figured out music."

Traci is still angry, but sits down in the one available chair. I'm beyond miffed, wanting to take my journal back to the privacy of my bedroom and dive in. Why should my grandmother's secrets be shared with all these women?

"Tonight," Sylvia says, looking directly at me. "We will not argue." She's regained her poise and is in control of the situation as she perches herself on a stool, then unties the twine from the journal. "We're going to read you a bedtime story. So grab your cupcakes, and make yourself comfy. We have a story to tell."

She doesn't even bother to start at the beginning, just opens the book at random, nods to Madonna for a drum roll, and starts reading.

BOOK TWO

May 14, 1910
Ned is dead.

Forgive the tearstains and shaky handwriting of a widow in mourning. My world has turned upside down and backwards since I wrote here two weeks ago. And now, dear Diary, I write from the bottom of my heart and the depths of my soul. You will keep my secrets. When my dear sister Emily sent you to me, she expected me to document our efforts to tame the prairie. I have in fact done so. Documented our successes and frustrations. But where, if not here, can I express my grief over Ned's death? I cannot ruin the quilt his mother treasured, crying into it, destroying the last remaining piece of the five hundred pounds of bedding she brought in a covered wagon. Should I stuff my emotions in a flour sack; bury them under the cottonwood tree; plant thistle, quack, dander, or another weed to hide the hole? If only I could hide the hole in my heart.

I fear it was my fault Ned was thrown from his horse. In my head, I know this cannot be true. The horse was spooked by the storm and must have bolted when lightning struck the fence across the field. I saw the lightning and may have heard the horse's scream through the thunder, although I cannot be sure. I felt exhilaration at the sight, ran out from the porch to let the cold rain drench my body, and sighed relief because the temperature had finally dropped. The coming storm had hung over our heads all day, making the animals crazy and the humans crazier still.

Little did I know the lightning bolt murdered my husband. Ned had been riding back from the hen house, and I still marvel that, when I found him, the basket of eggs was intact, not a single broken shell, even though Ned's neck had snapped, and he was no longer breathing. I did not find him until late that night when the storm had passed, and the sky was overflowing with stars. The horse has not dared show her face here again.

I'm so sorry we had quarreled that afternoon. Ned declared he was ready to start a family and I proclaimed I was not. "I am only twenty-one," I told him. He actually raised his voice to me. "If not now, when? I want a son more than life itself. I want a boy I can teach to fish, who'll spend time with me, and ask me about the important things in life. You are so wrapped up in your dreams of a silly circulating lending library, you have forgotten your promise to make a family."

The truth is I have made no attempt not to conceive since the day we were married two years ago. Could something have been wrong? Should we have consulted with Dr. Brinkley, the Goat Gland doctor, who is rumored to implant goat gonads into men's private parts? Or is it my body that is deficient, and I cannot bear a child? I wondered that afternoon: would Ned soon be sorry he had not chosen Claire?

Claire wailed like a colicky baby at the funeral. It is the only time I have seen her when she was not radiant. She cried like a madwoman; her face turned purple, and her eyelids were so swollen her eyes looked like small shrunken peas rather than shiny jade marbles, as they usually do.

Her behavior stunned me so that I shed not a single tear during the entire service. I needn't have brought a handkerchief. Everyone else was sniffling and blowing their noses, but I was not. Not a single tear while the Reverend Hodges recited the 23rd Psalm nor even when Simple Gifts was sung. It was an abbreviated service, for the temperature had again risen to 110 degrees, and the mourners were eager to strip down to their cotton clothing, and to get home before another storm. They didn't even dawdle over the banquet in the church basement afterwards.

Everyone was shocked by my composure. The men—looking

like adolescent boys, uncomfortable in their heavy wool black suits, which showed too clearly where they had grown taller or put on weight—tried to mumble a few words of condolence. The women—in long black dresses and outdated hats—clenched their husbands for dear life and pierced my soul with their looks of sympathy. As they walked away from me, I could hear them whisper, "Poor woman, has she gone mad? Whatever will she do now? I cannot believe she is not hysterical, as I would be."

Everyone was shocked by my composure except Branford. He seemed to understand the crushing pain in my chest that makes crying both impossible and inadequate. He prevailed upon Claire's mother to take her home and insisted on escorting me, walking me back to the farm because I would not go near a horse, even to ride in a carriage. Eugene Lubbers owns the one automobile in town and I want nothing more to do with the funeral director. I would rather walk. I've always thought Lubbers a wicked man, even before he drooled on me while making funeral arrangements.

Branford kept his voice low as he talked to me, telling me how much Ned must have loved me, and listing the reasons why. He took my elbow first, then put his arm around my waist, all the while telling me how strong I am, how smart, how witty. Almost as if he were courting me. When he took my hand, I thought his would be smooth, for he is a gentleman, but as if reading my mind, he apologized, saying it was the lye he used in cleaning the print forms that gave him such blisters. He is educated as Ned was not, and the words he strung together were poetic indeed, far beyond those he writes for the newspaper. My reaction was inappropriate, but I wanted him to stay. I let my mind go to him, rather than suffer the excruciating pain of my loss.

May 21, 1910

I had confused feelings about going to the literary club meeting. The last week has seemed like a year, and I knew it was time to leave the house. At the same time, I dreaded seeing the looks of sympathy from my friends or hearing their well-meaning but meaningless words of condolence. When I arrived a few minutes late, I stood outside the door before entering Claire and Branford's house, eavesdropping as the women talked about me. "Do you suppose she'll go back home to Philadelphia?" It was Ada who asked. "No. This is her home now. Whatever would we do without her?" Hortense answered, far more certainly than I could have. They stopped talking altogether when I walked in, until Claire offered me a glass of cool lemonade.

Should I go back to Philadelphia? I've been asking myself that very question. Sister Emily certainly made it clear she would like me to return. She keeps reminding me of the beautiful new library in Chestnut Hill, built by Andrew Carnegie. So much more sophisticated than the Christian Hall Library where we used to go for elocution classes and magic lantern shows, while Mother and Father attended temperance meetings.

After all my complaining about my hard life on the prairie, I surprise myself by not wanting to rush back to "civilization and culture," as I've always thought of it. Yes, the pain of missing Ned is overwhelming, but he is still with me here in a way he would not be in Philadelphia. Philadelphia is where I was a child, and it is here in Kansas I have grown to be a woman. It is strange, but I fear in Philadelphia I would become "the Widow Sprint," whereas here there is little time for such designation. There, I would spend my time helping Emily with her household; here, I will be making a life of my own.

Hortense told me when her husband died she still had her daughters to be passionate about, and advised me to find my

*own passion. I know what it is. The thing I am most passionate
about is our lending library, and I won't leave before it's up and
running. It seemed like such an ambitious project when we first
conceived it. Now I understand it is what we are meant to do. The
exhaustion we all experience at home somehow lifts when we get
together as women friends and begin sharing our ideas. Even my
grief subsides the tiniest bit, although I know I'll never be happy
again.*

*I force myself to remember happiness. We were slightly giddy
that night last month, almost intoxicated, (but from ideas, not
liquor) when we decided to secretly start planning to build a real
library! They've had a circulating library in Kingman for almost
twenty-five years, when members of the Women's Christian
Temperance Union started it. Now they're approaching Mr.
Andrew Carnegie for a grant to build a building. The same man
who gave money for the library in Chestnut Hill. He's said to be
giving out grants like hotcakes and we're determined to get in
line.*

*At the meeting last month, we decided not to tell our hus-
bands yet, wanting to tell them all at once, in a unified effort.
Timing is important, and we worried they were so consumed
with their crops they would think our efforts frivolous. We knew
ultimately they'd be supportive but we wanted them behind us
from the start.*

*And so a plan was made. All of us laughed about how we
needed to butter up the men folk to get them to support our
library efforts. Ruth said, "A way to a man's heart is through his
stomach. I never ask for anything until I've baked my husband's
favorite apple cobbler." Ada laughed and said, "I won't even tell
you what I do when I want something." That led to a discussion
of the play Lysistrata and the women who withheld sexual favors
until their men stopped fighting and peace descended on Greece.*

"What if we did the reverse?" Ada asked. "What if we agree to make an effort to cook and to ... you know. Make our husbands happy. Then we can tell them about our library plans before we make a public announcement. If it works for us separately, it should work for us together." Even Claire said she'd do her part, and Hortense whispered she'd wager Claire would never even kiss her husband if she didn't want something. I hadn't giggled so hard since I was a schoolgirl.

Both Ned and I were exhausted by the time I got home that night, but I took care to freshen up. He was similarly inspired. We danced naked in the living room, singing Shine on Harvest Moon. What steamy passion on an equally steamy night. Ned kissed the top of my head first, then my nose, all the way down my face, my neck, my breasts. We fell into bed and it was beautiful and naughty and such a fitting celebration of our efforts to build the library. The memory of that lovemaking haunts me still, stabbing me with the want of more. I will look back on it as the happiest night of my life.

How I rage at the God who took Ned from me! My punishment for having wished I'd been smarter, stayed behind in Philadelphia and married Lyle instead. Tending his store sounded boring at the time, but then I came to think it'd have been so much more interesting, and certainly easier, than life on this godforsaken prairie.

June 1, 1910

The thing I should record about our Lysistrata night is that it worked. The men agreed to support our literary efforts. Although a few of them pointed out we're always complaining there's too much work as it is, in the end, every single one of them said they'd do what they could to help. Our "concerted efforts" certainly worked; it also doesn't hurt that the harvest looks to be bountiful. Ruth's husband has even donated a hog; at the County Fair, people will have the chance to guess its weight for twenty-five cents a try, the winner getting the hog and the library getting the profits. Ned had planned to donate a few good laying hens, but now I dare not give them up.

With the men's support, we decided to approach the Carnegie Foundation about a building. "Nothing ventured, nothing gained." If Kingman can have a Carnegie library, surely we can too. And because it was my idea, or maybe because everyone feels sorry for me or believes I have time on my hands, I was elected to write the letter.

It took me all week to write my letter to Mr. Carnegie, for I wanted it to be perfect. I've heard Carnegie and his secretary James Bertram support a whole new "American" language, with strange contractions of words to make them "more efficient." They use words like anser, bilding, and promis. I certainly hope they don't expect my letter to be written in a similar fashion. It's said Carnegie receives 500–3000 letters a day asking for money. Imagine all those letters sitting on top of Bertram's desk.

I took great care, telling Mr. Carnegie that we've already been circulating books, 797 volumes this year, but that our efforts have become too big a proposition for our club to care for properly. Fearing he may only know the bad things about the "Wild West," I reminded him that for some years now, books, schoolhouses, churches, and other evidence of culture and refinement have taken the place of cartridge belts, six shooters, and dance halls. Which is at least somewhat true.

I used my best stationery, monogrammed, careful not to make a single mistake, blotting it on my apron. Once the letter's mailed, we can only wait. Others say "we can only wait and pray," but I don't have much faith in prayer these days. How could a just and good God have taken a man like Ned? Is it me He's punishing, for wanting books so dearly? Eugene Lubbers implied as much when he brought his bill for undertaking. Does he think I will be able to repay it before he buries me?

June 9, 1910

Last night, Branford came in as the meeting was ending and told me he would be out today to help me find a new horse. "You simply must have one," he insisted. "We've collected the money. The Chases have a mare they have raised since she was a foal, a solid well-trained horse. We will give her a try, you and me together, and see if we cannot get you back on a saddle. You cannot live three miles from town without a horse." He tried to convince me I need a gun too, but I told him I'd make do with a second hatpin tucked in my hat. He told me Frank Chase had killed seven rattlesnakes with his Colt 38 last week. "You can't do that with a hatpin," he said.

Branford arrived on his own horse, Brandy, to take me out to the Chases. I could hardly refuse to ride with him, although I'm now terrified of horses. We rode into town first, so I could post my letter to Andrew Carnegie, Branford keeping Brandy at a slow and steady gait. After I'd posted my letter and as Branford pulled me up onto the saddle, he kissed the top of my head and gave me a squeeze to share my excitement at our library efforts. It made me proud, I sat a little taller, and with his arms around me, I forgot to be scared, or even sad. We spent the afternoon like that, first on Brandy and then taking Chase's horse Lady Godiva for a trot, and then back home on Brandy. We laughed about Lady Godiva and wondered if the Chases know the historical figure rode naked through the streets of Coventry in her protest against taxation.

"Would you do the same?" Branford teased. "For the library?"

"Only if you promise to support the library, front page and center in your newspaper," I teased back, blushing like a tomato I'm sure.

To thank him for his help, when we got home I opened a bottle of apple brandy we've had since last Christmas. I even poured a taste for myself.

He lifted his glass to me and asked, "Do you remember Emily Dickinson who said 'Dying is a wild night and a new road.' A wild night for Ned, perhaps. A new road for you, I hope."

Ned never would have made such a learned toast. He'd be shocked to see me drink at all. But I do feel as if I must start over, to find my way. I can't spend my life sobbing into the pillows, beating them until the feathers fly, wishing for him to come back. The pain is too enormous. That is why I should be forgiven for what we did.

July 12, 1910

I hope never to see hell, but if I do, I can't imagine it will be any hotter than it was here this afternoon. Will this heat wave never end? Is it my punishment?

The tumbleweeds are blowing across the plains in herds as if they were buffalo on the move. And the preacher who came through from Topeka said the temperature there hit 106 degrees. "It felt like 200 and the ladies were fainting," he said. "When I went by the dry goods store, the melting wax mannequins in the window provided a gruesome sight indeed. Their eyes were protruding and their jaws were hanging, demonstrating intense suffering. I'm haunted by them still."

Please, dear God, don't let the grasshoppers come. Last time they were a foot deep, ate clothes straight off the clothesline, curtains off our windows, bark off our trees, and wooden handles off our tools. Ate everything but the onions.

The heat made me so irritable that when I couldn't open a jar of pickles, I became enraged. That simple frustration made me miss Ned over every inch of my body. I wanted so badly to hand him the jar and have him twist off the lid—as he did for me a few hundred times when I used to take him for granted. Instead, I threw the jar against the washtub, and then had to squat down to pick up shards of glass and cucumber slices soaked in vinegar. The vinegar discolored the floor and will forever remind me of my tantrum. I started sobbing when the jar hit the tub, and then I couldn't stop for hours. I erupted like a volcano, after having convinced myself I could keep my pain in check.

My husband is dead.

July 15, 1910

When I got to the library meeting this evening, Claire, Rachel, and Ada went on and on about how miserable they'd been in the afternoon heat, and then all three confessed they think they are with child. It's been almost two months since our concerted effort to sway our husbands. Hortense told us there are tales of multiple deliveries nine months after a snowstorm, but couldn't cite an example of "conception as the result of a political act." Everyone had a good laugh imagining Doc Curtis might deliver a bevy of babies on the same night, nine months after we made our men happy before asking for support of our library. I pretended to laugh too, trying hard not to let my true feelings show. Trying hard to be happy for their good news. Hortense took my hand and said, "Looks like you and I will be doing most of the library work seven months from now, Amanda." She said it gently, but it still hurt.

I've actually missed my monthly, but I know it is jittery nerves, not a baby, that's caused the disruption in my cycle. How could I be pregnant now, after years of trying to become the mother of Ned's child? Claire was so full of herself for holding a child in her stomach that I wanted to run wild with Branford and make a child with him myself. Hopefully, it's only the heat that leads me to such mad thoughts. We had our one night together but that will be all. I cannot tolerate guilt any more than I can tolerate heat.

Guilt or heat, I must confess to not feeling well. Almost as if everyone else's condition is contagious. Am I having sympathetic morning sickness? If I'm not better soon, I will go see Doc Curtis.

July 22, 1910

Maybe it's the heat, maybe my nausea, maybe just plain homesickness, but I've been reconsidering my decision to stay in Kansas. It's too hard. And Hortense is right. There are things about this place that are just plain crazy. Even the crusaders who want things better have an edge to them. The doctor who preaches "Swat that Fly," and "Bat that Rat," has won his battle to have bricks imprinted with "Don't Spit on the Sidewalk," believing the expectoration leads to tuberculosis and other diseases. And even I think it's silly that the battleship Kansas was christened with water rather than the traditional champagne, thanks to Carrie Nation and her sort.

Are we all crazy here? Has the prairie made us a little "off"? Tonight we discussed a new book called The Wonderful Wizard of Oz, by Frank Baum, which we've been passing around. Claire insists this one book will make Kansas the laughingstock of the country, with its references to a girl swept away by a cyclone, from her dismal home in Kansas. I wonder if she actually read it all, got to the end. Because I came to a different conclusion. I came to see that even a place with challenges (like tornadoes) and people who remind you of witches (like Claire), even a place that can seem boring and ordinary, can become a home. A home to which you're fiercely loyal and want to make better even though the challenge is daunting.

Branford wrote an editorial reminding people how important the library is, because we've begun to hear doubts from the so-called town fathers. He cited several reasons, including the fact that a library is the best advertisement a town can have. "It is respectable to associate with books," he said, "even if you do not yourself actually read them." I can see his wide grin as he wrote, and it makes me miss him as well as Ned.

July 30, 1910

The letter came! I received our reply from Mr. Carnegie's secretary, Mr. James Bertrand, in his efficient English. He told us what we already know: the City of New Hope must commit to providing annual operating funds of 10 percent of the grant and we will need to abide by their requirements for construction. We have much work yet to do.

I am so relieved to have this project to occupy my mind. I cannot keep grieving Ned or thinking about Branford. Instead, I will throw myself into the work to be done.

Our ice cream social was a great success. The day was hot, and the parade was long, and everyone was eager to cool off with our delicious sweet vanilla ice cream. We couldn't crank fast enough, even with a dozen churns. We managed 144 gallons before the ice melted completely. People lined up to get a scoop and then sat on the curb in a line to savor it. Such a sharp contrast between the hot-and-tired waiting line and the cool-and-happy eating line.

The ice cream is the only thing that's tasted good to me in months and I let everyone feel sorry for me so I could lick the beaters.

All of us made cookies as well, and, at the last minute, I had the idea to collect cookie recipes and sell them too. Branford was most accommodating in printing them for us, and we sold our booklets for twenty-five cents apiece. (Even Claire shared her secret brownie recipe we've all been wanting; the secret ingredient turns out to be the addition of half a cup of sour cream or buttermilk.) All together, we are now seventy-eight dollars closer to our library.

Raising money for the library keeps me busy so I don't grieve Ned, or think about what may be happening inside my own body.

August 30, 1910

We wasted no time, fearing even Mr. Carnegie might run out of money, or change his mind. We submitted our plans to the Carnegie Corporation today. It will cost $6000 to build our library according to the Tilton Brother Architects. $6000! We went to work and made plans for fundraisers. And more fundraisers still. Even if Carnegie gives us the money for the building, we will need more to buy books.

This weekend was our Kaffir Corn Carnival. We are so excited about the Kaffir corn, which is supposed to be drought- and heat-resistant and can thrive in a place like Kansas. Imagine: it's a tropical African variety of sorghum that we can use to feed our cattle and poultry. The Carnival was a three-day celebration downtown with a parade, pageant, and contests. The boys made a triumphal arch of kaffir corn at one end of the street. Contests for men included fence-building and nail-driving. Women competed in chicken calling, geese plucking, and butter churning. Poor Branford couldn't win a thing, until it came time for turtle racing. Then the turtle he named

Quick won fair and square. Branford presented his medal to Claire,
but he was looking at me the entire time.

September 1, 1910

We're worried. *There's been a good deal of consternation about*
whether the City of New Hope will accept the responsibility of
providing operating funds for the next ten years, as is required
by the Carnegie Foundation if we are to get their support. The
request is for a mill levy, which will supplement the money we
raise through entertainments, ice cream socials, donations, and
the dog tax. We will circulate a petition to find the required
number of signers to put the proposition on the ballot. This will
be the first vote the women in the community are allowed to cast,
a monumental day indeed.

We've learned that a proposition to build a Carnegie library,
sponsored by the Women's Club in Liberal, was turned down a
few years ago. They hadn't yet given women the right to vote, so
members of the Club couldn't even vote for their own proposition,
which lost to sidewalks and a new jail. Ultimately, they were able
to buy a drab house to use as a library, but it certainly lacks the
stature of a Carnegie building.

As if we didn't have enough to worry about, we received a
letter from the Carnegie Corporation listing their concerns about
our proposal. There were two major ones. First, they don't think
our library can be built for $6000 and they will not accept our
proposal until they receive a statement saying no additional
funds will be solicited. The Tilton Brothers have assured us it's
not necessary to scale down the plans and have agreed to make
four blueprints and send specifications by the last of the week.
Carnegie also objected to the proposed front entrance, stating too
much space was wasted. All of this will delay the beginning of

*the building, when we are so very eager to get started. We want
our library to be completed before the one in Green Valley, so we
simply must make our case so that Mr. Carnegie will separate
himself from his cash.*

*Although I have been the one in charge of corresponding with
Mr. Carnegie's secretary, I fear my skills are inadequate to the
task, now that questions have been raised. For that reason, and
that reason alone, I sought Branford's counsel. Our meeting was
all business, of course, although I do admit my heart fluttered at
standing so close while we worked together. I wonder what he feels.*

*It's a matter of weeks before I will be showing, and the whole
town will know of my pregnancy. Hortense took me aside, she's
already guessed my condition, but the others have been oblivious,
seemingly unaware that even a widow can deliver a new life.*

*I wonder what she will be like, this baby I carry. I'm sure she
will be a girl. Claire has made it clear her daughter will never
be seen in a soiled frock or with a dirty nose, but I don't give
those concerns a passing thought. Will my daughter crave to be
educated, as I did? Will she learn to make a life on the prairie as
I have? I know she will be smart and want the answers to everything. Her upcoming arrival makes me more determined than
ever to build a library for her. She may not have the art museums
and operas of Philadelphia, but she will not live here without a
window to the greater world.*

— e —

September 8, 1910

*The waiting is driving us to madness so we've decided to pro-
ceed and find library space even before the Carnegie money is
committed. With our collection of almost three hundred books,
it is time to move the library out of Claire's house. Far past time,
as far as I'm concerned. There are books I want to read that I*

simply won't ask her for. And what if Branford learned what I was reading?

Jack, at Jack's General Store, has given us the use of his upstairs room. Our library will be open each Wednesday and Saturday afternoon, from 2–5 pm. We will stoke the furnace with coal during those times, necessitating an allocation of funds for both the coal and the fire insurance.

We were presented with a gift tonight, from Mr. Ronald Wells, a gift to the children of New Hope, which will be placed in the library. The gift was a souvenir of Mr. Wells' trip around the world and consists of a postcard album containing 200 colored views of Palestine and Egypt as well as an album of pressed flowers of the Holy Land and relief map of Jerusalem and the surrounding country. The flower album and map are bound in olive wood, beautifully polished. It was an impressive gift coming thousands of miles to the children of his hometown, given by one who has no children of his own.

His gift seemed to instigate philanthropic spirit among us all. Not to be outdone, Claire announced her intention of donating Charles Knight's pictorial edition of Shakespeare's complete works in eight volumes, "elegantly bound and beautifully illustrated." Then Hilda said the First Church of Christ would donate a copy of Mary Baker Eddy's Science and Health, and Nellie promised to provide A History of the Carnegie Steele, in hopes we will finally have our Carnegie library.

How I wish I had the means to donate. It's all I can do to gather enough eggs and pickle enough cucumbers to trade for what I need. When I die, I will request no flowers be given but rather friends express their sympathy by giving money to the library.

September 15, 1910

There is no doubt there is a baby in my belly, and she is making me more emotional than ever. The others are so wrapped up in themselves, and their own pregnancies, they haven't noticed my signs. It is just as well. They'd pity me all the more.

I survived the weekend. A level of loneliness set in that was beyond what I've ever experienced. All the grief of losing Ned came descending from above. How I raged at God. If I'm honest, I felt the "loss" of Branford too, as irrational as that is, for he was never mine to lose. Yesterday afternoon, I had to tear out the stitching on a simple nine-patch five times, because I couldn't see through my tears. My mind kept returning to our horseback ride and all that happened after.

The birthday package from Philadelphia, filled with fabric and books, and love, is the only thing that kept me going. Every night, after finishing my chores, I tucked myself into the rocker to read Tolstoy's Resurrection, which my dear sister Emily picked out for me. I tried to read carefully but kept rushing ahead. It is the story of a nobleman who seeks redemption for an affair he had years ago, an affair with a young maid who was then fired and ended up in prostitution. Is this the story of Branford and me? Could my dear sister know of my sin and be sending me a cautionary tale? At least I won't end up in a Siberian prison, living in a lake of human dung.

I was glad when I had finished it. Although beautifully written and certainly relevant in its exposition of hypocrisy, it is not the most optimistic read for a woman suffering kicks in her stomach promising the arrival of new life.

October 1, 1910

There is smallpox in town. We are all frightened out of our minds, including me, for the sake of the baby. I cannot risk her contamination, so even I agreed our club should not meet again after tonight, until the plague has passed. The library committee met to decide what to do about the books that are out in small-pox-ridden homes. The Coxes have three books checked out; the Chases two; and the Miltons another three. Those are the homes we know about. After much discussion, we decided to call the books back in and to fumigate the library. This means fumigating Jack's General Store as well. It will be expensive and we will have to close the library until the disease has abated.

I cannot imagine living without books in a time of such crisis so will re-read Resurrection. I have thought about it constantly and wonder if Branford is in mental agony over our time together. Does he suffer from stomach-wrenching guilt? I would not want him to think of me with anything but the utmost affection. I wonder if he wonders if this baby is his, since although no one except Hortense has yet spoken of it, there can be no doubt I am with child.

⸻ *e* ⸻

November 1, 1910

The conversation last month about the smallpox epidemic was tame compared to the one we had tonight about banning books. Claire's pregnancy is making her more difficult than ever, and mine is making me more impatient.

Claire got on her high horse about The Damnation of Theron Ware, a book about a Methodist minister who begins to question his faith as he comes across people with different opinions. "We cannot have it in our library," she insisted emphatically. "I would never want a child of mine to see."

I know these aren't Branford's views. He's an advocate of free-dom of speech and of the press, but I daren't mention that fact to her. Besides, I agree The Leopard's Spots should be banned, as it's such a distorted description of Reconstruction, touting as heroes the members of the Ku Klux Klan. There are KKK members in Marquette; they are despicable people, pretending to be on the woman's side in order to entice her to join their cause to discrimi-nate against colored folks, and we simply can't allow their views to spread. I certainly don't want my daughter to be exposed to them.

After we'd talked an hour, we voted to burn the banned books, so there is no question of their contaminating the community. We're more worried about what banned books might do to a per-son's brain than what smallpox might do to a person's body.

We carried on by discussing other books that might be suitable for the library but objectionable by some people on the grounds of being unfit for children, resulting in a motion to keep such books in a private place and loaned only to persons of mature age. We also determined to require payment to check out new books, which would be placed on a pay-shelf. Once that book is paid for, it will be moved to a free shelf. This will allow us to keep buying the most current titles.

And because we were obsessed with making rules tonight, we passed a motion requiring all transients and strangers to deposit the sum of two dollars before receiving the privilege of borrowing a book from the library. As if this town has ever seen a stranger.

May 1, 1911

I cannot believe how much has happened in the six months since I last wrote. Trevor Quinn, the light of my life, was born, February 1, 1911. Trevor Quinn, the wise one. All along I thought my baby would be a girl; I'd already named her Athena, the goddess of wisdom, so I was quite surprised when the baby who pushed himself out had a penis. A pinkie, I thought at first, but it was a penis. I want him to be smart, and that he is; his name will fit. And it is appropriate he is christened the same week we break ground for the library. New hope for New Hope. New hope for me.

Thank heavens Trevor Quinn looks like me, for there is still a gnawing doubt about paternity. I must believe Ned is his father, for I took such precautions on my one encounter with Branford. I was quick with the vinegar afterwards, but once I knew I was with child, I could not bring myself to use the rhubarb compound and pepper that midwives in Philadelphia touted. Instead, I choose to believe this child is the product of my lovemaking with Ned, the night we "conceived" our plan for the library.

Trevor Quinn was born on a clear, warm day and that itself was a miracle. We suffered such a wicked winter, with over four feet of snow in January. There were ten-foot tall snowdrifts and many of the ranchers lost cattle that could not find their way. As it is, by the time we came back together, we were more determined than ever to build our library, knowing how much those books soothed us on icy winter nights. Yes, the warm baby I cradle close to my bosom should be enough, but I want to hold a book as well.

May 15, 1912

A year has passed, and between my son and the household, the chickens and the library, I have fallen into bed each night far too spent to write even a few words in a journal. Today, however, cannot go unmarked.

We opened the Carnegie library with 1700 books. Astonishing. We are so proud of that fact, even though Green Valley managed to dedicate their library two weeks ago. They had to be first. Even though they'd collected only about a dozen books and had to beg

*people to bring more to the opening. A library without books?
Unfathomable.*

*We celebrated the dedication with a parade, including a
marching band led by Mr. Dickens at the high school. Then digni-
taries spoke, including our very own Robert Higgobottom, who's
running for State Senator. He was most eloquent, saying "Our
history is a sacred trust inherited from the pioneers, let us never
cease our efforts to preserve it." Eugene Lubbers went on and on
and on, as if he was the world's best orator, and as if we'd forget
he'd opposed our efforts. After he'd finished, we had more music.
Hundreds of people came, flags were out all over town, and no
one went to work. Trevor Quinn stayed awake through the whole
event, knowing it was momentous, and wanting to be a part. He
cried only a time or two when I forgot to feed him.*

*Branford has a new reporter at the paper, one who also has
a camera and will take photographs. He is the same Ronald
Wells who has traveled the world. Today he was documenting the
library dedication and took it upon himself to take a photograph
of Branford and me standing on the library steps, Trevor Quinn
in my arms. Branford stood so strong and straight, taking absolute care not to touch me, and as I looked into the camera lens,
I felt as if we were looking straight into the future. I don't need a
photograph to capture the moment. I know my legacy: a smart
son and a building that will encourage wisdom for the century to
come. It is plenty.*

TRACI

Something's changed. It's like Angie's grandmother's ghost is in the air. I run my hand over the windowsill and know she must've done the same thing. Maybe the first day the doors opened, she stood right here, looked out the window and thought about the hundreds of New Hopians who'd reap the benefits of her efforts, although I bet she never could've imagined all the people who'd come through these doors. How many lives would be changed. Even if I have to leave tomorrow, I'll never forget this place.

When Angie comes in, she hugs me like she'll never let me go. She looks tired, confused, and radiant all at the same time, like my roommates used to look after a night with a new lover. "You have no idea," she manages to blurt out before she bursts into tears. "Thank you," she sniffles, before she loses it again.

When the rest of the women show up, they're buzzed too. For the first time, the Hillians and Hopians are mixed up, not in segregated seating. They're gabbing among themselves, and I hear just scraps of conversation. "*Amazing to think they built this building before there were cars or telephones or even bathrooms in this town.*" "*You know we're all descendants of those pioneer women. We need to stand tall and carry on, follow their footsteps.*" "*They certainly left big shoes to fill.*" "*That pioneer DNA is in our genes too, you know.*"

As they settle into their handiwork, Gayle speaks up, loudly enough to make everyone listen, and the others eventually get quiet so she can talk.

"You know, I thought a lot about it yesterday, thought about it all night long when I couldn't sleep. Donna's right. We should go forward with plans for a Prairie Hill Cultural Center. We'll still come here for No Guilt Quilters, but we should have our own place in Prairie Hill. Maybe start with a knitting group called the 'Twister Sisters Knitters.' We need an arts center for ourselves. And a library. No matter what our husbands say."

Everybody's quiet while her statement sinks in. Finally, Sally breaks it. "Hope you're not suggesting the *Lysistrata* approach, because my worser half wouldn't even notice. It's not like we're young, hot, and hungry, if you know what I mean." She keeps her eyes on her knitting, like she's too embarrassed to look up.

"Me, I've worn out the meatloaf recipe. Will need new armaments," Donna laughs, as she waves a pair of scissors like a weapon.

Gayle regains control of the conversation, ignoring their protests. "There's no reason we can't call that architect at K-State and ask him to proceed. He was willing to do a preliminary design and mock-up for $10,000, much less than his usual fee; said we could see if we liked it before we went any further. We need to build a new library anyway; it makes sense to try to combine the library with an arts center."

Rachel brings a tray of iced tea as reinforcements, and the conversation stops while everyone tinkles their glasses.

"If New Hope can do it, don't you think we're up to the challenge?" Gayle asks. "Maybe that tornado was God's way of shaking us up. Literally. Reminding us it's time to take destiny in our own hands." She pauses to count her stitches. "Maybe we could even get Traci to be our artist-in-residence? After all, recycling is her specialty. And we'll certainly be making art out of trash. If nothing else, we have a lifetime supply of garbage out there at the dump."

"You can't have Traci," Mrs. Gene Lubbers says, as if she owns me. She's shown up again for help with her quilt.

It's a Hopian, Jennifer, who encourages the Hillians. "You can build a cultural center. *We* can. Let's start by making a quilt, auctioning it on eBay. There's a king-sized, cathedral window up there now that's already got a bid of nine hundred dollars. Has 1,921 pieces so we'd each have to do about a hundred."

"You'd help us?" Gayle asks.

"Don't we have our own challenges, raising money to keep the arts center open and the artist-in-residence program alive? We're up to our necks in ScARTlettes as it is." Mrs. Gene Lubbers throws her wet blanket on the conversation. Like she gives a crap about me or the artist-in-residence program. Like she's made a single potholder. She just shows up to demand help with her quilt, which she's making with a vengeance, determined to help the First Lady pick out her china.

Rachel throws her a glare. "We had plenty of help when we converted this building. Remember how the Arts Commission had statewide conferences then? Towns actually helped each other with good advice. Neodesha and Fredonia still fought over which had the best arts council, but I'll never forget the first time I shared a room with Mary Jo Lee from Prairie Hill. She told me about the Picture Lady Program. Bless her heart. I'm kind of glad she died before the tornado. Anyway, only fair to pass it on."

So suddenly they're going to take on the building of a cultural center in Prairie Hill, just as I leave town. Easy as that. Easy as that, but the timing sucks. I'm sorry. Would be fun to stick around and see what happens. Much as I hate to admit it, I like these women. They're as much family as I've ever had. And I can't even bear to think what it will be like to leave Thad, after I've finally found him.

Tomorrow at the latest, I need to tell Rachel about Sylvia's pregnancy and then Sylvia will tell Rachel about my lies. I thought about not telling on her; it'll all be obvious soon enough; it's not my problem. But then again, decisions must be made, and the earlier she gets help, the more choices she'll have. Sylvia can't wait another few months and then dump the baby in a garbage bin.

Everything will go on here, with or without me. The journal will stay here at the arts center. Angie doesn't like it, but Rachel convinced her it's like Solomon's baby. If she truly loves it, she won't tear it apart and spread it around to everyone who believes they own a piece of it, like me for finding it and Thad for having it on his land and Elena for the "common good" of the library. Pages scattered here, there, and every which way.

The journal inspired the Quilters to ramp up the ScARTlette factory. They're hoping for a hundred of them before they're finished, which will save the arts center for a couple more months. Rachel says every day we stay open offers the opportunity for a miracle. Brett said he'll run an article in the *Gazette* and try to get other newspapers in the state to publish it too, so New Hope can become known as the source for high-end gifts.

Even the Teens were inspired by the reading of the journal and have started working on a Kickstarter campaign to raise money. They want to sell their singing services, by doing "telegrams." For $25, they'll show up at your choice of place, to sing "Happy Birthday" or "Happy Anniversary."

As for myself, the popularity of the library quilt makes me think I could make quilts with other weird postcards—like jackalopes, the three-legged cow, and fifty feet high cornfields. They won't be a hit in Kansas, but maybe somebody like Freddy can sell them in a gallery. Ironic that I need to support myself just when the arts center is getting it together to pay me. If only I hadn't needed to lie.

I'm online, deep into my research over my lunch break, when Thad surprises me by dropping by to accuse me of stealing from his storm shelter. He already knows about the journal; in New Hope a secret can't be a secret for more than a nanosecond. After ranting about how he never gets to own anything, even anything found on his own land, he shrugs and admits the journal's probably not his anyway. What he wants to do is read that journal for himself.

We scarf down leftover pizza and wash our hands carefully before he scoots our two kitchen chairs together so we can read the journal together. We alternate reading out loud, one entry at a time, not stopping to comment. When we get to the part about dancing to *Shine On Harvest Moon,* he starts biting his lower lip, like he's afraid he'll cry. He slips his arm around me, and it stays there.

"Oh Traci, Traci, Traci," he says, as he pulls my chair out, forcing me to stand up. Putting one hand on my shoulder and taking my other hand, he dances me around, crooning like he was Frank Sinatra. After about three verses, which he's making up on the spot, he picks me up and carries me over to my bed, because there isn't another place to sit. We should be laughing at our silly behavior, but we aren't. It's all very serious.

Thad doesn't lay me down, like he did last time when I was sick, but instead props me up on the side of the bed and kneels on the floor in front of me and takes both my hands. "You really don't get it, do you?" he asks me, looking directly at me with his deep brown eyes. "You don't get how much this whole town loves you. Do you not see how everyone hangs out here, morning to night, just to bask in your presence? You've got hundreds of admirers, but I've proclaimed myself president of your fan club, because I'm the one who respects you most. Has it not occurred to you I never stepped foot in the building once it turned into the 'arts center?' Not until you got to town." He slips my sandal off and starts massaging my foot. "You don't get how much *I* love you," he sighs, handing me a button saying "I am loved."

Does he have any idea how long I've waited to hear that four-letter word? That four-letter word connecting me to a person I love back?

ANGELINA

"You knew? When did you know?" I attack Brett when I storm into his office, where he sits comfortably, feet on the desk. "Did you always know we're related? Why didn't you tell me? Why did you let me make a fool of myself?"

"Whoa girl." He smirks as he continues. "How did you find out? Happy Birthday, by the way." He hands me a card but I don't even glance at it.

"Traci found the journal and they decided to read it aloud to me at the slumber birthday party. No one else caught on, or maybe everyone in town already knew, but it's pretty clear your great grandfather mated with my grandmother to make my father. Did you always know?"

He takes his feet down from the desk and crosses his arms across his chest in a defensive position. "Nope. Not until I saw your grandmother's photo, with my great grandfather looking on, obviously smitten, his hands in his pockets to hide his physical response. My grandmother never did like yours and it all made sense. My great grandfather evidently took it upon himself to soothe a grieving widow."

"And you didn't tell me? How could you not tell me the minute you knew?"

Brett puts his finger to his mouth to shush me, motioning with his head to the pressmen in the next room. "Seemed like you had enough on your mind, what with finding out Thad was your half-brother. Another relative popping up seemed like it might pop your gasket."

"So you decided to withhold information?"

Is the list of secrets I don't know about my own family endless?

"Listen," Brett says. "I know this must be hard on you. But aren't you glad to know you have family? We're related, kiddo. That means forever."

I don't bother to tell him I'd hoped "forever" would take a romantic turn. How stupid would that have been? How embarrassing.

"You know, I had an idea," Brett continues. "You should come to work for the paper. Maybe become a partner. Your being one of the family and all. You know the printing business, and this whole town would love to have you stay."

"How kind of you," I say, with as much sarcasm as I can muster. "You don't really owe me, you know, just because your great grandfather conveniently committed adultery with my grandmother. Apparently, my father committed adultery too, at least once, when he made Thad. We ought to form a support group, not a business partnership. I don't need you to feel sorry for me, just because I don't have a clue as to what I'm going to do with my life."

I want to turn and stomp out, but not until I know everything.

"Hilda? Why do you have such power over her?" I ask.

With that question, his face turns to stone.

"You've got to know the answer to that one," I insist.

"Look, you can't tell anyone, okay? I shouldn't tell you, but you're family now."

He reaches across the desk and takes my hand in both of his.

"Hilda killed my wife and baby," he says, his mouth drawn tight. "Connie and William Allen, named after William Allen White. I always thought he'd sit behind this desk someday." His eyes start leaking but it's apparent he's angrier than he is embarrassed. "They were driving home from an AA meeting in Great Bend. The car must've hit the gravel road and Hilda must've slammed on the brakes. The car careened and crashed into a tree. By the time I got to the scene,

Hilda was nowhere to be seen and Connie and William were dead. William's head was a foot away from the rest of his body and both were drenched in blood."

Brett's face is beet red and sopping wet.

"How terrible," I blubber, unable to fight back my own tears. "What a tragedy."

"A tragedy indeed. Especially since it was my fault," he whispers.

"Your fault?" I don't see the connection.

"My fault."

He stops like that's the end of our discussion, then reconsiders. "I was the one who suggested Great Bend for AA because I knew nothing would stay anonymous here. I was the one who'd fought with Connie that afternoon because I was jealous of her AA sponsor, with whom she was talking more than she was talking to me. I'm the one who wouldn't give her the purple cashmere sweater she wanted, purple being the color for sobriety. Wouldn't give it to her until she stayed sober for a whole year. Here's the only thing I didn't do: build the bar between here and the AA meeting, which is where they got soused. I let the police assume Connie was the driver, which I knew she wasn't, because Connie had just called while nursing the baby. No need to put Hilda in jail. It wouldn't bring them back."

GAYLE

The journal made me see.

There's no way we can't rebuild Prairie Hill. Complete with a library, cultural center, and anything else we need or want. If our ancestors could do it with so little, there is absolutely no excuse for us. We'll be the new pioneers. Our houses are in pieces, but Prairie Hill was always a close-knit community and a great place to raise a family. And all those things we used to complain about? Now we can fix them. It'll take a lot of work, but we're worth it. Too many Kansas towns are dying as land gets bought by out-of-state mega-farmers. Prairie Hill deserves to thrive on.

These are the arguments I'd practiced in front of the mirror, knowing I'd need to make them in front of the whole town. I've never been one for public speaking, so I was scared one step past shitless, but Donna and Sally insisted it must be me to make the primary pitch. "Everyone knows you, and trusts you, from Yesteryears," they said. Yesteryears seems so far away. I try to tell myself we're on the way to Tomorrowland.

Tonight we had a town meeting in the Salvation Army tent, to try to determine who's coming back. When Tom Little stood at the chalkboard to take inventory, I surprised myself by being the first to raise my hand. "We're in," I said. "Mark and I have already picked out our new home, and I'm announcing the formation of a committee to build a new library and cultural center. Any and all are welcome to join us."

The whole room erupted in applause like I'd scored a touchdown.

Donna's was the second hand up, saying they'd rebuild, and my bosses, the Evertons, said they'll not just rebuild their home, they have every intention of reopening Yesteryears. That set off an avalanche of enthusiasm. Altogether, ninety people said they'll rebuild their homes, and twenty-five businesses said they'll be back.

Speaking to the community meeting, "com-meet" we call it, was both easier and harder than I'd imagined. I tried to create the perception we know what we're doing. My palms were sweaty and my heart beating too fast, but I managed to keep my voice even. I was doing an okay job until Les Stites got up and started quoting all the bad things he's read about the New Hope arts center, making Gene Lubbers sound like his brother. I could answer his arguments, except for the big one. Where the hell will we get the money?

TRACI

After I tell Rachel about Sylvia's pregnancy, she stays quiet for an eternity and a half. Finally, she says, "You did the right thing. We'll get her in to see Doc Simmons and take it from there. People don't need to know she's with child until she's made some decisions. At some point we'll need to involve her foster parents, but let's give her a chance to consider her options first, so she can make her own case for what she wants. No sense in making a bad situation worser still."

Rachel opens up a jar of oatmeal cookies, which she offers up like it's my reward for ratting out Sylvia. I'm too nervous to do more than nibble.

"There's one more thing," I tell her, my voice a squeak. "She didn't want me to tell you she's pregnant, and she'll know it's me who squealed. She threatened me. Told me if I told on her, she'd tell you the truth."

"Which is?" Rachel drops her voice almost to a whisper. This woman is the best listener I've ever met, treats everyone like they have something important to say.

"Which is. I lied to you."

"When?"

"When you hired me. I hadn't taught those courses, didn't even finish high school, and my references weren't real." I look hard at her face, daring myself to watch her reaction.

"Oh that. Never mind about that. That's water under the bridge, and I know you'll never do it again." Rachel stands up, as if the conversation is over.

"You're not shocked? You don't even seem surprised." As hard as I look, I can't tell what's going through her head.

"Oh honey, I already knew. I just thought you needed a fresh start. You didn't think I'd hire you to work with our kids without checking you out, did you? I figured it out the night we talked while you were still in New York. I thought about rescinding the offer, and then remembered how my father lied his whole life about coming on the orphan train." She pours another cup of coffee for herself, dunking her cookie into it after sitting down. "In fact, I Googled you the night we talked. Found the review of your show. Then called Freddy at the artZee Gallery. He must've asked me more questions than I asked him, was definitely checking us out to make sure we'd be good to you. Freddy's Aunt Peggy was a Pi Phi at KU and was there when they pledged Frank's sister. Such a small world. That's what sealed the deal. Anyways, Freddy told me you were one of the most talented artists he'd found this year. And that you have a heart of gold."

"So you knew all of it? My whole story? All along?" I ask.

"You mean about being found in a dumpster? Yes, ma'am, I read that too. But Moses was found in the bulrushes, and look what he managed to do. As far as I'm concerned, that's what you're doing with the Teens. Performing a miracle or two."

⌒℮⌒

I'm not used to seeing Rachel as anything but cool as a cucumber, as they say around here, but when she comes back after taking Sylvia to Doc Simmons, she's visibly shaken. Looks more like a pickle than a cucumber. Wrinkled and vinegary. I offer her a seat at my worktable.

"It went okay," she tells me. "But it's still really, really tough. I'm not sure what Sylvia will decide to do, but Doc Simmons was clear about her options. It turns out you made a lucky guess when you noticed her baby bump. She wasn't showing; she's still in her first trimester so that's a good thing. I'm taking her up to Planned Parenthood tomorrow for more extensive counseling. Then she can decide."

"And that's it?" I ask. "What about the guys?"

"Well, that's the beginning. With Sylvia's permission, Doc Simmons called Joe James, who's calling all the boys involved. And their parents. Not like we're going to press charges or anything since it's clear Sylvia was the instigator and sixteen is the legal age of consent, but Joe is adamant the boys need to work the rest of the year and pay for medical expenses. Whatever Sylvia decides."

"All of them? All the boys will pay?" I persist. It's not the question I want to ask.

"Yep. Turns out there's no need for a paternity test. Sylvia insisted most of it was 'French kissing and finger fucking and the only cock in my cunt was Nate Lubber's.'" Rachel blushes at her own language. "Pardon my French, but that's the direct quote. If that's not true, one of the guys will squeal. I hate that it's happened, but this is the best solution. Word will spread like a prairie wildfire, and these despicable acts will stop."

"Will Brett publish it in the paper?" I ask.

"Won't need to. As my father used to point out, if a boy commits a prank, his father will know before he gets home. He would greet my brother, 'Ready for the woodshed?' before he was through the front door. And that was before telephones."

I offer Rachel a refill on her coffee, and she starts to cry. "Look at you, how you've started to take care of us all," she says. "You know you've been an amazing influence on Sylvia, right? You should've seen her promise Doc Simmons she wouldn't do what happened to you, just drop her baby anywhere. 'How fucked up is that?' she asked him. 'Traci turned out okay, but she hardly had a chance.'"

"It probably didn't hurt that she heard about your father, and about

Thad," I remind Rachel. "She's got good examples of how bastard kids can make good after all."

I try to spread the credit around, and pretend I'm not pleased that Sylvia paid me a compliment. She thinks I turned out okay.

"*Never, ever, ever* let me hear you call yourself a 'bastard kid.'" Rachel raises her voice to make her point and actually wags her finger at me. And then she wraps me in her arms like I was her daughter. By the time we're done, we both could win Olympic gold medals in bawling. And it's not like either of us practices much.

When I ask Rachel about the ramifications on the arts center, if they'll figure out a way to blame me for Sylvia's condition, she says no way can that happen. "The facts of life indicate she was pregnant before the mural. Before you got here. It truly was a description of what she was going through. As for us, we're actually in better shape. Old Man Lubbers will no longer rescind his contribution here or his ad buy at the *Gazette*. He miraculously did a quick turnaround. Saw the light, if you will. He'll be doing cartwheels to prove what an upstanding citizen he is. Try to bury the fact he's raised a jerk of a son. That boy will spend time in jail if he doesn't straighten up, and the old man knows it. Wouldn't be good for his funeral home or for the reputation of a guy who's been calling for death for the promiscuous."

After Rachel leaves, I go back to my worktable, try to concentrate, wonder how I can design a border that can be used for the wide variety of baby quilts that are emerging. Will we need to make one for Sylvia too? It's the toughest of choices, and I almost feel sorry for her.

Over the years I've wondered about the woman who delivered me, then delivered me to the garbage bin, and imagined what she was like. I used to fantasize she was a famous actress, on her way to take the stage in a Broadway show right there on Times Square, when her labor pains started. Even now, some rich and famous Hollywood star might be wondering what happened to me, having lived in regret for twenty-six years, at her own stupidity and cowardice. Someday she might tell all to Oprah, and they'll call me to meet her. In my fantasy, I'm already a famous artist, as famous as the movie star, surrounded by adoring fans, and everyone will be amazed at my story.

In my gut I know that woman, my mother, must've been like Sylvia. Creative, with a rich imagination, desperate for a happily-ever-after ending. And scared shitless.

ANGELINA

Emotionally wrung out, I feel like a soaked dishrag. For all I've learned—about my family, about the libraries, about New Hope and the women who make it run—I have lost the thing that's meant the most to me. My PhD. Now I see my grandmother would have supported me. I've disappointed her too.

Wallowing in bed does no good, so I head to the arts center, which is where I always end up. The soothing chatter of the women provides my only home.

The women have their ScARTlette factory in full operation, more determined than ever to raise money. Connie showed us her new calluses the other day; Rachel told her it was time to use a thimble. Jennifer had to get a tetanus shot when she ran her sewing machine needle through her middle finger in her rush to reach her self-imposed quota of a dozen scarves. Gayle is soaking her hands in paraffin every night, to soothe the cramps from knitting, having decided she'll make a dozen for the New Hope effort before starting on their new fund-raising drive. Even with their hard work and enormous efforts, I know they can't make enough scarves to keep the arts center.

I half listen to the women's chatter as I wonder what comes next for me. Brett suggested I look at other PhD programs if I'm still "hell-bent" on getting those letters after my name. Go to the ends of the earth to find a university that will accept me. Australia, maybe? Why should I be so terrified when the Internet makes it no further away than Kansas was when my grandmother homesteaded here. I can pack the Carnegie library quilt Traci gave me and take it with me wherever I go, my own personal security blanket.

Rachel, always sensitive to everyone's moods, comes over to sit beside me, offering me a slice of carrot cake. "Would you ever consider staying here?" she asks. "We could sure use you in this town."

"But what would I do?" I can hear the whine in my own voice. "Where would I live? How would I make a living?"

"We could figure all that out. Wouldn't your grandmother be delighted?"

If only it were so easy. I've gotten a lot of positive feedback to the story I wrote for the *Gazette*, but I hardly see myself taking Brett up on his offer to work there. There are only so many library stories to be done and then I'd have to start covering crops and weather and politics. Definitely not my expertise.

Joe James called, telling me we need another meeting, so I head over there late in the afternoon, when the temperature has once again hit 98 degrees.

He doesn't even wait for me to sit down before he starts talking.

"Angie, I don't know where to begin. When we last met, I realized something was amiss. There was a piece of the truth you were lacking." He wastes no time with niceties, as if he knows his minutes on earth are limited. He's definitely old, but when he sits behind his desk, his voice gets stronger, and you can see him for the dynamic lawyer he must've been.

"To get to the point, I've gotten the impression you don't know you're the owner of your grandmother's land."

"What land? Thad's land?" Is he confused in his old age? Or is it me who's seriously baffled as to what he's saying?

"Thad doesn't own the land. He never bought it from your father.

True, that land went to your father after your grandmother died, but your father never sold it to Thad. The land was to go directly to you when your father died."

Joe James shuffles paper on his desk and places a deed in front of me before continuing. "When your grandmother died, your father told Thelma they could stay there indefinitely, but he never gave them the land. There was no legal agreement; he just said they could stay. Thad stayed on after Thelma died."

"But Dad died ten years ago. Why am I just now finding out?" I don't understand what he's telling me.

"We notified you as soon as we heard about your father's death and sent you a statement every year. When we never heard anything, we assumed the arrangement was fine with you, even though it was tough to see the land lie fallow. We figured you were holding off selling until land prices went up, which they have dramatically. Patience was a brilliant move on your part."

"I never got the letters," I say. "Obviously."

Joe James looks confused but carries on. "The first one would have come registered, required a signature. Could someone have intercepted them? It'd be a federal offense, but it's the only answer I can think of."

He looks through a folder as if there might be an answer there.

"No, of course not," I answer, knowing perfectly well my mother is the felon. Suddenly, everything makes sense. Why my father never worried about my making a living, why my mother didn't want me to come to Kansas, why Thad was so upset when I appeared. The situation is crystal clear.

"The point is you're a rich woman. Land's selling for over sixteen hundred an acre and you have over twelve hundred acres there. That's almost two million dollars. It's all grassland now, but it could be used for hunting or ranching or even alternative power. They're looking for places for wind farms."

I'm too overwhelmed to say anything and start doodling in my notebook as I've started to do when I'm nervous. A habit picked up from Traci.

"Take your time. There's no hurry," Joe James tells me as he looks at me patiently while I digest the news. "You do probably want to talk to Thad, though, so he can figure out what to do with his studio. He's going to be heartbroken after all the time and effort he's spent getting it just the way he wants. Or maybe he'll be relieved. I'll bet he's been on edge all summer, figuring your being here meant things would change. It'll be easier for him, once everyone knows what a good artist he is."

"From what I learned, he has every bit as much right to that land as I do." I don't know whether I should've said this, but it appears Joe James is my lawyer after all and I might as well deal with the situation.

"Maybe. But that's not the way the will was written. Your father never admitted paternity, Thelma never asked him to, and Thad's actually been pretty lucky to have a free place to live and work for a decade."

"And that's why Thad never sold to the Chases?" I ask.

"It wasn't his to sell," Joe tells me.

I get up to leave, but Joe James puts up his hand to stop me.

"Angie, there's one more thing. I had a call from an old college friend of mine, Henry Caine. He should've called you directly but he used the occasion to catch up with me. Probably to make sure I was still alive. We do that now, check up on each other to see if we're still alive. Anyway, he's on the board of the Kansas University Press. They'd like you to write a book, based on your summer here and your grandmother's journals. They love the story you did for the *Gazette*."

I'm dumbfounded, but Joe James has no trouble filling in the silence.

"Think about it. Your name, Angelina Sprint, will be on the spine of books in every Carnegie library in the state. There with Herman Melville, Henry David Thoreau, and James Joyce."

"And Willa Cather," I say, imagining row upon row of bookshelves. As I leave the law office, once again I don't know where to turn. Once again I barge in on Brett, firing accusations.

"So you knew Thad's place is mine, right?" I ask, kicking the door shut behind me, because I have no intention of keeping my voice down. "Is that why you asked if I wanted to become a partner in the paper? You figure I have cash to invest?"

"Whoa, sister. When will you ever learn to trust me?"

He swivels his chair so he's looking right at me with that intense look my father had. I plop myself on the chair in front of his desk, the chair I must be wearing out.

"I actually don't need your money," he continues, avoiding the question about whether he knew. "What I thought I made perfectly clear is I need your brain power. You're a damn good writer; that Carnegie story went AP syndicate, which never happens here unless there's a tornado. Both our advertising and subscription sales increased by 24 percent the week after we ran it. Maybe the economy's getting better, or maybe we've found a star reporter. Our own Lois Lane. Between that and your experience in running a printing press, you're the perfect partner. After all, you're the only person I've ever met who knows Dr. Seuss used the New Century Schoolbook font for *Cat in the Hat*."

"That font that's related to one they use for the briefs of the Supreme Court," I counter.

Brett's eyes light up. "And you think you aren't smart? You know Dr. Seuss wrote *Cat in the Hat* because grade schoolers weren't learning their vocabulary, because books were so boring, right? Someone made a list of 348 words kids should know, and Dr. Seuss used 236 of them in *Cat in the Hat*."

The man's pretty proud of himself for knowing this fact.

"Listen Angie," he continues, "the only devious part about my offer is I'd like you to stay in town. We should grow old together. That part is personal, and I cop to it. How I wish my son could've known you."

"What am I supposed to do? What exactly am I supposed to do with my one precious life?" I pick up the glass paperweight on his desk and cradle it as if it were a crystal ball. "I wanted to be smart, I wanted to be a librarian, I never actually wanted to be rich. To have enough, certainly, but 'rich' wasn't on my list."

"Oh come on. Everyone wants to be rich."

"Not me. My dad always taught me a dollar bill was just a piece of paper—and there are lots more powerful pieces of paper than a dollar bill. Like the Gettysburg Address and Anne Frank's *Diary of a Young Girl*. He gave me reams of paper every year for Christmas, so I could draw and write—and once a roll of butcher paper, truly infinite in its possibilities. 'You don't think paper's powerful?' he'd ask. 'Consider how much a paper cut hurts. Contemplate how the first thing a baby gets is a piece of paper called a birth certificate. Or the power of a love letter.'"

"So that's why you were so hell-bent on getting that piece of paper with PhD written on it. PhD's just a piece of paper after all. Seems like you've done more good by telling the story of the Carnegies in my paper—and certainly if you do the book for KU—than if you finished your dissertation so it can rot on an academic library bookshelf somewhere. Angie, you belong here, where the action is."

"Wait a minute. You know about the KU Press? Does everyone know everything in this town?"

"Pretty much." He turns to his printer and pulls out a story marked 'draft,' titled, 'KU Press to publish Angelina Sprint book.'"

I tear it in quarters and put the pieces in my pocket, my privacy fully violated.

"Do you also know what I'm going to do with that property? Do you have a press release ready for that? Because I don't know what I'm going to do. I know I don't want to hang onto it until the next Dust Bowl. The Chases would love to have the land, Thad would love to have the land, I'd love to have Grandmother's house, but …"

"No buts about it. You're smart enough to make it happen. You've got the best lawyer in five states; he can recommend a surveyor and get the deal done. You'll have cash for whatever you want, you can become a philanthropist yourself if nothing else. Follow Carnegie's example and do good work. Sounds to me as if the only question is whether you want to put your mother behind bars for mail fraud."

GAYLE

We got the architect, Christopher Fernandez, here on false pretense, since we don't have a clue as to how we'll pay him for the design let alone the building. Then there's the issue of maintenance, which Les Stites never misses the opportunity to bring up. Having watched the potholder brigade over at New Hope, having seen how they scrape for every dime, I have no illusions about how hard this will be.

Some people in town think we're insane, but if they could meet Christopher, they'd believe too. He certainly is the definition of charismatic. All the gals were flirting, trying to impress. Even Angie. I do believe he liked her back.

"So what was it like?" Christopher asked us. "What was the tornado like?"

We must've shuddered in unison, but Donna answered. "Well, we should've known it was coming by the way the cats were acting. The cats and the kids. We have a few thunderstorms every month and we get used to bad behavior when the barometer drops. Right after dark, the sirens went on and the electricity went off. We began to see funnel clouds in the lightning flashes." She gestured toward the tranquil sky. "A flash of sheet lightning and you'd see a funnel cloud, but you couldn't tell which way it was moving because the flash wouldn't last long enough. We were all lined up outside our houses, up and down the street, when we began to hear the roar. That's when we scrambled for cover, in the southwest corner of the basement, the way we were always taught. Stayed there with a rug over our heads, listening to what sounded like a staticky AM radio, stuck between channels, turned up full volume, getting louder and louder. Then, suddenly, we were covered with rain, and we realized the whole house had blown away. Nothing was left above us. It was all over."

Christopher looked horrified as he absorbed the power of the storm.

"At our house, we huddled under a ping pong table in our basement," Ann told him. "All six of us, me holding onto our cat Barney for dear life. When it was over, there was broken glass everywhere. That ping pong table saved our skin. Literally. We had to scramble to find two mismatched boots for Guy to wear. He'd come downstairs barefoot. Glass everywhere. That's a mistake he'll never make again."

"You know, it's weird," I said. "I've lived here my whole life, was born here, went through school here, but sometimes I can stand here and not know what street I'm on. Was this Main or Grand? All the landmarks are gone and it's disorienting. We do need an anchor, a reason to come back."

Later, at the arts center, Angie pulled out "Notes on Library Buildings" to show Christopher the standard plans for Carnegie libraries, and explained how the emphasis was on getting a bang for the buck, in terms of space for books. She showed him this could best happen with a rectangular-shaped building with a basement and one floor. The main floor would be twelve to fifteen feet high to accommodate book stacks, and the windows would be six feet up to allow for shelving. Bookcases could subdivide the rooms.

Christopher leaned over close to look at the sketches. When he asked about the landscaping, Angie assured him Andrew Carnegie had no interest in paying for shrubbery; his monies would go to the interiors not to exterior niceties.

Vic called before supper, and I filled him on our dreams. He could not have been more enthusiastic. Told me to ignore the small town politics. Said it sounded like we were building a beautiful building made out of love. Told me I'd shown him what it was like to be homeless, roofless, but not hopeless, a lesson he'd never forget.

Just as we were about to hang up, Vic blurted, "There's one more thing, Mom. You're building the kind of community that'll be a great place to live. The kind of environment we'd like to raise our kids. I was opposed at first, but Jill's right. You're going to be too busy to smother your grandchildren. You're going to continue being the strong, brave person we want them to know. We're looking for ways to move home."

TRACI

I can't believe Angie was up for camping out in front of the remains of the Carnegie library in Prairie Hill. She's crazy in love with it, but still. When she said she wanted me to take a million more pictures before they bulldoze, I suggested we do the photography over twenty-four hours to catch it in different light, and she agreed. I figured it'd be good for her to concentrate on something other than her failed PhD.

If anyone can divert Angie from the blues, it's Sylvia, who's come along as well. Sylvia wearing her tablecloth caftan, as if her baby bump were huge. Sylvia making a wisecrack a minute. Smarty-pants Sylvia, always the center of attention.

I'm madly snapping pics, having already told Angie I'll be manipulating the images, printing them on fabric for a crazy quilt. It'll be the last piece in the portfolio I'm sending to the Museum of Craft and Folk Arts, an exhibit Freddy arranged.

The midday sun is so intense it washes out the landscape, making for an artistic statement about drought and vastness and emptiness. Shows better than words ever could what it must've been like to build this library in the middle of the frontier. Later in the afternoon the shadows are dramatic, casting off from the library façade and the few lone weeds that have sprung up. A tumbleweed makes a dramatic geometric statement in the middle of a wide expanse of nothing, which contrasts with a close-up of an overgrown dandelion that shows the seeds protruding on thin threads. One minute I'm Ansel Adams taking the wide shot, the next Imogen Cunningham capturing the detail, like it said in the book Angie loaned me.

It's at least 104 degrees. We could enter a wet t-shirt contest on the strength of our sweat alone. Sylvia decides to whoop it up, sprays carbonated water on herself, starts dancing, acting like the kid I never got to be. Once I start snapping photos, she hams it up all the more, radiating maternal beauty.

We're starving by the time we're done, thankful for the humongous picnic Rachel sent along—ham and her famous sweet mustard, poached asparagus, chocolate chip cookies. No wine, in deference to Sylvia's age or at least her condition, but the lemonade is fresh squeezed and we drink gallons of it. Homemade and just sweet enough.

No clouds for the sunset, which is disappointing, but after dusk we're treated to a crystal clear night. No moon, so dark I'm not sure what kinds of images we'll get even if I adjust the F-stop and aperture, as we take more shots of the façade. So peaceful you'd never believe this same sky hurls thunder and lightning, hail, dust storms, and tornadoes. A gazillion stars in the sky. For the first time ever, I grasp the concept of infinity. Nobody could count so high.

Sometime after midnight, we stretch out on blankets and agree to try to grab a few hours of sleep before dawn when the light will change again. I'm so mesmerized by the stars I can't bear to close my eyes.

"Nighty night," Angie says. "Don't let the bedbugs bite."

I shiver, but my bedbugs seem one hundred million miles away. "Do you know it was bedbugs that drove me out of New York? I never could have made it as a pioneer woman, huh?"

"They hated bedbugs, too. Drove them nuts." Angie answers. "If bedbugs invaded their sod houses, they had to remove the bedding and bake it in the sun, then soak down the sod walls with kerosene."

"Boy, that could be dangerous if a guy threw off his match after lighting his cigar," Sylvia observes. "Ker-Boom."

"Or if lightning struck, which it sometimes did." Angie says. "Set thousands of acres on fire as the wind swept flames across the prairie."

The thought of the explosion makes me jumpy so I jerk when a star falls down. Jerk so hard I might have whiplash. And then another.

"Oh my god! Did you see that?" I gasp.

"Did you make a wish? When you see a falling star, you're supposed to make a wish," Sylvia tells me.

"It happened too fast."

"Not to worry," Angie says. "They call this Perseids. It's a shooting star shower. Happens in August. There should be another hundred or so falling stars tonight. That's why I wanted to sleep out. Time to make new wishes."

Time to catch a falling star.

We're quiet together, waiting for the next one, and we begin to breathe in unison.

"I know what I wish," Sylvia interrupts the silence. "I wish my baby will have two mommies. Mommies like Rachel and you and Angie." Unbelievable. When did she decide? I break out in goose bumps at her statement and wonder when this happened. Guess it's a compliment she wants someone like me to be mother to her baby. "I've decided I want my baby to be adopted by a lesbian couple," she continues, "because women really are the best."

"You what?" Angie sits up with a bolt. She takes a deep breath and turns on Sylvia, trying to keep her voice calm. "You're so lucky," Angie tells her. "You can choose a mother for your child. Who gets to do that? Who gets to place her offspring into the best possible situation? But don't you want a father too? I mean I loved my father. I *love* my father. In spite of everything."

"Nope. I've made up my mind. My baby's going to have two mothers." She thrusts out her lower lip to indicate her determination.

"Can we talk about this later?" I try to re-capture the peace and realize I sound like Rachel.

"Well, the parents, whoever they are, they'll be lucky," Angie says. "They'll have a beautiful baby with dark eyes, long lashes, and spunk. I'm absolutely sure about the spunk part."

"Hey, I like that word. Spunk," Sylvia says. "That's what I'll name my band."

A hundred wishes! What would I wish for? I didn't grow up wishing. It never occurred to me to wish for a summer in Kansas, to meet a bunch of housewives and another bunch of messed up kids. Would I dare wish for Thad? Okay, deep down inside I've always wished for a home, but I see myself as a turtle, a person who carries her home around with her, who can tuck her head in and out, depending on the circumstances. Now I've come to see a bunch of pals, really good friends, is what makes a home. Home is where the heart is and all that. Shouldn't I wish for world peace, or at least a truce between New Hope and Prairie Hill?

I drift off to dream of a tornado coming right at me, but instead of destroying me, it lifts me up, and I sail across the heavens, spotting Angie's Carnegie libraries and clicking aerial shots. Everyone's dancing around them. They sweep their arms up and down over their heads, as if they were doing jumping jacks, and I hold the shutter open to get images of snow angels. And then I dream of the bucket of gold at the end of the rainbow, gold attended not by leprechauns but by prairie dogs standing on their haunches, protecting the treasure.

ANGELINA

Thad and I walk through the fields surrounding his studio, following the footsteps of our great grandparents who homesteaded. Joe James has arranged this meeting between the two of us so Thad knows I'll soon be making decisions. He points out a camouflaged meadowlark nest made of woven grass. "Meadowlarks are ground-nesters," he tells me. "They perch on a fencepost to sing, cackle, and claim their territory, usually about seven acres per bird. They're the Kansas state bird, members of the blackbird family, you know."

I didn't.

"Can I show you a secret?" he asks, taking my elbow and walking me back up toward my grandmother's house, stopping just this side of cottonwoods planted as a windbreak many decades ago. "See here? I do believe this is the remains of the soddy our ancestors built. You can almost see the outline of the foundation."

Shivers run down my arm, and I kneel down to run my fingers over the packed clay, sniffing the earthiness of my fingers. "Consider the courage it took to build here, in the middle of nowhere, with no more resources than hopes and prayers," I tell him. He pauses while I wipe tears with the back of my sleeve. Their DNA is penetrating through the clay to my heart, providing a psychic connection.

It takes me a while to compose myself, but when I do, we walk over to the storm cellar and then search it, to make sure there are no treasures still hiding. Nothing but pickles and jams and a few hundred cobwebs. We go into Grandmother's dilapidated house and find my artwork in her kitchen, yellowed, but still there. Thad's artwork is there too, which would serve as proof of our kinship if I needed any. Also proof he's always been the better artist.

He invites me into his trailer, and I see it's a nest of its own, a bachelor pad for sure, but certainly more comfortable than what I'd imagined. At his insistence, I sink into his recliner and he perches himself on the ottoman at my feet, like he's ready for a serious talk. After all this time, he still hasn't told me what he knows about my grandmother and the library. "Did you ever talk about it?" I ask, desperate for crumbs of stories.

He shakes his head. "Remember, I was just five when she died."

I'm disappointed but I guess I knew this answer.

"You know, I don't know why you're so interested in being a librarian anyway," Thad says, as if this will somehow comfort me. "Aren't libraries all going to electronic checkouts, self-service, becoming just warehouses for books? A librarian's main job becoming that of asking the stinky homeless men to leave so they don't offend the literary elite?"

"You can't believe that!" I almost scream. "Don't you know librarians help with reference searches, homework, job and resume assistance, children's story times, school class visits, summer reading programs, genealogy, book clubs? Did you know more than two billion books are checked out every year?"

He's laughing at me!

"You goaded me on," I accuse him.

"That's what brothers are for, right? Brothers were put on this earth to harass their sisters." There's an edge to his voice; I'm not sure if he's teasing.

"You love the library," I tell him. Suddenly I'm sure of this, and his grin confirms the fact.

He thrusts his hands in his pockets and says, "Well I was the kid who undoubtedly had ADD. They didn't call it that. But I had the attention span of a cat in a mouse farm, so I was always in trouble for daydreaming or acting out. The teacher would send me to the library, which was like heaven for a kid like me. Two things that still trigger my ADD like crazy are libraries and hardware stores. No matter what was on my mind, there was fascinating stuff on the shelves. Widely diverse and seductive distractions. Art books or architecture, motorcycles or mysteries, CDs. I devoured every one of Tony Hillerman's mysteries, then started in on the art books. Me and Traci both like Rauschenberg, you know. I was never in serious trouble, but I did continue to make life miserable for my teachers so they'd send me to the library for quiet time. "

"Please, please, please don't throw me in the Briar Patch?" I ask.

"That'd be it," he says. "And that's what Sylvia and her homies are doing with Traci. Getting into just enough trouble to be sent to the arts center to hang out with her."

Thad gets up to look out the window, standing so his profile is in silhouette, his strong chin thrust forward in determination. He's gazing out over the pasture, toward his studio. "Have you decided what to do with this amazing hunk of land you have here?" he asks, his voice breaking in spite of himself.

"I have."

"And?" His voice quivers in even that one syllable.

"I've decided to keep Grandmother's house for myself, and, as of this morning, enough of the land to incorporate the sod house foundation. That should not be destroyed. I'll see if someone can restore the house; if not, figure out a way to bring in a small structure that can serve as a retreat for me. I don't want to live here full time but I want to be able to come back. Often and always. Right now, it looks like I'll need a place to stay while I do some writing. I might bring in another trailer."

"That's great," he says, although it's apparent he doesn't mean it. "And the rest?"

"Joe James is calling a surveyor and lining up a realtor. Once we have an appraisal, I'll see if the Chases want to buy."

Thad's face falls instantaneously, once again showing the temperament of the artist he is. He starts pounding his right fist into his left hand.

"There's one other thing," I tell him, fearing this guy will break down in front of me. "I'm deeding the studio and two acres around it to you, so you can move your trailer back there and still have room for both vegetable and sculpture gardens. I hope that's okay?"

He pulls me out of the recliner and dances me around his living room, which isn't easy, given the number of half-done art pieces, scattered all over the floor.

EPILOGUE
Nine Months Later

TRACI

⚊⚊⚊e⚊⚊⚊

Yikes! I can hardly get through the front door, after running over to Jack's for another package of paper napkins. A herd of people have gathered for the unveiling of the model for the new Library and Cultural Center, on this, the one-year anniversary of the Prairie Hill tornado. When the weather turned iffy, they decided to do the honors here, meaning the whole crew stayed half the night to sweep up threads and polish floors. It smelled like ammonia when I left but now the hot sweat of human life is the scent de jour. Everyone's mingling and I can hardly make it to the back of the room where the Guilters have set up a table to serve punch and gingersnaps and to sell potholders and ScARTlettes. Sylvia is rapping a new piece on her guitar, a riff on "Over the Rainbow," but you can hardly hear her over the din of conversation. When I give her a thumbs up, she stops long enough to show me a new video of her baby boy, who was open-adopted by a straight couple in Denver, and is wearing a blue beanie Sylvia crocheted herself. She and the band members are all wearing upcycled men's shirts, decorated with floral pockets.

I look for Angie in the crowd. Surely she won't skip the architect's announcement, no matter how sad she is that the final wall of the Prairie Hill library is about to come down. The photos we took of the old Carnegie library last summer are brilliant. We caught it at sunset, under the stars, at daybreak, and high noon. The photos should be enough, right? Still, neither of us can bear to see the razing of the final wall. She's been subdued the last few days, despite the fact her book is almost finished and she'd begun to get excited about writing her next one.

Angie slips into the seat beside me just as the architect, Christopher Fernandez, in dress shirt and tie and sweating profusely, clears his throat and taps on the pedestal for attention, which is followed by the sound of scraping chairs. People tussle for front-row seats, so they can get a good look at the model when, or make that *if*, he ever gets around to pulling off the white sheet. "C'mon," he tells the crowd, trying to sweet-talk them into obeying. "You can look at the model all morning. You can come up close and put your nose to it. But let's get this show on the road."

When more or less everyone is seated, he clears his throat again. "First of all, I want to thank you for giving me the opportunity to work on this most important building. We're delighted with the results and hope you will be, too." He shuffles index cards as he speaks. "We appreciate the hospitality the New Hope Arts Center has offered us today; we'd hoped to do this unveiling on site, but, no one knows better than you guys, you don't try to outguess Mother Nature."

Everyone tries to laugh, but you can tell they don't think he's so funny.

"I need to tell you we had completed a set of plans several months ago, and then threw them away and started over again after I had lunch with Angelina and Traci. Traci cooked but it was still an expensive lunch for me, as I came away with a new appreciation of what the Carnegie libraries meant to this state. I've done not one other thing since I left here, hardly eaten, scarcely slept. I threw everything out to start over." He's nervous, speaking each word distinctly, like he's determined to get it right. There's a lot of impatient squeaking chairs.

"As you will soon see," he continues, "we have met the standards for the highest LEED rating. The Prairie Hill Library and Cultural Center will be the first completely green public building in the second completely green town in Kansas. We will make use of everything from low-flush toilets to solar panels to concrete flooring and ... "

"Can we just see the model?" Thad yells from the back.

The architect tries to laugh him off. "Impatient, are you? Can I please tell you ..."

"We've waited long enough." Thad yells again, "Take it off." I join in and soon the whole crowd is yelling in unison: "Take. It. Off." Hands clapping after every word.

He looks around the room, then shrugs and pulls the sheet off with a flourish.

The room becomes dead quiet. The building is magnificent. Positively awesome. He shows us the front, the length of the building, a glass wall, overlooking a garden of sunflowers. "This side, with its wide open windows, looks to the future. We've done it in Pittsburgh Corning's new safety glass, so you can see outside, but it's strong enough to sustain tornado-strength winds and the debris they can throw."

He pauses to turn the model on its pedestal.

"On the backside, we've used red bricks to represent the solidity of the past. We'll purchase new bricks, but also integrate as many of the old ones as we can salvage. By placing the bricks in a vertical formation, the wall will look like a huge bookcase, reminding us of the library's original function. To underline the message, we can burn titles into the spines of some of the "books," reminiscent of the "Don't Spit On Me" bricks from Coffeyville. I thought we might do *Little House on the Prairie* for Angelina.

He catches her eye and she responds with her palms together in a bow. I can see tears in her eyes, and that triggers my tears. Angie will be losing her library once and for all. Etching *Little House on the Prairie* on a brick won't change that.

My head is buried in my bag, digging out a rumpled tissue, when I hear the crowd gasp. I see why when I look up. The architects have kept the front wall, the façade, of the Carnegie library, kept the portico and Corinthian columns.

"We decided we could reinforce this wall and save it," Christopher says. "And it definitely should be saved. You know, I'd like to say I would've come up with this on my own, but I wouldn't have without Angelina's commitment to the Carnegies and Traci's love of all things old and her dedication to saving them. Can I thank these two women and the women of these two towns who make miracles happen on the Plains?"

He comes into the audience and takes my hand, and Angie's, and raises them in a victory pose like we're prizefighters. The whole room explodes in a standing ovation. Thad snaps a picture and shows me myself with a giddy grin.

It seems like every single person in the room wants to give me a hug; a few even want me to sign their programs. I'm so giddy I might float away like a balloon.

After each and every person comes up to congratulate me personally, like I was the one who did it, the Teens and Quilters stay to clean up the library, but can't bear to leave. Jen pulls out a bottle of champagne she'd been hiding in her bag, and we all get a sip.

"To Traci," Rachel says, offering a toast, making me the center of attention yet again. "To Traci who found her heart in Kansas, like the Tin Man. Who basically saved the arts center with *love* and inspired Prairie Hill to build a cultural center of their own."

A little hokey, but I'll take it. Why not? I might as well play along.

"To Angie," I lift my glass to her. "Who found her brain and just how friggin' smart she is."

"If Angie got the Scarecrow's brain and Traci got the Tin Man's heart, who's the lion? Who got the courage?" Sylvia asks.

"Oh that's easy," says Gayle. "We all did. Everyone said we were courageous after the tornado, but that wasn't courage, that was animal instinct. We didn't have a choice except to run and hide and pull a rug over our heads. Literally. Deciding to put our hearts and souls into building a cultural center, that's courage. Standing up to those who disagree, that's courage. We are lionesses all."

"Amen, sister." The room laughs at Sylvia's enthusiastic response.

"Stop it. I get pretty tired of the *Wizard of Oz* references. Ever since I moved out here, my family teases me endlessly about being 'Dorothy from Kansas.' I hate being a stereotype," Jennifer says. "I've thrown away my red shoes."

"But see, that's the whole point. They're not 'stereotypes' but 'archetypes.'" Angie argues. "Everyone thinks the *Wizard of Oz* stays popular for its psychedelic colors and whimsical music, but our insecurities are universal. We've all got self-esteem issues."

"All I can say is I am so grateful Angie found the pot of gold at the end of the rainbow," Rachel says. "And now she's the first philanthropist since Carnegie to donate to both Prairie Hill and New Hope. To think we might have had to shutter this place."

There's total silence as everyone considers how much we've made happen. Total silence is a rarity in this group.

Finally, Jennifer speaks up. "The thing is, it was us who found the pot of gold. Not money, but each other. I've lived here for almost twenty years, and it's only now that I feel like I belong."

"You know how Rachel always reminds us 'hope' is a verb?" Gayle continues. "Well, 'home' should be a verb too. We make ourselves a home, wherever we land, no matter what the obstacles. Home-making means a whole lot more than sweeping out the cobwebs and washing dishes. 'Make yourself a home,' should be our slogan."

Sylvia provides a drumroll to underline the statement.

There's no place like home.

ACKNOWLEDGMENTS

M y parents always insisted my first words were "Thank you." I've certainly had reason enough to use them, especially in writing this book. It may take a mere village to raise a child, but it took the equivalent of the population of Kansas to support this effort over the last few years. Thank you!

Gratitude to librarians everywhere, especially those at the Kingman, Great Bend, and Lincoln libraries in Kansas and the Chestnut Hill library in Philadelphia for help in research, and those at my own Bach branch of the Long Beach (CA) Public Library, who handed me about a thousand books during the time it took to write this one. More gratitude to the American Library Association, which granted permission to quote George S. Bobinski's fine book, *Carnegie Libraries*. Allen Gardiner's book, *Carnegie Legacy in Kansas*, was both inspirational and invaluable.

I cannot praise the UCLA Writers Program enough. Gayle Brandeis led me into the program—by being such a fine writer, calling my bluff, encouraging my writing. This book was workshopped through classes taught by Caroline Leavitt and Robert Eversz. Numerous students provided valuable insight, most especially Carol Starr Schneider and Kerry Fisher.

Early readers included Goody Cable, Lois Gilbert, Tony Quintana, Kathy Lazarus, Heidi Durrow, Erin Hart, Jenn Stroud Rossmann, Helene Harmatz, Connie Hiett Delgado, Terry Winer, Jennifer Pooley, Ann Hood, and Sue Ann Robinson. It should go without saying, but it won't: I appreciate all who take time to read my story. Readers, especially of first novels, play a critical role in our cultural ecology.

So much hospitality and encouragement were offered along the way from the dearest of friends, including but not only: Ellen Morgan, Don Lambert, Troy Botello, Art Warren, Diann Spencer, Patricia Mitchell, Peggy Cornelius, Doreen Bauman, Ramona Carlin, Rosina Didyk, Patti Walters Wells, Mike Thompson, Michael Levitan, Ana Steele, John Clark, and Ingrid Kidd Goldfarb. I have been luckiest in friendships, rich in inspiration from the creative people around me. You know who you are.

My own women's groups provided support as well as material and insight, including my book club of twenty-five years, the LitWits; my knit sibs of Wednesday nights, StitchnBeach; and six women who shared a life-changing week at Djerassi, the NunBoxers.

Thanks to Brooke Warner and She Writes Press, who saw merit in my novel and gave me the confidence to keep at it. Her team, including Lauren Wise and Julie Metz, have delivered this book with expertise. Caitlin Hamilton Summie (Hamilton Marketing & Publicity) has worked magic in promoting it.

Always grateful for my family, the Eisenstarks. My father taught me to read and so much more; my brothers provide inspiration, grounding, and humor. My mother is on every page.

Most of all, I'm indebted to the women of Kansas who hired me as a very young woman, straight out of graduate school, to ride circuit around the state as the executive director of ACAAK (Association of Community Arts Agencies of Kansas). They taught me, nurtured me, paid me to learn from them, and told me their stories. That hiring proved to be one of the most important events of my life. They still inspire me, decades later and counting.

ABOUT THE AUTHOR

© Rachael Warecki

Romalyn Tilghman is a freelance writer and consultant in arts management. She earned BA and MS degrees from the University of Kansas and has studied writing through UCLA's Writers Program. *To the Stars Through Difficulties* is her first novel, inspired by her work as Executive Director of the Association of Community Arts Councils of Kansas, and then as Regional Representative for the National Endowment for the Arts. Since then, she has consulted with private foundations, government agencies, and performing arts groups, and served on national boards and panels. She lives in Southern California.

For more information, visit her website: www.romalyn.com

SELECTED TITLES FROM SHE WRITES PRESS

She Writes Press is an independent publishing company
founded to serve women writers everywhere.
Visit us at www.shewritespress.com.

A Cup of Redemption by Carole Bumpus
$16.95, 978-1-938314-90-2
Three women, each with their own secrets and shames, seek to make
peace with their pasts and carve out new identities for themselves.

Center Ring by Nicole Waggoner
$17.95, 978-1-63152-034-1
When a startling confession rattles a group of tightly knit women to its
core, the friends are left analyzing their own roads not taken and the
vastly different choices they've made in life and love.

Shelter Us by Laura Diamond
$16.95, 978-1-63152-970-2
Lawyer-turned-stay-at-home-mom Sarah Shaw is still struggling to find
a steady happiness after the death of her infant daughter when she meets
a young homeless mother and toddler she can't get out of her mind—and
becomes determined to rescue them.

The Rooms Are Filled by Jessica Null Vealitzek
$16.95, 978-1-938314-58-2
The coming-of-age story of two outcasts—a nine-year-old boy who
just lost his father, and a closeted young woman—brought together by
circumstance.

True Stories at the Smoky View by Jill McCroskey Coupe
$16.95, 978-1-63152-051-8
The lives of a librarian and a ten-year-old boy are changed forever when
they become stranded by a blizzard in a Tennessee motel and join forces
in a very personal search for justice.

Again and Again by Ellen Bravo
$16.95, 978-1-63152-939-9
When the man who raped her roommate in college becomes a Senate
candidate, women's rights leader Deborah Borenstein must make a
choice—one that could determine control of the Senate, the course of a
friendship, and the fate of a marriage.